A Gravely Troubling Discovery

Hannah Hendy lives in a small town in South Wales with her wife, their daughter, and two spoilt cats. A professional chef by trade, she started writing to fill the time between shifts. She now writes cosy crime fulltime, a dream job! She is the author of the bestselling cosy crime series, The Dinner Lady Detectives, published by Canelo Crime and Canelo US. Hannah is represented by Francesca Riccardi at Kate Nash Literary Agency.

Instagram - @hannahhendywrites

Facebook - @hannahhendywrites

Twitter - @hendyhannah

Website – hannahhendywrites.com

Also by Hannah Hendy

The Dinner Lady Detectives

The Dinner Lady Detectives
An Unfortunate Christmas Murder
A Terrible Village Poisoning
A Frightfully Fatal Affair
A Gravely Troubling Discovery

A Gravely Troubling Discovery

HANNAH HENDY

CANELO CRIME

First published in the United Kingdom in 2024 by

Canelo
Unit 9, 5th Floor
Cargo Works, 1–2 Hatfields
London SE1 9PG
United Kingdom

A CIP catalogue record for this book is available from the British Library.

Print ISBN 978 1 80436 472 7
Ebook ISBN 978 1 80436 473 4

Cover design by Ami Smithson

Cover images © Shutterstock and istock

Look for more great books at www.canelo.co

Printed and bound in Great Britain by Clays Ltd, Elcograf S.p.A.

In loving memory of Angela MacTaggart

Prologue

Monday mornings were nearly always ghastly, even with the false confidence of the warm sun rising slowly in the sky through her office window.

In Rose's humble opinion, summer always came a little too early. By the time she had bullied Seren into swapping out her winter wardrobe for her warm-weather one it was almost always nearly over. Still, it was early enough in the day that the students and teachers were all on their way in, and she was hidden away in her tiny office. She had meant to spend her first few hours of the week going through some of the Year Eleven mock exam work or even arranging to call a few parents – the work of a deputy head was never done – but instead, she found herself reaching over behind the laptop and pulling the ring binder from the shelving unit where she kept her most important files and folders.

It didn't look like much from the outside – just a plain old ring binder – but inside was a veritable treasure trove of intricate plans and schemes. Years' worth of information carefully curated by herself and filed away to preserve the delicate knowledge inside. She peeled back the front cover and delved in with red marker pen. Of course, she usually planned everything on the computer, using the internet to search for the exact thing she wanted. But planning a wedding this important, Rose reasoned, couldn't be constrained by the confines of a few pixels and underground phonelines. The binder was a carefully constructed bible of wedding plans tailor made for Rose's best friend Seren and her fiancé, school security guard, Gary Matthews. Put together by Rose obviously, but she did occasionally ask for Seren's approval. Most of the time anyway.

The catering had been easy to sort out; the school canteen would provide. Rose would never tell any of them how much she enjoyed their wares, however, lest Clementine Butcher-Baker's head grew too big to fit through the doorway of the kitchen.

But all the same, a meal cooked by the canteen staff was a much better prospect than a boring roast dinner at a chain hotel. There had been tricky intricacies to fathom with that – it might not be entirely practical to use the school canteen if the venue was too far away from it. And of course, they would have to leave plenty of time between the ceremony and the wedding breakfast to ensure that Margery and her team of Education Centre Nourishment Consultants could attend both. Seren would have the day off from kitchen duties of course. Rose was sure with a bit of careful preparation they would manage it. She hadn't yet mentioned it to Margery, but she had already blackmailed Mrs George and the rest of the English department into working for the day as the waiting staff. Mrs George had folded at the mere mention that Rose knew she had supplied her form group with shop-bought cakes and pastries, aiding them in the winning of the Christmas bake sale competition. Rose hadn't even known it was a sure fact when she'd made the accusation, only noticing that the edible gingerbread diorama of *The Crucible* looked far too perfect to be homemade.

The dress was the most difficult piece of the puzzle, of course, aside from the ever-illusive venue. Rose felt as though they must have trawled most of the country now looking for the perfect dress and place. A few times during this search, Seren had appeared happy with some boring plain dress or other – even the occasional smart trouser suit – but Rose knew that the right dress simply hadn't revealed itself yet. Seren had done a lot for her – still did a lot for her – and it all needed to be impeccable.

Through the window the sound of drilling began again, and Rose winced. They seemed to be taking forever to finish the new playground. Really, how difficult could it be to drag it all up and then re-lay it? And did they really need to start it all so early – it was barely ten past eight. She had said as much to James that morning, but he had rolled over in bed and told her that it shouldn't be too much longer. She hadn't wanted to bother him much more than that. There was a big school-wide inspection coming, and she knew that as headmaster he was concerned about the outcome. Privately, she was too, and the drilling wasn't helping matters. The builders had already been here for three days the week before. Every time she began anything in class it seemed that they would start drilling again, and the students would all act up as per usual. Any new thing set them off into a frenzy. After the disaster with the swimming gala last week there was even more reason for them to run rampant. It was even worse that it was happening right outside her office window. If she opened it and reached out, she would have been able to touch the tools the workmen were using.

Ignoring the interruption, she began to delve into their next point of contention – the flowers. Seren had said Gary didn't mind if they didn't even have flowers, and she would be happy with a bunch of carnations. Rose scoffed out loud in the silence of her office at the memory. Of course, Gary Matthews didn't give a fickle fig about the flowers, or any of the other décor she had suggested. She had known he didn't care for the finer things in life the day she had interviewed him years ago for the security guard position, when he'd arrived eating a bag of prawn cocktail Wotsits, but that didn't mean that they shouldn't have them. Anyway, Seren couldn't be expected to hold a droopy bunch of carnations for the best photographer in Ittonvale, could she?

Rose ran a finger through her notes. They would need to find a florist that could meet expectations. She had considered dried flowers instead of a traditional bouquet, but then if they were going a non-traditional route, why not choose non-traditional flowers? Black orchids for power, Scottish thistle for loyalty. Maybe they would make the bouquet too dark though. They were getting married in August. Sunflowers would be in season. Yes, that was it! A simple flower, like Seren had said she wanted. It was perfect. Rose took the lid off her pen and wrote down a few notes on the page opposite.

The drilling stopped. She realised that she had become so accustomed to the noise that the silence sounded loud and rattling in her head, her thoughts bouncing around inside it and becoming distracting in themselves. She got up and went to the window to open it and let some fresh air in and examine their progress in the playground. She tried to gauge how many more days they would be blessing her with their presence, by the holes they had made. The man who had been holding the drill leapt back as though it was suddenly on fire and the man across from him peered down into the depths of the hole. There was something in it and they both stared down into the crevice they had created.

Rose found herself holding her breath, before releasing it in a gasp as the man dragged at the tarpaulin that had been revealed beneath the concrete, and pulled up the human-shaped figure that had been wrapped inside.

Chapter One

They had lived at number twenty-two Seymour Road for so long, that Margery could barely remember living anywhere else. Not that she would want to. The little two bed terrace was perfectly big enough for the pair of them and their two cats. They were close enough to the school canteen to walk there if they had to, though they preferred to get the bus to avoid the hill up to the school, and close enough to the town centre for shopping and the very occasional visit to the Bell and Hope pub. The little town of Dewstow was a usually calm and quiet place, and the last few years of murder and mayhem had sometimes made Margery feel like she had fallen into an alternate universe, though that all seemed to be over.

They sat at the kitchen table and lazily ate the last of the crumpets. A peaceful Sunday morning was a wonderful thing, especially after all the chaos of yesterday. Margery didn't know what the headmaster had been playing at, but the catering needed form usually required a minimum of seventy-two hours' notice. Which he had known of course. He had seemed dreadfully upset when he had arrived in her office on Friday morning to tell her he'd forgotten all about the charity swimming gala and Margery had wondered what on earth could be important enough to make him forget about it. They had barely had a day to prepare, and Margery had counted her lucky stars that she hadn't yet missed the cut-off time for a Saturday fruit delivery and that her team of dinner ladies could all attend.

It had been hard enough to get Karen and Sharon to come into work on the weekend; Saturday was usually parkrun day. And Margery's second in command, Gloria, usually went to church on a Saturday so she could have a lie-in on Sunday. As it was, they had spent the better part of the morning segmenting oranges and whisking up flasks of cheap, barely soluble coffee for the teachers and parents, along with weak jugs of lemon squash for the students. The entire thing had been much too citrus heavy, but it was all Margery had been able to get at such short notice. Usually, a swimming gala was meticulously planned down to the last detail. Last year's had included a wide array of swimming appropriate aquatic themed snacks and drinks. It was lucky in a way that they hadn't needed any of it at all, though now their small kitchen was drowning in leftover sandwiches.

Their elderly tortoiseshell cat – Pumpkin – joined them in the kitchen, snoozing softly on the rocking chair in the corner. Her younger sister Crinkles wasn't around this afternoon. Margery knew that if she stood up and looked out of the kitchen window, she would see her lounging on next door's shed roof in the sunshine, her long white fur unmissable. Margery was just about to suggest to Clementine that perhaps they should do something distracting, like try and finish the new 2000-piece jigsaw they had picked up from the charity shop, or organise Clementine's collection of interesting bells. It would certainly be more exciting than hearing again about Clementine's theory that if giants existed then they would own lions as pet cats. Before she could say anything there was a sharp rap on the door, the noise reaching them in the quiet kitchen. Clementine looked up from her plate with a start, and they both exchanged a worried look.

'Who could that be?' Margery wondered out loud.

Clementine brushed the crumbs from her hands and stood, pushing the chair back under the table. 'I really hope it's not the headmaster, Margery. He might see the washing-up liquid we've stolen from the school and have us arrested.'

Margery smiled as Clementine left through the living room to the front door in the hallway. There was indeed a five-litre bottle of industrial strength washing-up liquid sat on the windowsill above the kitchen sink, but she didn't think the headmaster or anyone else would think much of that. Though she found herself praying that it wasn't Rose, coming with the good news of the rescheduled swimming gala date.

She could hear Clementine talking to someone for a moment and then whoever it was had decided that they were coming inside the house. Mrs Mugglethwaite, who worked at the post office and may as well be the CEO of the town's rumour mill, was suddenly standing in the kitchen with another much older woman. Margery recognised her as Mrs Redburn, part of Mrs Mugglethwaite's gang on the number sixty-four bus they used to get to the school every weekday morning.

'I told you they'd be in, Evelyn,' Mrs Mugglethwaite said, the woman behind her looking around the cluttered kitchen, at all the knickknacks Margery and Clementine had acquired over the years. 'The dinner lady detectives! They'll help sort you out, don't you worry.'

Clementine reappeared behind them both, sharing a bemused smile with Margery. The kitchen suddenly seemed even smaller with the two visitors inside it, both wearing huge raincoats and carrying large canvas shopping bags.

'Hello,' Margery said, trying not to show her bewilderment at this unexpected visitation. 'How are you, Martha?'

'I'm great,' Mrs Mugglethwaite said, her face a horrible mixture of triumph and glee. 'It's Evelyn who needs sorting. Her husband's having...' she lowered her voice to a whisper, though Margery couldn't for the life of her work out for whose benefit, '...an affair!'

'He might not be!' Evelyn squeaked shrilly.

Mrs Mugglethwaite rolled her eyes and scoffed. 'He almost certainly is,' she said. 'But you're right. Let's let the detectives sort it out. Where shall we sit?' She pointed at the single chair at the kitchen table. Margery still occupied the other.

'Shall we go into the garden?' Margery suggested, looking longingly at the free space and fresh air outside the kitchen window. 'We've got a four-seater garden table.'

'Ooh excellent!' Mrs Mugglethwaite said, reaching for the back door immediately and unlocking it.

'I'll make a pot of tea,' Clementine said, shaking her head with confusion at the sight of Mrs Mugglethwaite struggling with the door handle and finally managing it. Margery considered Evelyn as she followed them both out onto the patio, leaving Clementine to make the drinks. She was a bit older than Margery, Clementine or Mrs Mugglethwaite, with short light hair cropped in such a way that it curled around the bottom of her neck.

Mrs Mugglethwaite flung off her raincoat, and laid it carefully on the back of one of the garden chairs before lowering herself into the chair with a tired thump. She dropped the shopping bag on the floor next to her, and whatever was inside clanked as it hit the hard concrete patio. Evelyn took the chair next to her, sitting up straight with her hands balled tightly together in her lap. She didn't look as though she wanted to be here at all, Margery thought. It was very possible that Mrs Mugglethwaite had dragged her here. Margery was too tired to argue with any of it, deciding privately that Martha and Evelyn's presence was as good as any other distraction would be. She hoped neither of them would ask for the canvas parasol that sat above the garden table to be opened. Clementine had only recently taken it back out from its winter hibernation in the shed, and Margery worried that once it was open a rain of spiders would be revealed. Still, the day was proving to be a lovely one and Margery always felt better when the sun was out – all her worries melting away like ice in a drink.

Mrs Mugglethwaite always seemed to know all the town's comings and goings, though Margery had never been able to work out exactly how. She had always assumed it was a combination of the gossip she overheard all day at the town's only post office and the fact that her husband, Arthur Mugglethwaite, was on the town council. He probably heard many of the darker rumours and tales that swirled around Dewstow and passed them on to his wife. The other town councillors were not known for their ability to keep secrets, either. In fact, Margery thought that Mr Fitzgerald would be more likely to shut up his local oddities shop, sell it all, and move away to Spain, than be able to keep a secret for more than ten minutes, unless it was his own.

Evelyn didn't respond. Instead, she stared out at their small back garden. It was not much of a garden, all be told.

Just the small strip of patio they sat on, then a slightly raised wall across with a step in the middle that led to a patch of lawn that Clementine would occasionally mow when she remembered. The lawn mower had not yet been woken from its winter hibernation, so the grass was currently a mess of dandelions and other weeds. A flower bed ran either side of the grass and then at the back of the garden sat their old leaky shed, which was filled with tools and Argos catalogues. Margery had carefully painted the fence a few years ago and it still looked relatively nice, except for the small, cat-sized hole by the back garden gate, which Clementine had cut out when Pumpkin had begun to find the jump up onto the fence too much. Crinkles was still on next door's shed roof, rolling around in the sunshine, her fluffy legs in the air.

Evelyn took all this in, her mouth twisted into a disdainful grimace as they sat among the weeds poking up through the concrete patio slabs. Clementine broke the silence, arriving with a tray of tea things.

'What can we do for you ladies?' she asked them as she doled out teacups and bourbon biscuits. 'I'd offer you a Quality Street, but we only have the coconut ones left. We weren't expecting visitors.'

They hadn't been, especially after the relaxing morning they'd had. If they hadn't known that Martha was likely to spin it into something more nefarious, Margery would have had the mind to ask her to leave, she always felt that it was best not to invite any extra drama into their lives. Especially of the gossip laden chaos that Martha usually brought with her. Mrs Mugglethwaite bristled anyway.

'I emailed you yesterday!' she explained, waving her hands around. Margery worried for the teapot. 'It's not my fault you don't check your website.'

'We don't have a website,' Margery said, looking to Clementine for confirmation. 'Do we?'

Clementine almost looked embarrassed for a moment. It was a rare sight on her face. 'Well… I might have asked media studies group B to set us up a little one, just somewhere to put our long list of achievements, a few photos of us, maybe an assortment of newspaper clippings, that sort of thing.' She busied herself with the tea things again. 'We may or may not owe them one hundred pounds. I told them, "The internet was always free in my day," and they insisted that it couldn't possibly have been invented in my day. I said, "Well I am nearly sixty-five, I could have invented the internet for all you know," and she said—'

'Evelyn suspects her husband is having an affair,' Mrs Mugglethwaite interrupted, as though she couldn't keep the information in for any longer, the words spilling out of her mouth and into the air between them. She didn't wait for Evelyn to respond before continuing. 'He keeps leaving the house for hours at a time.'

'All right,' Margery said, taking the cup that Clementine handed her with a grateful smile. 'That's not good news, I suppose, but… well…'

'What on earth has that got to do with us?' Clementine finished Margery's sentence, plonking herself down next to Margery and reaching over to the table for a custard cream.

'For Christ's sake, this was all in my email,' Mrs Mugglethwaite scoffed. 'You're the dinner lady detectives are you not?' She added a cube of sugar to her teacup. 'Don't you remember when you helped me find my missing shoe?'

'Yes, but the shoe wasn't actually lost Martha,' Clementine said, giving her a withering once over. 'You'd just forgotten you'd put it in a different cupboard.'

'You can't tell me you're only doing murders now.' Mrs Mugglethwaite ignored Clementine entirely and put her cup down in horror so she could jab her finger towards them accusingly. 'Are you too good for a good old-fashioned crime? You found those ladies having an affair last year...'

'I'm not sure adultery is really a crime...' Margery began.

Mrs Mugglethwaite scoffed again. 'Well, it certainly isn't compared to all those murders!' she laughed. 'But you've got to help Evelyn. She's got money. She can pay the going rate.'

'What is the going rate?' Margery said.

'One hundred pounds, like your website said, of course!' Mrs Mugglethwaite cried.

Clementine avoided Margery's eye, so she didn't see the exasperated look Margery shot her.

'Surely he must have a reason to be leaving. Why don't you just ask him yourself?' Clementine asked Evelyn directly, ignoring Martha's outburst and Margery's wondering how on earth the going rate for investigations could possibly have been calculated.

Evelyn bristled at the audacity of the question. 'He says he's been at golf,' she explained, in a haughty voice that didn't match her face. 'But he simply can't have been.'

'Why not?' Margery asked.

'Because he hasn't been using his clubs,' Evelyn said, 'and his clothes aren't dirty like they are when he plays golf. Pristine, like he hasn't even been to the golf course.'

'But why would that mean he's having an affair?' Margery asked, stirring sugar into her teacup.

'Because I've been doing his washing for decades,' Evelyn said, as if that was the most obvious thing in the world. Margery thought that if she was having an affair, it would take much more for Clementine to find out. They had always split the responsibility of the washing, taking it in turns to throw a load into the machine.

'Okay?' Margery said finally, Evelyn had finished huffing and sat looking sadly at the table. 'Well, I suppose the golf thing is a bit strange but—'

'We'll see what we can do,' Clementine said, reaching over to pass the woman a biscuit in a comforting manner. 'But we can't promise anything.'

'Excellent!' Mrs Mugglethwaite cried, beaming at them both. 'Now, tell me what happened at the school gala yesterday... I heard that one of your Education Centre Nourishment Consultants fell into the pool and got the whole thing cancelled. Surely that can't be true?'

It was true. Margery grimaced, remembering the look on Seren's face as she had slipped across the shiny surface of the swimming pool floor in her new trainers and slid into the water. Which she might have got away with if not for the fact that she had been carrying an enormous tub of orange segments that had all tumbled into the water with her and sunk to the bottom. The gala had been cancelled immediately and the children evacuated from the pool while Mrs Wiggins, the head of health and safety, screeched about citrus contamination.

It had been Summerview Secondary School's year to host, against fierce rivals Ittonvale Comprehensive School. They had been taking turns to host since just after the second sunset on Earth, as far as everyone was concerned, although, in reality it was probably only four or five decades. It was a good chance for the headteachers of both schools to fundraise, each student paid two pounds to turn up and race. So, it was incredible that Mr Barrow had managed to forget. Especially as he had already paid for the renovations on the top playground that the gala was supposed to be paying for to begin with. The dinner lady team weren't thrilled about the playground below their kitchen window becoming a noisy construction site, but they all agreed that it needed to be done. Especially after Seren had tripped on one of the many potholes lining its surface and her lunchbox had smashed open on the floor, Babybels and satsumas rolling all over the place. That seemed very ironic to Margery now.

Summerview's deputy head, Rose Smith, had immediately begun planning a do-over of the gala, but Margery secretly hoped that it would all fall through before the end of term. It had all been too much drama to begin with, though she knew that many of the teachers would be upset if it didn't go ahead again. She really wished she had a pound for every time the prodigiousness of the gala was brought up in the weeks building up to it – she'd have a fortune now. She could tell just by the way Martha was eyeing her that word would have spread all over town by now and she hoped something would arrive to overshadow it soon enough.

'All that and poor Ittonvale School has been missing their PE teacher, haven't they?' Mrs Mugglethwaite said with a disapproving tut. 'Lord knows where she's run off to, leaving them in the lurch like that. Maybe Summerview School should just let Ittonvale win this year, out of sympathy?'

Margery decided to go inside and get more biscuits. Getting through the rest of the afternoon with Mrs Mugglethwaite was going to take something sweeter than a party ring.

Chapter Two

'I still can't believe you said we'd help, Clem,' Margery said, for what felt like the hundredth time. Even though they'd had the rest of Sunday afternoon and evening to argue about it, Margery was still a bit annoyed.

'Why not? It solves the problem of us owing the children one hundred pounds for the website, doesn't it? Not that they used actual money, they probably paid for it in beans or internet coins,' Clementine said as they swiped into the school's front entrance with their pass cards and made their way to the canteen. 'Anyway, Lord knows it's been a bit too quiet around here; we could use the excitement!'

'Have you forgotten that we were at the scene of a horrible death just a few months ago?' Margery asked. They reached the canteen and shuffled through. Margery got her keys ready.

'Well,' Clementine said as she waited for Margery to unlock the kitchen door. 'This is different. Evelyn's husband is definitely alive if he's off having affairs in his golf clothes.'

Margery nodded in agreement as she swung the door open, and they crossed the threshold into the kitchen. 'I suppose you're right Clem. Evelyn did seem like she needed our help, didn't she?'

They put on their hairnets, washed their hands and began their usual Monday morning routine. Margery filled in the fridge temperature paperwork while Clementine turned on the gas and had the usual argument with the stove top while trying to get it to light, her Midas touch with it always a saving grace. Margery looked up at the clock and realised that they had better get a move on if they were going to get breakfast club done in time.

She began getting the kitchen ready, but was interrupted almost immediately by the arrival of the team. Officially titled Education Centre Nourishment Consultants, they preferred to be colloquially known as dinner ladies. Under Margery's watchful kitchen-manager eye, they fed 1200 students, teachers, and support staff lunch daily during termtime at Summerview School. It was not an easy task, especially when breakfast club and extracurriculars were involved, but they somehow always managed it. The last time they had almost missed a lunch deadline was because the meat delivery had failed to arrive after the driver's van had burst a tyre, and that was a good few months ago now. Anyway, Sharon and Karen had quickly run to Tesco and back, saving 'Bangers and Mash Tuesday' from failure.

Margery heard her team long before she could see them. They arrived through the doors to the canteen in a gaggle, their voices filling the empty room and bouncing off the pink plastic topped tables. It was immediately obvious that they were arguing, but it was the kind of argument that Margery associated with being part of a large dysfunctional family, more than anything else. It reminded her of growing up with her siblings in the small home they had shared, and was always oddly comforting.

'Please go home,' Gloria was begging Ceri-Ann, who was waddling along in front of the group, ignoring the hand Gloria had wrapped around her thin wrist. 'Your due date is next week. We've only just had that new mop head delivered. You can't be having the baby here.'

Every day for the last three weeks Margery had banned Ceri-Ann from coming to work in the school kitchen, and every day Ceri-Ann arrived, anyway. She kept insisting that as Symon wouldn't be able to take his parental leave until the very last moment, there was no need for her to rush off on maternity. The entire team had tried to explain on several occasions that this wasn't at all the point, but it was no good.

'I want to be here, mate. I can't cope at home, everyone fawning all over me,' Ceri-Ann said, her hands resting on her baby bump, which was almost comically round on her slim frame. 'And, there's nothing wrong with me! Loads of people work till their due date.'

'Most of them have nice little sitting down jobs though, not kitchen work. Anyway, how many children are you carrying Ceri?' Clementine said. 'Because it looks like you're having triplets from over here.'

'Should have gone to Specsavers, shouldn't you?' Ceri-Ann scoffed, but she only made it as far as the nearest canteen table before having to sit down. 'God, what if they missed one on the scan, though? This can't just be one massive baby.' She looked down at her feet sadly. 'I keep having to buy bigger shoes. And my mate Chantelle said that her hair's never gone back to normal after her second baby. I can't afford wigs now, can I? Or even the Taylor Swift concert – I had to sell Chantelle's Eras Tour tickets. Livid she was.' She shook her head in sorrow at the memory. 'We've got to spend it all on nappies and tiny shoes and that. I can't even buy a new phone. I smashed the screen on mine, and now all the TikToks I watch look like jigsaw puzzles.'

'Well, if you won't go home, will you let me give you an easy job today?' Margery suggested, leaving the kitchen entrance to sit next to Ceri-Ann on one of the uncomfortable canteen chairs. 'You can sit on Clementine's chair in the kitchen and peel potatoes for tomorrow at your own pace. No rush.'

'Yeah, let me do the potatoes, please, mate. I don't want to be on my own,' Ceri-Ann said, shifting her gaze from Margery's with the admittance. 'Symon's well busy at work, so he's not about.'

'What about your family?' Margery asked, trying to think back to the last time she had met a member of Ceri-Ann's family.

Ceri-Ann rolled her eyes. 'God, don't even talk about them. My mum is doing my head in. Keeps flapping about.' She groaned. 'We never should have given her a spare key. Sy's mum is just as bad. It's like they've both decided to be as insane as possible. They're already arguing about whose house the baby's going to go to at Christmas. Not us. Just the baby!'

Before they could discuss the matter any further, the canteen door slammed open and Karen and Sharon rushed in — Karen gasping and pointing to the canteen while Sharon staggered behind her weeping.

'What on earth!' Clementine cried, as they lurched through the canteen. 'Did they cancel the half marathon or something?'

'Murder!' Karen shrieked back at her still pointing towards the kitchen. Sharon stumbled to the table beside Ceri-Ann and slumped over it, still weeping.

'What?' Clementine said again, as Margery followed Karen, who stumbled past them and into the canteen kitchen. She made it to the window before collapsing against the metal sink, tapping against the glass with her index finger. Below them on the ground floor the drilling had stopped, and a crowd of students had joined the builders, the teachers trying to regain order.

Karen turned to Margery, her eyes wide with panic. 'They've found a body!'

'What?'

'Gosh,' Clementine gasped, Margery hadn't even heard her arrive behind her. 'It's not a student, is it?'

'Is it really a murder?' Margery found herself asking out loud after Karen's outburst. She wondered if past events had made her a little too open to the possibility. Anything could have happened, but here she was jumping straight to the idea of foul play.

Margery turned from the window to look at the rest of the team. Gloria had turned very white, clutching her chest and staring out at the playground with wide eyes.

Seren, who had been busily getting the breakfast club ready, had nearly dropped the box of own brand cornflakes onto the floor in surprise, but she'd managed to catch them and was now gripping the box tightly. The cornflakes inside being crushed under her grip.

'No,' Sharon said, wiping her eyes, 'I heard the police say it was an adult skeleton by the size.'

'What happened?' Margery asked Karen. 'Did they say how they died? Or who they were?'

'No, they don't know yet,' she shook her head. 'They don't know anything. The builders just dug it up twenty minutes ago. We were walking past when they were doing it.'

Margery was suddenly struck with the horrible thought that you could live your whole life surrounded by people, by students and other teachers, and you could still be buried in secret under a playground. The thought sent a shiver down her spine.

'It could be a joke skeleton?' Margery wondered aloud. 'One of the students put the plastic one from the science lab there overnight, or something like that?'

'I don't think so,' Karen said, her eyes haunted. 'It's all wrapped up in this like blue tarpaulin thing, you know? It looks old...' She lowered her voice to a fraught whisper, 'It's got holes in it.'

Another police car pulled off the road alongside the school and began to drive onto what was left of the playground tarmac. The students all took a collective step back as the officers emerged from the car and made their way over to the hole. Mr Barrow was already standing at the side waiting for them, his hands behind his back clenched tightly together.

There wasn't much time to process any more horrible thoughts. Lunch still needed preparing, as did the headmaster's tea trolley, assuming he still had time to drink it. Sharon and Karen were too upset to do it, while Seren and Gloria were fully invested in slapping together lasagnes for the lunchtime rush. It fell to Clementine to sort out, which meant that Margery had to help if not for anything but co-dependency.

They set up the tea trolley in a well-practised routine; they had been setting it up for the past twenty years after all, and even the shock discovery of a corpse wouldn't throw them off their stride. Margery arranged the biscuits and self-serve portions of Kenco coffee sachets, tea bags and stirrers and Clementine filled the accompanying thermal flasks with hot water and cold milk. Then they trundled it out of the canteen, leaving the others to finish the prep for lunchtime, careful to mind the trolley's persistent wobbly wheel which Margery had never been able to find the budget to fix. The entire thing would have to collapse into a pile of crumpled metal and plastic before she had any hope of buying them a new one.

'Well...' Clementine said, while the trolley careened on its wobbly wheels through the endless school hallways. 'This is probably worse than the vending machine breaking that time.'

'It's certainly not good, is it?' Margery said. 'That poor person. I wonder who it is?'

'If it's just a skeleton, then maybe it's completely innocent,' Clementine guided the trolley over a particularly bald piece of carpet, the wheels rattling along it. 'Maybe they were buried there a hundred years ago, a king or something.'

'I'm not sure, wouldn't a king be buried properly?' Margery asked.

'Well, they found Richard the Third under a car park, didn't they?' Clementine said. 'What if it's King Arthur?'

'I'm sure King Arthur was mythical, and even if he wasn't I don't think they had plastic back then,' Margery said, thinking of the blue plastic sheeting she could see from the kitchen window. 'But I bet the police will find out.'

As deep in thought as she was, Margery pushed open the headmaster's office door without thinking and regretted it when Rose and her guest were revealed, sitting in Mr Barrow's office. Rose sat in her husband's office chair with her hands together primly on his desk and the stranger in the special visitor's chair in front of it.

'Hello Mrs Butcher-Baker,' Rose said, her voice seemingly full of cheer, although Margery knew her well enough to tell that it was strained. 'Is that the tea trolley? That's good… lovely, even.'

'Yes, apologies for not knocking, Mrs Smith,' Margery said, trying not to wince at the cold stare from the stranger, who remained perfectly still in his chair. 'We thought you might have been at the… outside…'

'Yes, I'm not needed there quite yet,' Rose said. She smiled at her gently, but her eyes gave away her distress. 'Listen, Mrs Butcher-Baker, you've reminded me. There's an emergency assembly at eleven. I've told the teachers, but you need to be there too really. Could you let the cleaning team know on your way back to the kitchen?'

'Of course,' Margery said, nodding and feeling her eyes open wide. She pushed the trolley into the room further and began to wheel it into its usual place along the bookcase at the back of the room.

The stranger didn't wait for her to leave before continuing their conversation. 'As I said before, this is all just a matter of formality,' he said. 'Just a few weeks and then we can give our full report to the board. I'll need access to your books and records of course, and we will be reviewing lesson plans and classes in general. Though I'm sure there won't be a problem there.'

Margery left the trolley and slipped out as quickly as she could, not having time to wonder any longer about Rose's worried look or ask her about it.

'When you say weeks, Richard, how long do you mean exactly?' Rose said, as Margery shut the door again with a soft click. Clementine stared at her wide-eyed.

'What was that about?' she whispered.

Margery shook her head. She didn't know, but she wasn't sure she liked the sound of it at all.

Chapter Three

They gathered at the back of the school hall, as they usually did during assemblies, and watched the lines of students pour in. It was always strange to be back in here. It had been completely renovated after the terrible case of arson a few years ago, yet it somehow managed to look the same as before; a ghost of its former self.

Margery often found herself feeling nervous during assemblies or meetings in the room, though she doubted that something so horrible could happen again in her lifetime. Rose stood to the front of the hall next to the portable CD player, which was playing what Margery was sure was supposed to be calming ocean noises, but always put her on edge since she had nearly drowned. She closed her eyes and tried to picture the garden, but it didn't work, and she found herself digging her nails into her palms. Instead, she tried opening her eyes and looking for five things that she could see. She breathed in deeply as she did so and felt the weight lift from her chest enough that she wouldn't have to leave the room. It was not quite enough to calm her breathing entirely.

The headmaster finally arrived, followed by the stranger from the headmaster's office. Mr Barrow whispered something to Rose as the stranger took a seat to the side of the hall and then he waited by the CD player. When he realised that the noise of crashing waves and dolphins whistling was not likely to stop soon, he reached forwards and turned it off. Mr Barrow waited for the chatter of the staff and the babbling of Year Sevens to calm down and then he cleared his throat.

'Thank you all for joining me at such short notice.' He looked around the room at all their faces, his own drawn tightly, the forced smile not meeting his eyes. 'As you will all have heard this morning, the building team discovered something unusual while they were working hard on the building renovations.'

'Unusual is putting it lightly,' Margery heard Gloria murmur to the side of her.

'There was a skeleton found on school grounds. And so, we have no choice but to avoid that area while the police and construction team carry out an investigation.' Mr Barrow looked close to tears. 'All areas outside the school building are now off-limits during arrival and departure to school and during break times.'

There was a collective groan from those assembled.

'Unfortunately,' he continued, 'of course, this means we'll all miss out on the nice weather. But needs must I'm afraid so the police can investigate.'

The hushed whispers resumed, and Mr Barrow looked around desperately, catching the eye of the strange man who was watching him carefully, one hand wrapped around a thin wrist. The man's large grey eyebrows raised as the headmaster glanced in his direction.

'Also,' he continued, his eyes flitting desperately around the hall, as though someone would save him from what he had to say. 'Summerview School is having a little inspection, which is absolutely nothing to worry about at all, in fact, I'd even go so far as to say it's a very good thing.' He chuckled nervously in a horrible manic manner, before getting a hold of himself again. 'So if you see our new friend, Mr Monroe,' Mr Barrow gestured to the stranger, who took a step forwards and nodded to them all, 'or his team, then please feel free to say hello. He will be joining us in a few lessons and that sort of thing. Nothing to worry about at all.'

The gathered students and teachers in the hall began to murmur among themselves. Margery and Clementine exchanged a worried look.

'Now,' Mr Barrow said, slapping his hands together. 'Let me pass you over to Miss Morgan, who has some details about the upcoming swimming gala redo... which as you all know will be held at Ittonvale School.' He gestured for Miss Morgan to join him and she pushed her way past the staff lining the walls of the hall and made her way over. 'We have arranged for minibuses to transport all attending from the front gates to Ittonvale School straight after lunch next Tuesday. Please make sure you're all ready to go and have your parental permission slips with you.'

Miss Morgan finally made it to the front, and even from the distance Margery could see the upset look on her face, her eyes watery and her mouth pulled into a scowl that reminded Margery of a sad clown.

'The swimming gala trophy has been stolen!' Miss Morgan screeched as soon as she arrived in front of the headmaster. The gathered students and school staff gasped, and everyone began murmuring to themselves again. Mr Barrow winced and held his hand up for silence, giving Miss Morgan a stunned look of dismay.

The winning gala trophy was an enormous monument to athletic ability, both in size and aura. Ittonvale School had taken it home last year and Margery knew that the headmaster had been looking forward to it being back in Summerview's trophy cabinet.

'We don't know if it's been stolen,' Mr Barrow said as loud as he could over the cacophony and waved his hands in a plea for silence. 'Only that it's no longer safely in the trophy cabinet at Ittonvale School where it's been since Summerview's unfortunate defeat last year, or at Dewstow leisure centre, where it was held for the last gala.'

'It must have been stolen then! Who would do such a thing?' Karen gasped from Margery's right. Margery turned just in time to see Karen hand Sharon a tissue to wipe her eyes with before she burst into tears again.

'Are we sure it was definitely at the gala? I didn't see it, usually they have it on display.' Clementine whispered to Margery. 'Do you think it's been missing since before then? Surely they'd have known it was missing before then though?'

'We really don't need any more conspiracy theories,' Margery said, but it made a certain amount of sense.

'Maybe you've seen it,' Mr Barrow continued, taking over from Miss Morgan who looked like she really wanted to keep shouting about the missing trophy. 'Maybe one of your friends has accidentally put it in their locker or you've mistaken it for some sort of... erm... garden ornament... Regardless, it must be returned to the school. There will be no penalties for its return, as long as it's brought back before the second go of the swimming gala next Tuesday. Now, if that's all, please try and have a good rest of the day.' He reached for the CD player and the sounds of whales moaning began again.

'The headmaster must be dreadfully upset about the swimming gala trophy,' Karen said as the students piled out of the hall. 'He didn't even read a Rudyard Kipling poem.'

'He's probably upset about the skeleton they found,' Gloria said, her eyebrows raised comically high on her forehead at Karen's comment. 'Come on, let's get back to work.'

–

Back in the kitchen, the hours flitted past until only Margery and Clementine were left putting the till away and making sure the gas was turned off. They hadn't had a chance to discuss what they had been told in the assembly, but Margery wondered if the school was finally being audited after all the board of governors threats last year. The school had certainly not had an easy time of it recently, what with the murder the year before, and two more – unrelated – in the year before that. The school had spent much of the budget on a new security system when it had surely been most needed to update the science and technology department. It didn't look like things were about to get any easier with Mr Monroe and his team watching lessons. She turned the key to the gas switch and flicked the extractor fans off on the panel next to it, then began to do her usual last walkaround before they left. It was amazing how many times they had forgotten to do something silly like put the dirty tea towels into the laundry basket or cross off the jobs completed on the cleaning rota.

There was a noise at the kitchen window – so quiet at first that Margery thought that she must have imagined it. But the tapping didn't stop; Margery and Clementine exchanged a worried look. Margery wondered briefly if one of the dinner lady team had forgotten something. They knew not to come up the fire escape though, it was too much of a slip hazard. They all avoided it as best they could. Even when they took part in the monthly fire drill, they were very careful to all take the stairs one at a time, hands gripping the handrail and safety shoes on. Even the food delivery drivers didn't use it.

When Caroline had been kitchen manager, they used to drive around the back of the building and leave the boxes on the bottom steps, which meant the dinner lady team had to drag them all up one by one. Now the drivers parked their vans at security and then wheeled the wares through to the front entrance where they would remain until Mrs Wiggins radioed for Margery, who would get Karen and Sharon to check them and transport them up to the first floor in the school's only lift, which was located next to the reception.

Margery wondered if the tapping noise was a bird sitting on the window ledge and pecking away at the glass, though that seemed like a mad thought. Perhaps the commotion of the past few days was beginning to get to her. She left the sandwiches and went over to the window. Maybe the wind was blowing against it. It wasn't that long ago that they'd had it fixed after all. Maybe it was broken again, though it seemed unlikely now that Ceri-Ann had stopped smoking out of it. She couldn't see anything out of it as she approached – the large food wash sink got in the way – so instead she decided to pop open the fire escape and take a quick look outside. The window ran above it, so if it was broken, she'd be able to see it easily and could call for Pete the handyman straight away. She pushed the door open easily with the long handle that ran across it. It wrenched from her grasp as the gloved hands grabbed it by the side and pulled it back from her own. Margery stumbled backwards as the door opened fully and the man forced himself into the room.

The police officer stood before them, but he didn't look at them at first. Instead, his eyes glanced around the canteen kitchen, as though he was inspecting it. They had not met Officer Wilkinson before, not properly anyway. They had been briefly introduced at Officer Thomas's retirement party, but it had been very clear to Margery that the man didn't like them or their exploits and had given them a wide berth. Where Officer Thomas had been, if not completely willing, amenable to their helping with the string of murders that had plagued the town, Officer Wilkinson was not. In fact, Margery sometimes remembered the look he had given them at the party and shivered at the coldness of it. He finally finished looking around and turned to them, not bothering with any preamble.

'Ladies,' he said in a gruff voice, 'have you seen the headmaster?'

'No,' Margery said. 'He was down there with you, wasn't he?'

'He was this morning,' Officer Wilkinson muttered, glaring back at the fire door, which had already slammed shut behind him.

'You can't have lost him?' Clementine asked. He narrowed his eyes at her instead. 'Surely he's still down there somewhere? Or maybe in his office? Or calling someone to take the skeleton away?'

He looked like he might argue with her, but instead he leaned against the nearest counter so that he was at eye level with both of them.

'Listen, I know who you are,' he explained, his eyes narrowing. 'You've both had some success in the last few years…' He waved a hand in the air as he spoke.

'Solving murders, you mean?' Clementine interrupted him. Margery wondered where this was going in complete bewilderment. They certainly hadn't had anything to do with the body that had been found – in fact, they barely knew anything about it aside from what Karen and Sharon had said and the whisperings of the staff and students during the lunch hour.

'Yes,' he said, in a matter-of-fact way that reminded Margery of Clementine trying to explain to one of their cats why they couldn't have a second dinner. 'But you're going to leave this one alone, if you know what's best for you.'

Margery could tell from his tone that he thought them nothing more than a pair of ancient old ladies meddling in things that they shouldn't be and occasionally getting lucky. He could have only been in his early thirties, and had that hunger about him of a young man eager to do well in his career. She didn't think that she or Clementine had ever had that; they had both pottered through their lives nicely instead. There were no Michelin stars in their catering background, but they did occasionally visit the Michelin garage just off the nearby A road for new car tyres.

'So, it is a murder then? Who do you think did it?' Clementine asked him in the brazen manner of questioning that occasionally worked on lesser individuals. It was the wrong thing to say. Officer Wilkinson stood upright again. Margery watched enviously as he straightened up with ease, her knees felt like they could crack with jealousy at the sight of his easy lift.

33

'Just keep to your lane,' he said and turned to storm away, back through the fire escape. 'We don't need the old meddlers detective agency on this case.'

Chapter Four

Clementine shrugged off Officer Wilkinson's brief but troubling interruption immediately. 'Let him think what he wants,' she had said, 'and we'll get on with this affair business. Much more interesting than a murder anyway.' Though, after saying all that she had also repeatedly muttered about being called old meddlers, tutting under her breath that she was only nearly sixty-five and Margery only nearly sixty-four when she thought Margery couldn't hear her.

When they had finally got home, they had set up the whiteboard in the kitchen and written down everything Evelyn had told them about her husband and her suspicions on Sunday. Margery wondered why they ever bothered to put it away, it had helped them solve several cases now. Margery had written it all down in her kitchen notepad between recipes for traybake cakes and winter soups. Not that there was much to go off – Evelyn had been very tight lipped about how she really felt. The only real clue she would give them, was that she 'had a feeling' that he wasn't going to golf when he said he was. Margery didn't really think it was very helpful, but she sympathised. She couldn't help but find it quite dry after the murders they had solved, but it would have to do. It was better this way, staying right out of it. The last time they had tried to solve anything an innocent man had been arrested and nearly lost his job. They couldn't let that happen again. Officer Wilkinson, for all his terrifying bedside manner, seemed to have a handle on it all.

There was not much to go off apart from Evelyn's, 'strange feeling'. Martha Mugglethwaite had several other theories about where Mr Redburn could be when he said he was golfing, but Margery and Clementine had learned over the years to take anything she said with a huge great heaping of salt. Clementine's phone bleeped on the table, and she turned to look at the message rolling across the screen, taking the glasses from the chain on her neck and putting them on.

'It's Officer Thomas,' she said, her brow furrowing. 'I wonder what he wants?'

'It's just Nigel, now,' Margery reminded her. Nigel had retired from the police force the year before and now refused to go by his former title. They had been to lunch several times with himself and his wife since he had retired and had all become firm friends. Clementine had unlocked the phone and was reading the message in her usual squinting fashion, with the phone held at arm's length.

'He wants to meet us.' Clementine gave Margery a baffled look. 'He says it's really important.'

'Gosh, why are we so popular at the moment?' Margery asked, looking over to the calendar below the kitchen clock. It was covered in scribbles of blue biro and black marker pen. Their lives had been quite relaxed before any of this had happened, sometimes Margery missed the old days where the most exciting thing that ever happened was a parcel being delivered or Pumpkin bringing home a live mouse that would then disappear under a kitchen cabinet. She supposed though that in the time before, she and Clementine had been drifting along in a comfortable but boring relationship, and the spark that had diminished a little had returned full force now. The Clementine she knew from catering college, who had once told their head lecturer that the collective noun for a group of male chefs was called 'an ego', had reappeared.

'I know,' Clementine said wistfully. 'I'm going to need to get a new going-out cardigan, the sleeves on mine have gone all bobbly.'

'What does Nigel want to talk about?' Margery asked.

Clementine showed her the phone screen. 'No idea, but he asked if he could pop in.'

Margery looked around the untidy kitchen and their detective work board. The house really wasn't up for guests, even if Mrs Mugglethwaite had forced her way in the other day.

'Maybe we could meet him out?' Margery suggested, rather than embarrass themselves in front of the former police officer. It was one thing for Mrs Mugglethwaite to witness the washing hanging on the clothes dryer in the corner of the kitchen next to the cat food bowls, another entirely for Nigel to see their old socks. And anyway, it was probably for the best that the former officer did not see that they were investigating anything. Even something as innocent as the Mr Redburn's apparent affair.

'What if we meet him at the golf club?' Clementine suggested. 'They've got a bar, and I think he's a member anyway. Then we can ask a bit about Mr Redburn. The staff will certainly know him if he's a member. Nigel might even know him.'

It wasn't a bad idea, Margery thought. She was sure if they went to the club then they would probably catch Mr

Redburn playing golf, and the mystery would be entirely over before it could even begin. Officer Wilkinson was foolish to think they would risk their jobs by getting involved in another police case, she thought to herself. This time there was no risk of them getting dragged into anything to do with murder. After all, the Redburn case was sure to be a quick open and shut one, and there was no risk of murder where an affair was involved. The body in the playground must have been lying under their feet for ages so even if she wanted to, she couldn't investigate that. The thought made her shiver involuntarily and she pulled her cardigan closer to her neck.

—

They arrived at the country club entrance and drove down the long winding path to the main building. Margery had always admired the place when they drove past it, but they hadn't been here for decades. The grounds were lovely, the sprawling green of the golf course glowing under the setting sun. Golfers wandered along the grass, pulling their caddies behind them on their way back to the club before the sun set completely.

The country building was also a hotel. Margery thought it didn't look any different from the outside than it had when they'd last visited twenty years ago for a Christmas function. They pulled up in the car park, their little car looking a bit silly among the electric vehicles and big range rovers with custom number plates. They made their way into the main building and through the impressive foyer into the clubhouse bar, which was entirely wood panelled and made Margery feel like she was in an extremely spacious coffin.

'Mrs Butcher-Bakers!' Nigel beamed at them from the sofa in the corner, looking utterly relaxed, a bottle of wine in front of him and three glasses.

Margery had never been able to get used to the sight of him out of his police uniform and the sight of his knobby knees poking out of cargo shorts was almost too much. He had obviously been using the course today, and was still wearing soft spike golf shoes and a smart polo shirt.

'Hello Nigel,' Clementine smiled as they sat down on the sofa opposite him and made themselves comfortable. 'You're looking well.'

'I'm feeling well, thank you Clem.' Nigel smiled at them both. 'The wonders of retirement. You should both think about it.'

'The kitchen would burn down to the ground without Margery at the helm,' Clementine said. 'And that would just be me doing the toaster in the morning.'

Nigel guffawed. It was nice to see him so happy.

He poured them each a glass of wine and then cleared his throat. 'I heard on the grapevine…' he began. Margery knew immediately that the grapevine would be his wife Mary, who still worked at Dewstow police station as a receptionist. 'That you were involved in an altercation earlier.'

'Yes?' Margery said, as Clementine nodded. She sipped from her glass waiting for him to continue. 'How do you know that?'

'Eyes in high places,' Nigel said, and smiled in a way that told Margery he knew much more than he was letting on. He cleared his throat again. 'Well, I suppose I'm being nosey really,' he continued, taking a sip from his own drink. 'But I wondered what had been said. Did Mark Wilkinson say what was going on?'

'No,' Margery said, wondering where this was all going. 'Not really. He said that we weren't to get involved though, so I hope you're not going to ask us to.'

'Hmmm,' Nigel hummed to himself, reaching up to his face to stroke the moustache that was no longer there.

'You must have a reason to have asked us to meet you,' Clementine said. 'Not just for a gossip. Do you know who the body belonged to?'

'From what I heard the police are baffled by it,' Nigel explained. 'You say body but… And this is crude but… well… the head was bludgeoned. Something very nasty must have happened to that poor person. Their ribcage was caved in, they had probably been killed by great force – at least that's what the forensic people said.'

Margery found herself gasping and clutching her own chest as the full picture of the person's death arrived in her mind. There had been so much of it in the last few years, all much too close for comfort. She took a deep breath and tried one of the grounding techniques their therapist had taught her after the horrible incident the summer before last when they had witnessed the mayor of the sleepy holiday town they were staying in claw at his own throat as he died, asphyxiating at the table across from them in a hotel restaurant.

She tried to think of a calm place where she could relax, and in her mind's eye she could imagine the hammock in her grandparents' garden where she used to spend time as a child. Imagined the cool breeze on a warm day as it blew through the trees above her.

Sometimes, however, this technique would not work and instead of the garden her brain would transport her to her grandmother's kitchen instead, and she would be acutely aware that she would never see it, or her grandmother ever again. Today, however, it did work, and she felt the pressure in her chest ease a little. Enough to continue the conversation.

'I know,' Nigel winced as he broke the silence that had fallen over them all. Margery opened her eyes, feeling a bit better. 'Grim, isn't it? But it got me thinking. Why hasn't anyone come forward to claim they know who it is? This is a small community. A missing person case is a big deal... and yet...' He trailed off, lost in his own thoughts.

'What do you mean?' Clementine asked. Margery couldn't find the words yet. She was still recovering from her disgust at his description of the body. 'Who do you think it is?'

'If I knew that I'd tell the police,' Nigel said with a tut. 'But from what Mary said there's some confusion about it all.' He lowered his voice to a whisper and Margery found herself leaning in to listen. 'People don't just disappear. Not in this day and age, with phones and computers and social media. They didn't twenty or thirty years ago either. There was still CCTV then of course; it's everywhere these days. We're being watched right now probably.' He gestured up to the corner of the bar and though Margery couldn't see anything there, she still felt a shiver go down her spine. 'Someone must know who that body is.'

'Why are we here?' Margery asked, her voice feeling small under Nigel's gaze.

'I know you've told the police you won't get involved but, well... it's obvious that you will at some point.' Nigel smiled again. 'You always do. So I thought I'd lend a hand in your investigation.'

There was a long pause as they processed his words. They had already been warned away from the case by Officer Wilkinson and Margery and Clementine had both agreed to obey him. Margery wondered what on Earth Nigel was playing at.

'We really aren't trying to be involved,' Clementine said breezily. 'Honestly. We've got no intention of it.'

'I know you don't,' Nigel said. 'But it will probably happen, won't it? You can't help yourselves! And when you're ready I can get you into the police station to do some digging. You can find out what they know and in doing so you can figure out what happened.'

'Why don't you do it?' Clementine asked him. 'If you think it would be so easy? Or you could get Mary to rummage around in there.'

'If Mary or I got caught doing something like that, it would end very badly for us,' Nigel explained. 'Mary would lose her job and I might lose my pension. It makes sense for you to try. I can help you get into the building and guide you around the alarms and cameras.'

'What about our pensions?' Margery said. 'We could lose our jobs too! What about Symon?' Margery suddenly remembered Ceri-Ann's police officer boyfriend and Nigel's former number two. 'Can't he help you?'

'Symon's applied to train as a detective.' Nigel's face lit up at the mention of his protégé. 'Getting caught sneaking about could affect his career. He's doing very well at the moment, all told. It would be a shame for anything to go wrong for him.'

'Do you not think Officer Wilkinson can solve it?' Margery said. 'He seems very keen to win his stripes and he certainly doesn't want our help, in any way, shape or form.'

'I can see I'm not going to be able to convince you,' he said, picking up his wine glass again. 'It's just... I can't explain it. Mary said they've been going through old missing persons reports all day at the station. I just feel like there's something more to it all.'

'When will the autopsy come back?' Clementine said. Margery could feel her interest piquing, and realised with a sinking feeling that they might well be about to be dragged into something once again. 'And how does everyone know? It's not been in the news yet.'

'I don't think there will be much to autopsy, a DNA test is more like it,' Nigel said. 'But anyway, it's all over social media.'

'The Dewstow Facebook Community page has been going spare about it,' Clementine said, stroking her chin with her fingers. 'People are saying it's the body of that missing Ittonvale School PE teacher.'

'I think we're going to find out sooner rather than later,' Nigel said gently. 'This is what I mean about it being a big deal; you can't move on the high street for missing posters with Miss Hawthorne's face on them. If you had a friend or family member go missing, and then this body appeared, wouldn't you have been up the police station already to see if it's them?'

'They might have moved away,' Margery suggested. 'People move all the time, and if it's been that long then it's much more likely.'

'Perhaps,' Nigel said. But he didn't look convinced. 'I wonder if there are more bodies under the playground. If I were still in charge, I'd have them rip the whole lot up, all the playgrounds. And the sports grounds, every bit of it, anything that was built around the same time. Check we haven't got a serial killer on our hands.'

He suddenly looked sad. Margery imagined the wave of nostalgia that had washed over him at the memory of being on the force.

'Nigel,' she said gently, 'are you sure this isn't just a way for you to still feel involved?'

'Yes,' Clementine agreed, 'retirement can't be that boring yet.'

'I just think it's strange,' he said, but he couldn't look either of them in the eye.

'It certainly is,' Clementine said, 'but it doesn't need our help, and neither do you.'

They sipped their drinks in silence. Nigel seemed mollified by Clementine's words. Margery wondered how the police were getting on with it all. Surely they must have some sort of DNA testing they could do? No, it was much better to leave a couple of dinner ladies out of it.

'Do you know Mr Redburn?' Margery asked Nigel, trying to sound innocent. 'He has a golf membership here.'

'I don't think so,' Nigel said, his brow furrowing. 'I haven't been a member long though, only since I retired last year. You'd be better off asking one of the old timers. Is he a friend?'

Margery nodded at the same time Clementine shrugged. Nigel looked between them both in interest.

–

They stopped at the front desk on the way out, where they waited for a member of staff. The hotel reception was a big airy room, and the wind blowing in through the open front doors was giving Margery a chill.

She thought about the warning they'd received earlier from Officer Wilkinson. The police must worry that they were about to jump in and do something crazy each time something like this happened. It was a wonder that their faces weren't on a wanted poster down at the station. Perhaps they were. Margery had not been in there for a while.

'He needs to do his own dirty work,' Clementine said, tapping her fingers on the wooden top of the counter, more distractedly than impatiently. Her face wore the faraway look she sometimes had when she was thinking about suggesting they dive into something feet first or break into a locked building. 'Honestly, what does he take us for?'

'We do have a track record now,' Margery said, with a grimace. 'I'm surprised Officer Wilkinson hasn't set up a watch outside our house.'

'Well, from the sounds of it, he couldn't watch a snail without it eluding him,' Clementine said, the tapping increasing. 'Nigel knows we aren't doing any of that now, looking into murders and the like. It's always backfired on us whenever we've got involved. Remember when we accused the wrong person last year! I thought we'd never hear the end of it. I bet that playground body turns out to be that poor missing teacher and this whole affair thing will be much easier than anything else we've solved. We'll have all the answers we need before we know it, you wait and see.'

The receptionist finally returned from the back room and sat down at the desk, giving Margery and Clementine her best customer service grin.

'I'm so sorry to keep you waiting,' she said, clacking at the computer keys to get it to turn back on. 'What can I do for you?'

'We would like to know about one of your golfing customers,' Clementine said jovially, leaning on the counter with one arm.

'Are they a relative?' the receptionist asked, raising an eyebrow but quickly returning to the passive face she had worn before.

Clementine said yes at the same time Margery instinctively shook her head.

'Unfortunately, I can't disclose any information on our members,' she explained, not unkindly. But her voice was firm.

'Can you not tell us anything?' Clementine asked. 'His wife thinks he's here.'

'No, I can't.' The receptionist smiled, but it was a shallow interpretation of the one she had given them on arrival, and a clear message to leave.

Chapter Five

Whenever they decided to do anything like this, Margery thought to herself idly as she prepared the sprouts for lunchtime, it always seemed to involve climbing through a window or throwing themselves in front of a car and this time she was putting her foot down. After their small defeat at the reception desk last night, Clementine had performed a spectacular U-turn overnight on Nigel's terrible idea to break into the police station. Margery couldn't for the life of her work out why.

'No,' she told Clementine for the third time today. 'We aren't going to risk getting arrested on a whim for Nigel.'

'Come on, Margery, it'll be a bit of fun!' Clementine grinned. 'They won't arrest us. Just shout at us a bit.'

'They will arrest us,' Margery scoffed. 'Or worse.'

'The country club idea seems doable though,' Gloria said from her spot cutting up cucumbers and tomatoes for the salad bar. They were piled all around her as though she had fallen into the vegetable section of a supermarket and hadn't been able to escape.

'Does it?' Margery said in surprise.

'Yes,' Gloria nodded. 'As long as we can all plan a way to be there at the same time. It shouldn't be too hard to find something out. You could even ask Nigel if he wants to help. That will stop him being bored, won't it?'

'I think it's best we leave him out of this,' Margery said. 'I really don't like the idea of any of the police getting wind of Nigel contacting us about their business, and he was much too eager to tell us all their secrets last night.'

'They're digging it all up!' Ceri-Ann called from her makeshift seat on the windowsill, interrupting the conversation.

Margery didn't know how she had managed to clamber up to the window in her condition, but she was dangling both of her swollen feet into the food wash sink. She suspected that Karen and Sharon may have boosted her up there while she had been distracted in the dry store ordering next week's deliveries.

The team rushed from their workplaces to look at where Ceri-Ann was gesticulating. Through the kitchen window Margery could see the police supervising the digging, which had begun again in full force. They had taken the body away of course – they had done that very quickly the previous morning – but as Nigel had predicted, Officer Wilkinson was continuing to oversee the excavation across the playground and beyond. The entire thing was a criss-cross nightmare of yellow police hazard tape.

Margery dreaded to think what this meant for the dinner lady team. It would be even harder to keep students and teachers away from the canteen after hours now, let alone during the rest of the day. Usually, they were left alone unless it was lunch hour, or someone had forgotten to book a tea trolley. But since the discovery of the body, they had never been so popular. Already today Mrs George had, 'just popped in to see if you were going to have jacket potatoes on at lunchtime,' a clearly rehearsed question which she had asked without even looking Margery in the eye. Instead, she had spent the entire conversation half looking out of the window running across the canteen to see what was going on outside. It was infuriating.

And that was without the students' involvement, which was even more annoying than Margery could have ever imagined. The gang of Year Eleven students who had plagued Margery and Clementine last year had started arriving early to try and film through the window for their TikTok channel. Amelia had asked Margery and Clementine if they would please guest star on their podcast – *That's So Spooky* – again, but they had managed to dissuade her so far.

Gloria had brought in a copy of the local paper that morning and they had all read the ominous headline: 'Body found on school grounds, police search begins'.

Margery supposed it had made a slightly more interesting change from their normal kitchen chatter, which for the last six months had mostly revolved around a pregnancy phone app Clementine had bought to track Ceri-Ann's pregnancy for her. No one was sure what was wrong with it. Clementine swore she had got it from the normal app store, but it had done away with the usual baby size comparisons of fruit and was using much stranger comparisons. From the iris of an eye to a bottle of ketchup, and once – inexplicably – a Tesco 'Just Ham' sandwich. Last Friday, the app had told them happily that the baby was the size of an IKEA pendant lampshade.

'Do you think there'll be another body under it?' Gloria whispered as they watched the digger crack and pull up another chunk of concrete and soil, dragging it up easily like a spoon running through the top of a crème brûlée. Sharon began to wail at the sight.

'It's alright Sharon,' Karen said in a soothing tone while patting her on the shoulder. 'Skeletons are good luck, aren't they? Anyway, we've all got a skeleton, haven't we? There's nothing to be frightened of at all. Teeth are just bones that live in your head.'

Sharon just sobbed harder at that, but before they could try and console her, they were interrupted by the canteen door opening. Mr Barrow and the stranger who had been with Rose in the office stood in the kitchen doorway. Mr Barrow was obviously showing him around. Mr Barrow looked worried, Margery thought. His red hair was not neatly slicked back as it usually was, and he had forgotten to put on his cufflinks that morning.

'And this is our canteen of course,' he said, gesturing to the kitchen. Margery watched as the sleeves of his shirt flapped around his wrists in an upsetting manner. 'All state of the art of course.' He gave a nervous chuckle, while the other man scribbled on his clipboard and examined the ancient six burner hob, which was old enough that Margery suspected it had been rolled in second hand from some historical monument or other when the school had been built. 'Oh, and this is Margery, Mr Monroe. She's our kitchen manager. Margery, this is Mr Monroe, he's ahh… well…'

'As Mr Barrow kindly explained in the assembly yesterday, I'm an independent auditor hired by the board of governors. You can call me Richard,' Richard Monroe said in a squeaky voice, stepping forwards to grasp Margery by the hand with his skinny arm, and giving a firm shake. His cold bony fingers cut into the flesh on her palm. 'Now, tell me Margery, where do you keep your risk assessments?'

He cast an eye at the rest of the team who were still congregated by the kitchen window speechlessly watching him. Margery suddenly realised how strange and unprofessional the entire gathering must look as they gaggled in a group.

'I keep all our health and safety things in my office,' she said, gesturing down the hallway past the walk-in fridge. Richard nodded, his jowls moving with his head. He had the face of a person who enjoyed a sherry or two down at the club house after a round of golf, his face so wrinkled that it could have used a good iron.

'If you could get all your paperwork ready for me, someone from my team will come by at the end of the day to check it all over, and then I'm sure I'll be back over the next week or so to ask you all a few questions,' Richard said, making another note on his clipboard. The fountain pen making flourishes that told Margery that the kitchen was the very least of his concerns. 'Right, Mr Barrow, are we going to visit the Design Technology department next, before lunchtime?'

Mr Barrow nodded weakly and they left, leaving the dinner lady team to stare at each other with concern.

'What was that about?' Gloria asked, as the rest of the team got back to work. All except Ceri-Ann who continued to stare out of the window at the police's progress. 'He isn't really going to come and watch us work, is he? Surely they must have better things to watch than us peeling onions.'

'I suppose it depends on why they're here,' Margery explained. 'It's all a bit odd, what do you think he's really looking for?'

'With the audit?' Gloria asked. 'Well, it's obviously to see if everything's running properly, but I can't understand why.'

'It's because of Mr Weaver's death,' Seren piped up from where she was breaking eggs into the large stand mixer for the Victoria sponge cake. 'Rose said the governors hired him to check the safety of the school. Rose is livid, she said it's going to interfere with our Easter holiday plans.'

'Why?' Gloria asked.

'Because we were supposed to be trying to visit every theme park in the country for my hen do,' Seren explained, her face falling sadly. 'Now she's got to stay here and support Mr Barrow.'

'No, I mean why did the governors hire him?' Gloria asked. 'Surely they're better off waiting for OFSTED to arrive?'

'Maybe they're trying to pre-empt whatever they think OFSTED will find,' Clementine said grimly.

'Well, all I know is that Rose says it's ruining my hen party, because we're only going to manage to get to Thorpe Park and Peppa Pig World,' Seren said, with an ease that told Margery she didn't really agree.

Margery was already sick of Seren's upcoming nuptials to Gary the security guard, though she had tried not to show it. Since Rose had started to involve herself in the planning, the wedding had evolved from sensible civil union in a registry office to an elaborate festival of events. Worse still, when Seren was asked questions about her own wedding by members of the catering team, she was unable to answer them. Margery had a sinking feeling that Rose was planning the whole thing, and she dreaded what the final result would look like. Mrs George, the head of English, had already been down last week to demand

Margery share the canapé menu with her, and Margery had been too afraid to ask her why. She worried that their gentle truce with the English department might come to a sudden and bloody end if Rose had involved them in Seren's wedding too. The apocalyptic fallout from Mrs George using shop-bought cakes during the Christmas bake sale competition long forgiven, Margery didn't want to go back to arguing with Mrs George about why she needed to fill in a trolley needed form every time they had an after-school meeting.

'And obviously the body they found has made everything worse,' Seren continued. 'Mr Barrow thinks this might be really terrible for the school.'

'And terrible for our plans,' Rose said, dramatically swooping into the kitchen and causing everyone to jump out of their skins. She picked her way through in her heels, helping herself to water from the hot water boiler, filling her mug and lifting the herbal tea bag by the string in and out to help it steep. 'Has Seren told you all? We were going to be the first school staff to ride every ride at Thorpe Park. And now look at us: reduced to nothing.'

'I'm sure that's been done before, there's billions of schools in the country. Someone must have done it,' Clementine scoffed. 'No need to call the Guinness book of world records.'

Rose tutted, but she didn't even correct Clementine's mad exaggeration, continuing to swirl the tea bag in the cup by the string.

'You're looking stressed Rose,' Margery said, 'is everything all right?'

Rose grimaced. 'As you can probably tell, I'm not having the easiest of weeks, Mrs Butcher-Baker.' Rose smoothed her silver bob back behind her ears. She joined them properly, leaning back against the sink where Ceri-Ann was sitting with an exasperated huff. 'God knows how we'll get through the inspection with the children the way they are – terrible. And don't get me started on the teachers. I've had to get Mr Knight to take down his entire classroom display. He just couldn't understand why *Saturn Devouring His Son* was inappropriate for the art room walls.'

Margery agreed with Rose that the painting depicting the Titan biting the head off a child might not be quite appropriate for a school inspection.

'We'll do our best in the canteen,' Margery said, trying to reassure her. Rose looked worn out, with the sort of exhaustion that only usually showed around exam season. They were a few months away from that yet. Easter half term was on the horizon, but there were still a few weeks to go.

'I know you will,' Rose said, but as she brought her hand to rub her forehead, Margery was convinced she didn't believe her own words. 'And you're still on for the swimming gala rescheduling? Please tell me you are, you have no idea how many strings I've had to pull to get it sorted, missing trophy or not. But we need the money, especially now.' Rose lowered her voice to a faint hiss. 'The school is having to pay to have every bit of that school tarmac all ripped up, including pavements, and twice as fast as that single playground was supposed to be done – all the builders are on overtime. It's going to cost a fortune. James is beside himself.'

'But have they found any more bodies?' Clementine asked, misreading the room. Rose groaned and glared at her, as if she were interrupting a very private conversation and not chatting openly in the middle of the kitchen.

'Don't even get me started on that!' she said, turning back to Margery. 'I told James we should have spent the money on new library books in the first place and then none of this would have happened. Why are you asking? What stupid thing are you planning to do?'

'Nothing to do with the body!' Clementine scoffed before Margery could even get a word out. 'We... er... well... we may or may not have a stupid thing planned for something else.'

'The country club?' Rose smirked. 'To see if your friend's husband is where he says he is?'

'How did you...?'

'You're not very quiet people,' Rose said.

Clementine nodded in understanding as Gloria laughed.

'I don't think your plan will have many legs the way you're thinking of going about it.'

'No,' Margery agreed. 'We can't just waltz in there, can we?'

Rose's face lit up in a grin. She put her mug down next to Ceri-Ann, reached into the folder she was holding under her arm and pulled out a glossy magazine, holding it up with her other hand to show the model in the white dress on the cover. 'You can if you're planning a wedding.'

Chapter Six

Their tiny kitchen at home was much too small for the frivolities going on inside it and they'd had to bring the garden chairs into the kitchen, so everyone had some-where to sit without their neighbours overhearing the planning. Sharon and Gloria had still ended up standing around the kitchen table, there not being quite enough room to also drag in the living room chairs. Ceri-Ann had used all her graphic design skills to print off an A3 copy of the country club's blueprints, though where she had got them from Margery had been too afraid to ask. They were using the pieces from the battered monopoly set that they usually kept in the living room bureau, as stand ins for what their real-life positions would be. A small fight had nearly broken out when Karen and Sharon both wanted to be the Boot.

'So,' Clementine began, once they had written most of the details down on the whiteboard. It was so full of scribbles that most of it was barely legible, and Clem-entine kept having to squint closely at it before reading anything out. 'Karen and Sharon, you'll be pretending to be interested in joining the gym…'

'While getting to try all the fantastic equip-ment,' Sharon beamed over Karen's shoulder. 'Honestly, Dewstow Leisure Centre's only got one treadmill now – and it only goes two speeds. It's easier to run on the spot.'

Clementine gave them a withering look before continuing. Karen and Sharon were often the reason for a withering look in the small canteen kitchen. They were both in their late thirties, with the same mid-length mousey brown hair with blonde highlights and the same taste in outfits. They often joked that they were 'sisters from another mister', though Gloria usually referred to them as 'the twins from the shining'.

Clementine continued, 'Ceri-Ann and Gloria, you'll be having Ceri-Ann's baby shower afternoon tea in the hotel restaurant. See what you can find out there.'

They had already hosted Ceri-Ann a real baby shower the month before. The entire school staff had been invited to the canteen for cake and cups of tea and coffee, with everyone bringing gifts and vouchers for Ceri-Ann and the baby, which at the time had been the size of a bag of satsumas according to the app. It seemed like a very long time ago now.

'Will they not think it's weird that there's only two of us?' Gloria asked. Ceri-Ann looked up from her phone and shrugged.

'Maybe I don't have any mates, mate,' Ceri-Ann said. 'Ooh or we'll say you're my mum!'

'I'm only ten years older than you!' Gloria scoffed, but then wrinkled her forehead, thinking about it. 'I guess I am your work mum anyway. All right, then.'

'What if you give birth before then?' Karen asked, quite reasonably Margery thought. Ceri-Ann narrowed her eyes at her anyway.

'Then it'll be a welcome to the baby party!' Gloria said, patting Ceri-Ann on the shoulder. Ceri-Ann had gone very quiet, and she looked as though her thoughts were elsewhere.

'Seren, you're with us,' Clementine continued. 'We'll pretend to plan your wedding and Rose will advise us through the special spy equipment Ceri-Ann has provided…'

'Bluetooth headphones from Argos,' Ceri-Ann said, holding up the set so they could all look at them. They all oohed.

'I don't understand why Rose can't come in with us?' Seren asked, twisting the engagement ring around her finger. 'She's basically planned the wedding anyway. I don't even know what flowers we're having. She keeps telling me that it's a surprise. All I know is that we're going to Alton Towers the week before and we've got fast passes for all the rides.'

'Rose is a member of the golf club, so they'll recognise her if she turns up with you. It might invite unwanted attention,' Clementine explained. 'But it means she knows the layout of the place so one of us can sneak off and look at their records. That's the plan anyway.'

'I still don't think this is a good idea,' Margery found herself squeaking for the third time in the hour. 'Will it not be obvious that Clementine and I aren't real wedding planners?'

'We'll dress up.' Clementine waved a hand dismissively at Margery's plain cardigan and linen dress combination. 'We'll wear wedding planner coats or something.'

'What on earth does a wedding planner coat look like?' Margery asked, but before Clementine could answer there was a knock at the door. The dinner lady team looked around at each other. Margery felt her mouth go dry.

'Who could that be?' she found herself asking, as Clementine got up to open the door, dusting biscuit crumbs from her lap. 'We're all here.'

'If it's a ghost, hit them with that big gardening book Dawn gave us,' she hissed, gesturing to the tome on gardening that their neighbour had left the last time she'd visited to complain about Crinkles digging up her garden.

'I don't think you can hit ghosts,' Seren whispered back, wringing her hands together. 'Aren't they transparent? The book will fly right through them.'

'Sometimes... but I saw a film where they were all around you, and you couldn't see them unless you wore special glasses... but they could see you all the time,' Ceri-Ann said knowingly. 'And then someone let them out of the special ghost prison cells and then the ghosts murdered everyone.'

Seren gasped, putting her hands to her mouth as Clementine finally left to open the door. She disappeared through the living room and then reappeared a minute later with Mr Fitzgerald, a large binder under his arm and his dog Jason on a piece of string acting as a lead by his feet. Jason immediately plodded under the table to hunt for crumbs. Pumpkin glared at him from her seat on the rocking chair but didn't bother to get up.

Mr Fitzgerald was a very well-known fixture of Dewstow, having owned the local oddities shop since before most townspeople could remember. His age had never been determined, but he'd been old since Margery had been young, and that in itself gave him a mysterious air.

'Hello, all,' he said, stumbling into the kitchen with his long legs and throwing off his travelling cape onto the back of the chair Clementine had vacated.

Jason seemed to realise that Pumpkin was in charge, and meekly lay down under the table next to Mr Fitzgerald's Doc Martens. Mr Fitzgerald put the folder he was carrying down on the table. Margery felt sure she could smell the faint aroma of whisky as he made himself comfortable in the chair across from her, his long beard almost drooping into Gloria's teacup unnoticed.

He gave them all a wide smile. 'I must say, it's a pleasure to see you all outside of school grounds and away from the shop for once. We can have a proper natter. Ceri-Ann, I'm very much looking forward to the Taylor Swift concert.'

'Oh, no worries,' Ceri-Ann smiled back at him.

He sat back, lacing his fingers together and began to hum to himself tunelessly.

'Can I get you a drink?' Clementine asked, not forgetting her manners even in the strange circumstance of the visit.

'No, thank you,' Mr Fitzgerald said, eyeing the whiteboard scribblings, apparently with great interest. Margery was sure they were just indecipherable enough to look innocent. 'I've been at the Bell and Hope too long tonight. No need for any more.' He put a hand on the folder on the table. 'I've come to show you something.'

He looked around at the rest of the team as if wondering if he could talk freely with them there. Margery suddenly remembered that Mr Fitzgerald was a member of the school council, and though they had known him a long time she wasn't sure he would like members of the school estates team planning something so strange. Even if it was outside work hours. As if reading her mind, Gloria cleared her throat.

'Well, I think we've discussed all we can about Ceri-Ann's baby shower, haven't we?' she said, picking up her handbag from where it had been swinging on the back of Clementine's chair. It was a lie made of the truth, so

Margery didn't feel bad about it. 'We'd all better get back home. I've got to feed Caroline's snakes anyway.'

They all followed her lead and left together in a group, the gaggle of hushed voices disappearing out through the living room and outside.

'What did you have to show us?' Margery asked when she was sure they were alone again, her voice unable to hide the confusion she felt at Mr Fitzgerald's presence in their home on a random Tuesday evening.

Mr Fitzgerald pointed to the ring binder folder he'd set down in front of him. Margery stared at it. Clementine leaned forwards, sliding her chair closer to the table.

'I thought I'd give you a hand in your investigation,' Mr Fitzgerald said, gesturing at the folder. For a moment Margery wondered how he knew about their infiltration of the hotel, and then realised that he was not talking about that at all.

'We're not investigating the body found in the playground—' she began to say, but he cut her off with a dismissive waving gesture. He turned the folder to face them and then opened it so they could see what was inside, revealing row upon row of neat handwriting. The first column was names and the next dates.

'Well, I'm sure that you're already investigating the missing Ittonvale School teacher, Miss Hawthorne? No?' They shook their heads. Margery had seen the 'missing' posters about her, and heard the rumours floating around the school, but she hadn't really paid it much mind. Mr Fitzgerald didn't seem perturbed by their response. 'This is Dewstow and Ittonvale's missing persons record,' he explained, seeing the confused looks on their faces. He eyed them carefully, his beard drooping onto the table and covering the top of the pages. 'Well, not official you see. But I've been keeping track for years.'

'What do you mean?' Margery said, unable to keep the surprise from her voice. 'Surely there hasn't been that many missing persons?'

'Unfortunately, I think you'll find that there have,' Mr Fitzgerald said, gesturing to the folder. Clementine took the folder and began to rummage through it. Margery found herself leaning away from the book of names and bringing her hands tightly together in her lap. If Mr Fitzgerald was telling the truth, then there were a large number of pages in the folder, and indeed she could see they formed a heavy wedge that rivalled that of a telephone book. Margery felt her eyes widening in shock. Surely there hadn't been that many missing persons in such a small place; it was awful to think about. Where had they all gone?

'Well then, why haven't you given it to the police to look at?' Margery folded her arms. Mr Fitzgerald tutted.

'I'm an anarchist at heart, my dear,' he said. 'Anyway, I can't go telling the police I've got records like this can I? They might come around to the shop and see what else I've got records on.'

'This one's for your dog,' Clementine scoffed, running her fingers over the name, Jason Fitzgerald, carefully written in fountain pen ink. 'And so's this one.'

'Well, he has gone missing a few times,' Mr Fitzgerald shrugged as Clementine continued to flick through the folder. 'That's why there's a return date next to the missing one.'

'We're in here!' Clementine cried, stabbing her finger to the page so severely it nearly tore. 'That's the week we went on holiday last year.'

'I didn't know if you were coming back!' Mr Fitzgerald said.

The fright suddenly went out of the book of names. Lots of the missing persons, if they could really be called that, also had a return date next to their name. In fact, there were only a few true missing persons, and they couldn't be sure from the way Mr Fitzgerald had documented it, that those people hadn't just moved away to another town. Margery suddenly found herself feeling very tired.

'What do you want us to do with this?' she found herself asking. Mr Fitzgerald almost flinched at her tone.

'My dear, I thought it might help you both find the body's owner,' he said, frowning. 'Apologies if I've brought you any distress, that wasn't my intention.'

'No, it's quite alright,' Margery said, wondering whether to explain why she had reacted how she had. 'It's just quite a lot has happened over the last few years, and we thought we'd stay well away from this one. It needs professionals. Forensics and the like.'

Mr Fitzgerald nodded in understanding. 'I see, well you probably won't be interested in my list then. I'll leave it with you though, just in case you change your mind.'

The look on his face told Margery he was entirely sure that they would.

'Do you not think the body was Miss Hawthorne? The missing PE teacher?' Margery asked him, interested to hear his thoughts.

Mr Fitzgerald shook his head. 'Perhaps, but even if it isn't her, I'm sure I would have met them at some point. I've lived here a long time, and I know everyone.'

Margery and Clementine nodded grimly at that.

Chapter Seven

They found themselves outside the Redburn house in Ittonvale just before four o'clock the next day, having managed to get away from work on time, despite the general chaos at the school. For all their planning, they hadn't managed to arrange anything for the hotel until the weekend. They had managed to book everyone in for Saturday, at least, and the days leading up to the event had gone by as normal, although every morning, when they entered the canteen, they found the same group of teachers and estate staff watching the continuing demolition of the playground through the window.

The body was still a hot topic at the school, even with the audit in full swing. Amelia and Oliver and the rest of media studies group B from Year Eleven had continued to film the excavation in the playground on their phones, and Margery didn't have the heart to ask them to stop.

Ceri-Ann had made each of the canteen staff a new email address to book into the hotel for their part of the scheme and Clementine had already forgotten their password. Margery had wondered if they might be suspicious of a wedding planners' email address that began with 'weddingplanners1', but Ceri-Ann had shrugged and said she didn't think they'd even notice. Another very minor thing they had overlooked was that none of them had ever met Mr Redburn and wouldn't know who he was if they bumped into him at the golf course. Margery and Clementine decided that they would go to Mrs Redburn's house after work and ask her for a photograph so they would be able to pick him out of a crowd. Not that Margery thought he would be there. In her opinion, once someone had begun to have suspicions of their partner it could never end well.

Margery drove the car through the wooden driveway gates and onto the gravel in front of the large bay-windowed house. They were on the outskirts of town and the street leading to the house was more of a lane, the nearest neighbour barely visible through the trees lining the front garden. Across the road lay nothing but fields and woodland that led back to Dewstow by footpaths carved in the ground over the years by hikers, these in turn leading to the clearing where Margery and Clementine had found a body resting under a tree the previous year.

Margery shook the thought away. It wouldn't do to relive that memory right now. Both Margery and Clementine had benefited greatly from the counselling they had once a month, but Margery wondered if it was possible to ever really forget a thing like that. She had learned to deal with the feelings the memories brought, even how to cope with them, but it would have been better to never have lived them at all. Though she found that the more time passed, the further away everything seemed to get in the rear-view mirror, until she could pretend that it was all okay.

'I've been thinking about that list Mr Fitzgerald gave us, Margery,' Clementine said as they clambered out of the car. 'Some of the names on the list were still unaccounted for. Surely there must be town records of people. Census results and the like? Maybe we could cross reference and see if any of them are likely to be the body they found.'

'I thought we weren't getting involved?' Margery reminded her, shutting the car door and turning towards the house.

She could see now why Evelyn hadn't seemed impressed with their own small home and garden. The Redburn house would have been an impressive family home when it was built, and it still was. Margery was sure that a big house like that would be worth a small fortune now. It was merely a stone's throw from Ittonvale town centre and Ittonvale School. Although it must have been quite old, the building was in fine condition. One of the Redburn family obviously enjoyed gardening – the grass lawn to the sides of the property was laid with sleek lines that clearly took time and effort to perfect. Much unlike their own grass at home after Clementine had dragged the lawn mower across it.

'I just think it's interesting,' Clementine said. 'And it makes a change from a fresh dead body, doesn't it?' Margery winced at the thought.

Evelyn opened the front door. She had heard the sound of the car driving over the stones and came out to greet them, folding her arms over her chest and eyeing them warily. When Clementine had rang her to tell her they were coming, she had not seemed best pleased. Margery wondered whether she really wanted to know where her husband was going when he said he was elsewhere. Maybe Mrs Mugglethwaite had talked her into it, and she felt like she had to entertain these unwelcome visitors. However she really felt about it, she invited them inside anyway. Margery took a moment to admire the open entrance hall before Evelyn led them through the dark living room and into the bright conservatory. The open doors lead out to the sprawling expanse of green grass, a summerhouse over to one corner and a pond in the other.

Evelyn disappeared for a moment and then brought out a pitcher of fresh lemonade and put it on the table with the glasses. She sat down opposite them and helped herself.

'What can I do for you?' she asked as she poured. Margery watched the beads of condensation running down the glass pitcher and onto the place mat underneath it. She could also see Evelyn's feet tapping a beat onto the floor through the glass table, although Margery decided that she was probably doing it unconsciously.

'We wanted to know a bit more about your husband so we can help you with your issue,' Clementine told her. 'We realised we don't know what he looks like.'

Evelyn inhaled a deep breath. There was a creak from somewhere in the main house and Margery looked over her shoulder, feeling nerves settle into her bones. Though she didn't know why.

'He's here,' Evelyn whispered. 'So you'll have to keep it down.'

She got up and took a picture from the bookcase behind her, passing it over to Clementine. She looked at it and then passed it to Margery. The photograph showed an older gentleman with white hair sitting next to Evelyn. They were both dressed for a formal event. Evelyn was smiling widely, while Mr Redburn didn't look even half as pleased, though Margery couldn't quite put her finger on why that was. He wasn't frowning as such, but he didn't seem like he really wanted to be sat at the table with Evelyn's arms thrown around his neck either.

'My birthday party last July. Don hates having his photo taken,' Evelyn said, smiling at the photograph. 'Look, I think this might be a mistake...'

'What might be a mistake?' Mr Redburn appeared from behind Evelyn. He stepped down the stair from the living room into the conservatory and held out his hand to Margery and Clementine.

'Don Redburn. Nice to meet you,' he said as he shook Clementine's hand with gusto. 'Are you the ladies from the church?'

'Yes,' Clementine said, the lie slipping past her lips easily. 'We're trying to get your wife to join... er... the church committee. We're doing a huge bake sale, cherry bakewells, Victoria sponges... er... banana loaf... chocolate tiffin...'

Margery gave her a nudge under the table to stop her naming cakes. Don didn't seem to notice, though Evelyn's eyes flicked over them, and her face pulled back worriedly.

'Gosh, you can certainly try,' Mr Redburn smiled at them both. It was a warm smile. He was much more charismatic than Margery had thought he would be from the photograph, though she supposed that she hadn't known what to expect really. Maybe some spineless person who cheated on his wife. She supposed his charisma could make him much more likely to cheat, or at least make it easier. He was of average height and build with shoulders that had probably been strapping in his youth but were fading now, his stomach jutting over the waistband of his cargo shorts made more pronounced by his tucked in linen shirt. Mr Redburn looked to Evelyn and continued. 'You should consider it, dear. It would be good for you to get out of the house a bit more. Evelyn is a real homebody, aren't you darling?'

Evelyn gave him a nod and he reached down and gave her shoulder a squeeze.

'Right, I'd better be off,' Mr Redburn said, 'a late afternoon spot of golf. Don't worry about food darling, I'll eat at the club.'

Before they could say much more than a brief goodbye, he had gone, leaving them in an awkward silence. From the other side of the house, they heard the front door slam.

'You are still alright for us to investigate?' Margery asked Evelyn as soon as she was sure that Mr Redburn had actually left. 'We really don't need to if you've changed your mind. You seemed to be reconsidering a moment ago.'

'Yes,' she said, crossing her arms across her chest as tightly as a straitjacket. Her feet shuffled again underneath the table and Margery watched them return to the rhythmic tapping motion she'd noticed earlier. 'Well, I suppose I need to get to the bottom of it. Where could he possibly be going?'

'Are you sure he isn't going to the golf club?' Clementine asked.

Evelyn gave a small smile. She stood and beckoned for them to follow her back into the main house and through the kitchen. Evelyn opened a door, revealing a cool utility room where she must have been doing her ironing before Margery and Clementine had arrived. The ironing board and iron were still out waiting. She opened a cupboard and showed them what was inside it.

'I took his golf clubs out of his car last week,' she said. They all looked at the caddy. 'And he hasn't noticed yet.'

'Gosh,' Margery said. 'And you really have no idea where he's going?'

'None,' Evelyn said, her voice small and frightened.

'We should just follow him now,' Clementine said, gesturing in the direction of the front door. 'He can't have gone far.'

'No,' Evelyn said quickly. 'He mustn't see you following him. Just find out for certain if he's going to the club or not.'

'All right,' Margery said, though she knew Clementine would like nothing more than to disappear off into the ether, barrelling after Don in their car. 'We have a plan for that.'

Evelyn nodded, breathing an unmistakable sigh of relief.

'So, you'll really do it then?' she asked. Margery and Clementine shared a look. Margery could see the excitement in Clementine's eyes already at the prospect of starting another case.

'Yes,' Margery said finally. Clementine smiled at her.

'One hundred pounds you said it was, didn't you?' Evelyn reached into the handbag hanging from the back of the utility room door and pulled out her purse. 'I went to the cash point just in case you did agree to do it. He won't think to ask about cash if he looks at the bank statement.'

For a second Margery thought about telling her that her money was no good here, but Clementine had already reached out and taken it. Margery supposed that even if it all ended up being a simple open and shut case, there would still be petrol and other costs involved. She wouldn't mention it for now, but decided that now they were charging for their detective skills they really ought to talk about how official they were planning to make it all. If they were planning to involve the dinner lady team, then they ought to pay them for their services too. At the moment Margery knew that they all jumped in to help for the fun of it, but if this was going to become a paid endeavour then they should pay fairly for people's time.

'How did you both meet?' Margery asked. Clementine leaned in eagerly, her nosiness getting the better of her.

Evelyn smiled as she remembered better times. 'He came over to my mother's house and offered to sort the garden out. He had his own little gardening business then, which grew and grew of course. He sold it a few years ago.' Her eyes shone with the memory as she spoke. 'I just thought he was so handsome. He ended up coming over and doing lots of odd jobs in the house – my mother was beginning to struggle to do it all on her own, you know?' She stopped and smiled, thinking of it.

'I was so bold back then, I just marched straight up to him one day and told him he was going to take me out.' She laughed uproariously, and Margery and Clementine smiled too as her demeanour changed, the worried woman from a moment ago disappearing into the ether. 'And the rest is history really.'

The spell was broken. Evelyn's shoulders slumped back down again. Margery wondered when Don and Evelyn had stopped being happy. If it had happened all at once, or – as she knew was more likely – a trickle at a time.

Chapter Eight

They all pulled up at the country club at eleven on Saturday morning, driving down the long driveway in a convoy and stopping in the same car park. If the club had been expecting a heist, then it would have been particularly obvious what was about to happen. As it was, Margery and Clementine were counting on the fact that they were not expecting one, so that they could achieve what they came to do. She had worried all night about it, and so she hadn't slept well at all. She was concerned that they were overstepping some imaginary line again, as they had done so many times in the past. Clementine had no such concerns.

'It just makes sense,' she assured Margery as they climbed out of the car. 'We're all here for nice, normal reasons that no one could possibly have a problem with. And we're paying for it aren't we?'

'Ceri-Ann and Gloria are paying for their afternoon tea,' Margery said. 'But Karen and Sharon are having a free gym trial. And *we* certainly aren't paying for this wedding planning appointment.'

'That is true,' Clementine rubbed her chin in thought. 'Maybe we should charge Seren for the session as wedding planners.'

'I'm already paying for a venue though,' Seren reminded them as she got out of the back seat of Margery's car. 'Well, it's just a marquee and I don't know where we're going to put it yet, but it won't be as expensive as this place. I bought a new jacket specially because I didn't know how posh it would be and they forgot to take the security tag off.' She raised the sleeves on her new white jacket to show them the metal tag still attached to one arm.

'Gosh, I really don't know how we're going to find anything out here Clem.' Margery wrung her hands together. 'It all seems so silly.'

'We're going to try and spot Mr Redburn while Ceri-Ann and Gloria break into the front desk computer,' Clementine said, not even trying to remove the grin that had spread over her face.

'You just said that there would be nothing but normal reasons for being here!' Margery scoffed.

Clementine clapped her hands together, looking gleeful with all the excitement. 'Perfectly normal… with a few extra steps, Margery!' she said, grabbing her phone out of her bag.

'You all right with them earphones?' Ceri-Ann called over as Clementine handed Margery an earbud. 'Don't forget to put your hair over your ear to cover them!'

'This is a terrible idea,' Gloria said, and Margery began to open her mouth to agree. 'We should just try and steal the computer, save all this messing around eating cakes. We do enough of that at work.'

Margery closed her mouth again. If Gloria was fully on board with the situation, it wouldn't do much good to argue against it. Besides, they were all here now and the plans were all in place.

'I'll eat all the cakes if you feel like that mate,' Ceri-Ann laughed. 'Anyway, we won't be able to carry a computer out in my condition, probs. You'd have to carry it out for me.'

'Oh, now you care about carrying things,' Gloria scoffed. 'Where was that attitude a few weeks ago when you tried to put the potato delivery away? You know you're not supposed to lift anything heavier than an orange while you're pregnant.'

There was no time left for Margery to do any more worrying, now. Instead, she let Clementine connect the phone to the earbuds and dial Rose's number while she watched Gloria and Ceri-Ann head into the club, arguing about the weight of a box of potatoes as they went.

'We'll head in, too,' Karen said, picking up her gym bag. Sharon followed suite. Margery had a sneaking suspicion that they were both only in it to use the gym facilities and had no intention of helping, but the plan was so wishy-washy anyway that she couldn't blame them.

'Hello Rose?' Clementine said, a finger on her earbud as though she was playing the main part in a spy film. 'Come in Rose, are you there? Over.'

'Hello,' Rose said, sounding amused on the other end of the line. 'Of course I'm here! Now shut up and get inside.' Through her earbud, Margery could hear a soft crunching sound and wondered if Rose was eating popcorn while she listened.

'Come on, Seren,' Clementine said. 'You've got to pretend to be the bride now.'

'I am the bride,' Seren said, her voice wobbling with uncertainty.

They made their way across the grounds and into the main building, entering through the large double doors. Karen and Sharon were already checking in at the main desk and a man in sportswear was watching over them as they both filled in a form on a clipboard.

'Where are you?' Rose hissed loudly, causing Margery to wince. Somehow it was even worse to have her inside her head than if she had been standing in front of them, and the voice being in only one ear made her feel out of sorts and unbalanced. She tucked her hair over her ears again.

'This must be the entrance hall, Seren,' Clementine said, loud enough that a few guests waiting to check in turned and looked at them. She winked at Margery, in a way that said she was incredibly pleased with herself. 'You'll be in here in your, er, wedding dress and eating cake in no time!'

'You must be Seren? I believe we spoke over email?' a young woman in a smart black skirt suit said, stepping forwards to greet them. Her blonde hair was slicked back so tightly to her skull that Margery thought it must be horribly uncomfortable, and the perfect ballet style bun must take forever to achieve. She couldn't imagine having to put herself together so properly before work. Even if she had the bun would have been squashed to death by the hairnets that they wore all day.

'Oh yes! Hello Nadine.' Seren took the woman's hand, and they shook. 'Nice to meet you in person.'

'Yes, lovely,' Nadine said, turning to smile at Margery and Clementine. 'You must be Seren's wedding planning team?'

'Yes,' Clementine said, not missing a beat. 'We're Picca-lilli Paula wedding catering... ah, er, but obviously we do much more than catering, hence why we're here! We do it all, tablecloths, champagne glasses... erm... assorted confetti...'

It was too much bluster, but Nadine didn't seem to notice, ignoring Clementine as she rattled off different wedding themed items. Margery heard Rose scoffing over the line.

Karen looked up from the form she was filling in, and gave what she must have thought was an inconspicuous wave.

'Well, we do have our own recommended caterers here,' Nadine was saying, 'and I can't say I've ever heard your name, but of course that's no problem at all.' She smiled widely in the way that Margery associated with estate agents and people who had to tell you a bit of bad news they weren't really sorry about.

'Tell her you're a new business,' Rose's voice hissed into her ear. 'Tell her that Seren wants to see the kitchen.'

'We're a new business,' Margery said, feeling bad about the lie, but acting automatically on Rose's demand. 'We catered a wedding last year and it went so well we decided to open our own company.'

It's not really a lie after all, Margery thought to herself in alarm. After all, they had catered for Rose's huge hen party and their own wedding. And Rose had technically asked them to lend the school kitchen for Seren's wedding. Margery didn't like the idea of owning a real events company though, it seemed much too much hard work.

'Right, that's great,' Nadine said. 'Well, if you'll follow me, I'll show you the kitchens. And then we'll give you the full tour of the ballroom and grounds.'

From across the room, Margery saw Karen give her a thumbs up at the same time as Rose's disembodied voice told her to remember to ask to see where they kept the glassware. She just knew somewhere deep down in her soul that this was all about to go wrong.

Nadine ushered them out of the foyer and led them down one of the long hotel hallways, talking all the time and pointing out different décor that had been left over from the last refurbishment and the history of the photographs on the walls of golfers of times past.

'Outside caterers can use our kitchen equipment for a cost of course,' Nadine said cheerily as she frogmarched them. 'Saves you having to bring your own oven and stove.'

As Rose talked over Nadine, giving instructions in such a rush that Margery would have seemed mad if she were to repeat them all, Margery thought longingly about taking the earbud out and chucking it into the nearest bin. Only the thought of Rose's wrath stopped her from doing so.

Nadine opened a set of double doors and led them into the ballroom. The large room was full of round tables with starched white tablecloths, and wooden chairs tied in ribbon, as though Seren and Gary could turn up and get married immediately. Margery's eyes were drawn to the floor to ceiling windows that took up one entire wall, and were swathed in long cream curtains.

'Mark Twain once said, "golf is a good walk spoiled",' Rose said through the earbud, chomping away on something crunchy again. Margery clenched her teeth tightly together. Rose sounded like she was having the time of her life. 'Ask the woman if champagne is included in the welcome drinks, or if it'll be some ghastly sparkling wine or other. I can't abide cava, Margery. I just simply won't have it. I know it's prepared in the same traditional method as champagne but—'

'That's not what we're here for,' Margery hissed under her breath, interrupting Rose.

Nadine whirled around to stare at her. 'I'm sorry, did you say something?'

'No,' Margery squeaked.

'As I was saying,' Nadine turned back to Seren and Clementine, 'the club is situated on three hundred acres of grounds. Perfect for wedding photos. And we have two guest apartments and a ten-bedroom lodge house only a quarter of a mile away for your guests to stay. The onsite staff can provide breakfast in the morning and night cap drinks in the evening on their return and of course we provide a minibus service at a cost. You and your fiancé will have the bridal apartment of course, which comes with an excellent amenities package and balcony hot tub...'

Her sales pitch was immaculate, Margery thought. Seren was gazing around the large room in awe, and even Clementine was nodding and writing things down on her clipboard.

'Mrs Butcher-Bakers!' Rose demanded over the line. She was in Margery's ear, but she may as well have also been inside Margery's brain. 'Ask her if they charge extra to bring your own Frangelico! It's not a wedding without a hazelnut liquor.'

Margery ignored her, instead following Nadine as she showed them the grand bar across the left wall. The radio attached to the back of her skirt buzzed and Nadine put a finger to her ear. 'Oh gosh, I'll be right there,' she said, her eyes widening in alarm. Margery wondered if Ceri-Ann's plan was working. 'Would you excuse me a moment please ladies?'

Before anyone could say another word, she was already crossing the hall in great strides. She marched out into the hallway again, slamming the door behind her.

'What's happening now?' Rose asked. 'Tell her we'll need a discount on the rooms.'

'Seren isn't really getting married here,' Margery reminded her, feeling thankful that she could finally speak freely to Rose. 'The wedding is in a few months, there's no way this place isn't already booked. You need to stop asking so many questions, there's no way I can ask them all without seeming strange, and you don't even really need to know the answers!'

'I just think we should have the option,' Rose scoffed. 'We can always push the date back if we need to.'

'Who are you talking to?' Clementine asked, arriving at Margery's side, a quizzical look on her face.

'Rose, of course,' Margery spluttered. 'What do you mean—?'

'Oh, I took that out ages ago, couldn't stand her going on and on,' Clementine explained, taking the earbud out of her pocket. 'Do you want the other one so you can listen to her in stereo?'

'No,' Margery said firmly, regretting not having the foresight to join Clementine in a lovely, Rose-free morning.

'Is that Clementine?' Rose asked. 'Get her to Face-Time me this instant so I can see what's happening. I want to see what the ceiling looks like for the wedding photos. I'll hang up now, call me back.'

Margery pulled the earbud out. So much for being spies. So far, all they had managed to do was have a tour of a nice room and look out at a golf course.

'Rose wants you to call her on the video,' Margery said, gesturing to Clementine's bag.

Clementine took her phone out. She struggled to open a video call, clearly unsure of how it worked. Margery found herself looking at all the photographs lining the walls of the ballroom. Many were of black-tie events, dating back decades. A very busy photograph of a largish group stood out to her. The partygoers were lined up in a row in front of the ballroom's huge windows. She peered at the faces until she spotted Evelyn, who smiled radiantly out at her from the middle of the row. Don was on her right, looking about as cheery as he had in the photograph Evelyn had showed them earlier. The bottom of the frame had 'Billy and Vivian Black's Golden Gala 1999' written in gold lettering. Margery assumed that Billy and Vivian were the older couple on the right, standing just in front of everybody else and dressed to the nines, both in fur coats. She scanned the row of faces again and saw Richard the auditor peering out from behind Don and Evelyn. She wondered if they regularly threw such grand events.

Her thoughts were interrupted by Seren finally calling Rose on her own phone after Clementine had clearly given up trying to manage it.

'Hold me up so I can see Seren!' Rose demanded the moment she answered. 'What took you so long?'

'I can't get married here, Rose!' Seren protested, but she held the phone screen up and outward so she could see the room. 'A wedding here probably costs more than ten years of my wages.'

'Where are you?' Clementine asked Rose before she could answer Seren. Margery leaned forwards so she could see the phone screen too. It looked like Rose was in her car, her head wrapped in a white headscarf and her eyes covered by sunglasses. 'You're in the car park, aren't you?'

'Never you mind,' Rose said, ignoring the question entirely. 'Hold the phone up so I can see the room.'

Seren did as she was told, twirling slowly on the spot so Rose could take it all in.

'Ooh, yes, it's lovely, isn't it?' Rose said. Margery folded her arms and wondered what else they could be doing at home instead. Surely a better use of a Saturday morning would be reading a good book in her favourite chair, or finishing crocheting the bear for Ceri-Ann's baby.

'Wait, what does the man look like? Is it Mr Redburn?' Rose asked. Margery couldn't see where she was looking under the sunglasses, but she had turned towards the driver's side window.

'He's older, grey hair, average height...' Clementine rattled off, counting out the very boring details of Don Redburn on her fingers.

'Moustache?' Rose asked.

'Yes?' Margery said curiously. 'Why?'

'He's going to the golf course now,' Rose said, pointing at her window. 'You might be able to confirm if you go after him. Pink polo shirt, you can't miss him.'

Clementine didn't waste a second. She was halfway out of the fire escape before Margery could stop her. Margery fought with herself for a moment internally and then followed as well. At least this would feel like they were doing something. Seren plodded behind them, still on the phone to Rose. From immediately outside the ballroom, they could see the car park and Margery almost laughed to herself at the sight of Rose's huge range rover sat in one of the spaces closest to the club. She spotted the man in pink just as he drove away across the green in a golf cart.

'What are you waiting for?' Rose cried through Seren's phone speaker. 'Get after him!'

Outside the little golf hire building was a line of stationary golf buggies waiting for golf members to use. They jumped into the nearest one, Clementine sat next to her in the front and Seren on the back in the rear-facing passenger seat. Margery fought with the keys, forcing them into the ignition and starting the engine. Their take-off down the course after Don Redburn was nowhere near as graceful as his was, but somehow, they still managed to make it to the green before he disappeared.

'Follow that cart, Margery!' Clementine said, excitedly stabbing a finger towards the buggy in front of them.

'I am,' Margery countered as she followed Don Redburn's cart out onto the golf course, desperately thinking of what they would say when they finally caught up to him. She supposed that they could just say that they were here for a spot of golf, though she wasn't sure how believable that was or why she would chase him down to tell him they were here.

'Oh no,' Seren cried, still holding her phone and clutching onto the golf clubs next to her on the back seat. 'Security are following us!'

Margery turned her head just in time to see the security guard following them in his own cart. Nadine was sat next to him and her charming hostess act was gone. Now she was pointing at them angrily and yelling, though she was too far away for Margery to hear what she was actually shouting.

'Hold on,' Margery called to Clementine and Seren, before turning the cart wildly to follow Mr Redburn. It veered away to the right. The buggy whirred as Margery put her foot down on the accelerator as hard as it would go. A pair of golfers ambled past them and overtook.

'Christ, they're catching up!' Seren cried.

'Seren, please do not swear!' Clementine called. 'Margery, can't you hurry the bloody thing up? We're going to lose him and get caught!'

'I think the buggy is too heavy with all of us on!' Margery cried back.

'Seren, get off!' Clementine reached back to try and poke Seren from the back of the buggy. Seren tried to bat away her hands with her phone. Rose screeched through the speakers.

'Get rid of the clubs Seren!' Margery called, thinking of the extra weight in the back seat.

She clenched her hands tighter around the steering wheel, following the buggy in front determinedly, her knuckles going white. Seren did as Margery asked, pushing the entire bag of clubs off the seat. The buggy sped up a very small amount. Margery turned to see if the security guard was still following them, and saw that they had run over the bag of clubs, the wheels of the pursuing buggy becoming entangled.

'We've lost them!' Clementine cried, turning to Margery in triumph. Margery beamed back. Clementine turned to face forwards again and her face fell into a frown.

'Watch out Margery!'

Margery turned just in time to see the sand bunker coming, but not in time to turn the buggy away. They thumped into the bunker, the impact throwing all of them forwards with a horrible crunch.

Chapter Nine

Once Margery had realised that no one had broken anything, they climbed out of the golf buggy with tremendous effort, so stuck it was in the sand. Seren had come out the best of them, Margery thought, as she watched Seren dust herself off, waiting for them on the side of the bunker. Her position on the back of the buggy had thrown her further out of harm's way, and her trainers would probably not be as full of sand as Margery's poor loafers.

Margery and Clementine followed her with difficulty, Seren reached out and dragged them both up. Nadine and the security guard met them, huffing and puffing with the great effort it had taken to chase them. Their golf cart was still in the distance, tangled in the bag of clubs.

'We've called the police!' Nadine shrieked as they arrived. The security guard was doubled over, panting and coughing.

Margery looked around and realised that a small crowd had gathered all staring down into the bunker at the golfcart still submerged. The man in the pink polo shirt was there, and although he did have a moustache, he was definitely not Don Redburn.

Her heart sank. All that for nothing. She didn't know what Rose had been thinking.

'Oh, we won't need the police thank you,' Clementine said, dusting the sand from her knees. 'It was only a little crash, we won't be reporting the golf club for any damages, don't you worry.'

Seren laughed. Nadine glared at them both, opening and closing her mouth like a goldfish. Officer Symon was sauntering towards them across the golf course. Margery could see, when he got closer, that he found the whole thing very amusing.

'Hello,' he said cheerily, his smile somehow making him look even younger than he was. 'I don't think I need to ask what the matter is.'

Nadine immediately rattled off what had happened before Margery or Clementine could say a word.

Another golf cart was coming towards them, Margery could see it on the horizon, puttering along the course. She almost laughed out loud though when she saw who was on board. Rose was driving, with Gloria, Karen and Sharon all squished into the passenger seats and holding on for dear life. The golf cart arrived with great aplomb, braking hard on the grass, and stopped just before they fell into the same sand trap. Even Nadine stopped talking to Symon and turned to see what was happening.

'Mrs Smith!' she cried, her cheeks going red. 'I didn't know you were here.'

'I am,' Rose said, swooping off the golf cart and taking her sunglasses off to push them onto the top of her head. 'Now, what's all this?'

'These ladies tried to...' Nadine began, but Rose instead glared at Margery and Clementine.

'What are you doing here without a vehicle? Did you test the golf cart?' Rose demanded to know. 'How will we know how trustworthy it will be to transport Seren in her dress if you haven't tested it?'

Clementine gestured to the golf cart in the sand dramatically. 'Unfortunately, it didn't pass the test.'

'Are they with you?' Nadine asked incredulously, looking between them all. 'Are you planning this wedding?'

'Yes,' Rose beamed, 'it's my wedding... well... wedding planning, of course.'

'Aren't you just a teacher?' Nadine mumbled.

Rose narrowed her eyes at her. 'Margery, take the others and go back to the car,' she said in her best deputy head voice. 'I think there's been a little misunderstanding between us here.'

Margery and Clementine didn't need to be told twice. They scuttled over to the golf cart and squashed in next to Gloria, who took the wheel this time. Seren stayed behind with Rose, wringing her hands as Rose spoke.

'What happened?' Margery asked, as soon as they were far enough away from Nadine and Officer Symon, the cart whizzing along.

'Ceri-Ann pretended to go into labour,' Gloria chuckled. 'It was brilliant. She was rolling all about the place! We made her wait in the car, though. Obviously golf carts aren't very safe.'

'Did you get anything on Donald Redburn?' Margery asked eagerly.

'Er... well, no,' Gloria admitted. 'They thought that she was in labour, so I had to stay with her and pretend to be her mum. Then we just left before they rang an ambulance.'

Margery groaned, so this had all been a waste of time.

'We got something,' Karen said, looking over her shoulder at the three of them in the front seat. She held up something metal to show them.

'What's that?' Clementine asked.

'A USB stick!' Sharon grinned.

–

They didn't wait for Seren and Rose, instead they high-tailed it straight to the nearest dinner lady's house. Karen and Sharon lived across the street from each other in the little estate just before the border where Dewstow met Ittonvale. Karen's house was slightly closer, so they all piled inside. It was nice to sit in someone else's kitchen and eat their French fancies for a change, Margery thought, as she sipped from the mug of tea Sharon had made her. The house was well lived in, signs of life everywhere you looked, from the children's drawings on the fridge door to the overflowing laundry basket next to the washing machine. It gave Margery a warm and cosy feeling.

She took a deep breath, glad that all the excitement was over. The heist had not been a good idea by anyone's measure. In fact, it had probably got them into the most trouble they had been in – for a while anyway – and although they seemed to have got away with it for now, she was sure that there would be unexpected consequences in the future. There always seemed to be something else waiting for them, lurking in the shadows of the future.

'Where's Jack, Karen?' Gloria asked, sitting down next to Margery at the kitchen table. Sharon did the washing up, while Karen turned on the laptop.

Margery found her eyes drawn to the rabbit cage on the floor lined with old *Dewstow Freepress* pages. Miss

Hawthorne, the missing PE teacher, peered out from the front page that was underneath the water bottle. The rabbit in the cage sat and stared up at them, unconcerned, chewing on the vegetables Karen had put in when they arrived at her home.

'He's taken the kids to his mum's,' Karen said as she clicked at the keys of the computer. 'Thank God! They've been doing my head in this week. Izzy had headlice and gave it to the rest of us, and Noah's been clattering about the place breaking things. It's nice to have a break.' She seemed to feel the worried look Ceri-Ann gave her from across the table. 'Oh, don't worry, Ceri, there's loads of nice bits about children, too. One of them painted their foot and made it into a Christmas card at nursery once.'

Ceri-Ann didn't look soothed at all. In fact, she had gone the same colour as the milk bottle in the middle of the table. Margery wondered if she ought to have a chat with Ceri-Ann soon. She knew the woman well enough to know when something was bothering her, but this time she couldn't tell exactly what it was that had her worried. Maybe the impending arrival of the baby had her stressed out? Ceri-Ann was certainly not her usual jovial self at the moment.

'This is so exciting,' Karen said, interrupting Margery's thoughts. 'It's even better than the day I bought that jumper and then realised it was reversible – basically two jumpers for the price of one!'

She slotted the USB drive into the computer, and then tapped gleefully at the laptop. The others waited with bated breath for what she might find.

'How did you get this anyway?' Clementine asked, gesturing to the USB drive sticking out of the laptop. 'We thought you were just messing around trying all the gym equipment.'

'We did!' Sharon said, drying her hands with a tea towel and coming over to look at what Karen was doing too, standing behind her. 'They had two step machines!'

'Do you not have steps in your house?' Gloria asked.

'Well, yeah, but it's much more exciting doing it on the spot,' Sharon explained.

'We came out of the gym just as Ceri-Ann was doing her labour bit,' Karen said. Ceri-Ann grinned. 'The personal trainer ran off to give her first aid, and everyone else was distracted, so I jumped behind the desk and copied all their files onto the USB.'

'Whose USB is it?' Clementine asked.

'It was all my in-laws' holiday photos originally, but I deleted them,' Karen said, still looking at the laptop screen. 'No one needs two thousand photos of the same bloody timeshare and I just had a feeling it might come in handy.'

Margery sat back in her chair, impressed by Karen's foresight.

'I'm in!' Karen said jubilantly. They all leaned in to hear what she had found. 'Ooh well, this might take a while! There's loads of random stuff on here.'

'How do you know how to do this?' Gloria asked, looking between Karen and the computer incredulously.

'I'm not that old, that's why. I know my way around a computer,' Karen explained. 'Did you not have a MySpace page Gloria? It's how everyone used to learn to code, isn't it? If you could do your own MySpace page, then you could code a website that was just photos of you and your mates at a park and took hours to load.'

Gloria shook her head as Karen continued to search through the files.

'Ooh I used to love changing my MySpace profile page song,' Sharon said, gazing wistfully out of the kitchen window. 'You could really bare your soul, especially if you changed your screen name on MSN to the lyrics as well. The chorus to a My Chemical Romance song or something…'

'Are you telling me that you could have made us our website for free?' Clementine said. 'We wouldn't have to be doing this affair malarky if we didn't owe the children—'

'Is there anything useful to us?' Margery interrupted them all before the conversation could disintegrate any further. She leaned over to look at the screen. 'How about where it says members?'

'Ooh yes,' Karen double clicked the document, and it loaded up a screen of names and numbers. 'It's got to be in this Excel spreadsheet.'

'Look for the name Donald Redburn,' Clementine said, trying to stick her hand around onto the keyboard to do it for her. 'Or maybe Don Redburn.'

Margery watched Karen type the name into the search bar. The name popped up. 'It looks like he's a member, but he hasn't paid for months.'

'Would they let him in the club if he hadn't paid?' Margery said to herself out loud.

'I doubt it,' Gloria said.

It was almost certain then, that Don wasn't going where he said he was. Margery wondered for the millionth time where he could be going instead. Evelyn's affair theory was looking more and more likely to be true.

'It doesn't look like he paid for it anyway though,' Karen said, squinting at the screen again as she scrolled along the document. 'Someone called "V. Black" used to pay for it. But they obviously haven't been paying for it for a few weeks. You probably aren't allowed in without a paid-up membership.'

'I wonder who that is,' Margery said out loud. 'V. Black, hmmm. I recognise the surname from somewhere.'

'Maybe he can't go to golf because whoever this V is was paying for it, and now they've stopped he can't afford it,' Clementine suggested. 'A membership like that can't be cheap.'

'No,' Gloria agreed. 'It was £42 each for that afternoon tea… and you only got one scone.'

There was something to that, Margery thought – it must have been dreadfully expensive to even hold a membership there. They would simply have to find out who V. Black was and see why they had stopped paying for it. Perhaps they had been sponsoring Don, but something had made them stop, and Margery wondered if that might hold a clue as to whether he really was having an affair.

Chapter Ten

'You must be right. We don't think he's been going for months,' Clementine told Mrs Redburn as she sat opposite them at her kitchen table a few hours later. 'He stopped paying for his membership in January.'

Margery watched through the window as Don plodded up and down with the lawn mower, large headphones on, oblivious to the fact they were discussing him. She didn't know how they could have mistaken the golfing man for him now at all. Margery vowed that from now on they would carry their glasses with them everywhere.

'Since January?' Evelyn gasped, her eyes flitting to the side of the table. She straightened up again as if nothing had ever happened.

'Can you think of anywhere else he could go?' Margery asked Evelyn. 'Or anyone he could be with?'

'I have my suspicions,' Evelyn said. She reached behind her to the side of the chair and rummaged inside her handbag, pulling out a leather embossed notebook. She opened it and took out a page that had already been filled with neat handwriting.

'Firstly,' she said, consulting her own scrawl, 'he's very friendly with our neighbour. She's a young widow.' She said the word with a disapproving lilt, as though the woman shouldn't have married someone who was going to die. 'She's two doors down, her name is Emma. She's been all over him recently, asking him to do all sorts. Change a lightbulb, help her mow the lawn, that sort of thing.'

Margery thought that they sounded like quite normal things to ask for help with, but obviously she didn't know the whole story.

'Has she done anything else that would make you suspicious?' Margery asked.

'No, not really,' Evelyn admitted, her cheeks flushing red. 'She always invites me over at the same time, I suppose. There wouldn't be much time for them to be alone together.'

'Alright,' Clementine said, making a note in her own notebook. 'Do you have anything else to go on? Or just that?'

'He's very close with his former coworker, Karis,' Evelyn said. 'You can find her down at his old taxi agency. He sold it a few years ago but she still works there – she owns it now.' Her face crumpled in defeat. 'But I just don't think she would. She's very religious.'

'Okay, well that's something to go off, anyway,' Clementine said, writing down Karis's name. 'I think we should start with the neighbour. Will she be in just now, Evelyn?'

'What are you going to do?' Evelyn said, her brow suddenly furrowing in suspicion. 'You won't do anything that'll make me look stupid?'

'Of course not,' Clementine assured her, while Margery nodded in agreement. 'We'll be very discreet.'

'As discreet as you were at the golf course?' Evelyn raised an eyebrow. 'I've heard nothing but madness about that.'

'Sometimes, things are er... out of our control,' Clementine said, in what Margery knew was supposed to be a reassuring voice but came out more strained. 'Like golf carts.'

Evelyn didn't look convinced in the slightest, but they dropped back into silence while they finished their coffee. Margery looked around the kitchen at the photographs that ran along the windowsill. There were so many of Evelyn and Don; Evelyn beaming out from them. Margery found herself hoping with all her might that he wasn't really having an affair. It would crush Evelyn under the terrible burden of loving someone who loved someone else.

'Is there anything else you could think of at all?' Margery asked, breaking the quiet. Neither of the leads seemed to have much to them. Evelyn must really have been grasping at straws to create such a scenario. Perhaps Mrs Mugglethwaite had got under her skin and now Evelyn was searching for strawmen everywhere she looked, expecting sinister shadows to jump out of every skirting board. Margery hesitated to bring it back up, but she felt that to get to the bottom of it all, they would have to ask. Even if the conversation that followed wasn't a nice one.

'Evelyn, were you aware that Don doesn't pay for his own golf club membership?' she asked. Evelyn bristled visibly.

'Yes,' she said, before Margery had even had the chance to close her mouth after asking the question. There was a silence as they waited for her to give them a morsel more information. She tutted.

'Our friend pays for it,' she said, as though that were explanation enough. 'It's part of the deal with his membership of the Golden Circle.'

'What's the Golden Circle?' Clementine asked. Margery remembered where she had heard the name before. On the photograph at the golf club.

There was another photograph of the same group on the kitchen windowsill, sitting among Evelyn and Don's marital shrine. Margery's eyes snapped up to it now, although she couldn't make out any of the faces from this distance.

'It's a secret society,' Evelyn said, in her haughty manner. Eyeing them as though she wasn't sure whether to trust them with the information. 'Well, not really secret. Just a bit of fun.'

'Can we join?' Clementine asked, beaming at the very idea of having to learn a secret handshake.

'No,' Evelyn said. 'Membership is reserved for people Vivian and Billy used to deem worthy. Gosh, that sounds awful now I've said it out loud.'

'Well, who are Vivian and Billy?' Clementine asked. 'I'm sure we can woo them, eh, Margery?' She nudged Margery with her elbow, who shook her head at the look on Evelyn's face.

'Billy has been gone for a few years now,' Evelyn explained. 'He was Vivian's husband. They used to run the club together. I'm not really sure how it all started... you'd have to ask Don for that. Billy's father used to run it and then his father before him, always from Dewpond, just outside Ittonvale. Billy could probably have traced his family tree back a hundred generations there.' She suddenly looked awkward, and began to play with her fingernails. 'Vivian is my best friend... was my best friend until recently, you know how it is. The sort of friendship where you buy them the same perfume for Christmas every year, more like family really.'

Margery and Clementine waited politely for her to continue.

'You know, before you go upsetting my neighbours, you might as well go and give her a piece of my mind,' Evelyn said, her face darkening. 'She's obviously stopped paying the membership out of spite. I'd bet she's decided not to tell me. I'm sure she wants me to be the first to go crawling back, but not this time.'

There was something to that, Margery supposed. It all seemed very plausible.

'But why would she stop paying out of spite?' Clementine asked, her brow furrowed.

'We had a falling out recently,' Evelyn explained, but she didn't try to elaborate further. Instead, she got up and led them back through the house, showing them to the front door and opening it.

'Wait here a second,' she said. She disappeared for a moment and then reappeared, thrusting a gift bag towards Margery.

'You might as well give her her birthday present for last month,' she said. 'I'll text you Vivian's address.'

No sooner than they had stepped outside, Evelyn slammed the door leaving them on the doorstep, blinking stupidly. They exchanged a surprised look. Margery looked into the bag and found a bottle of perfume.

'What do you think they fell out about?' Clementine hissed.

Margery raised her eyebrows. She didn't know Evelyn enough to speculate.

On the driveway, Don was already in his car. The engine roared to life, and he gave them a little wave before he started to reverse, backing out of the drive, the gravel pinging away from the car tyres. He disappeared down the lane.

'Where is he going?' Clementine asked as he disappeared into the afternoon.

'Certainly not golf,' Margery reached into her bag and grasped for her car keys. 'There's only one way to find out.'

'Really Margery?' Clementine said in faux outrage. But she couldn't hide the smile that spread over her face. 'After we were nearly arrested for the exact same thing this morning?'

'That's true,' Margery said, looking down at the keys in her hand in surprise, astounded at her sudden audacity. Clementine was right. It wouldn't do to be caught in a compromising position again. She was sure the police would come down on them very hard if they did.

'I wish I'd stuck my GPS fob under the wheel arch,' Clementine tutted. 'I'll do it next time, we'll be able to see where he goes, even if we can't go with him.'

'Is that overstepping a line, do you think?' Margery asked – speaking to herself as much as Clementine.

Clementine raised a hand as if to say even if they were, that didn't matter much.

Margery had forgotten all about the GPS fob Clementine used on her keys so she wouldn't lose them. It didn't have a good battery life, but it did have a good range.

They got into their own car and Margery started the engine, which launched into life in a rattling cough.

'Where is he going, do you think?' she asked Clementine as she pulled out of the driveway.

'It doesn't matter. We'll never catch up now,' Clementine said.

They shared a long look.

'Let's just go to Vivian's,' Margery said, in defeat. 'But I think on second thought, that you're right about the GPS fob. It would be a great help. I wish we'd thought of it earlier.'

Clementine nodded grimly. Margery manoeuvred the car away from the house.

Chapter Eleven

'Are you sure this is the right place?' Margery hissed as they crept up the driveway. 'This house is enormous.'

Clementine looked down at the phone app in confusion. If the Redburn property had been impressive, Margery had not expected this place to top it. Just outside Ittonvale in the tiny village of Dewpond stood the stunning house, set back from the village and surrounded by acres of land. The path down to it was barely passable in the car and their little Nissan struggled along until they reached the building. The frontage was Georgian, but Margery wondered if the house itself could be from the Jacobean era. Rose would know. Margery made a mental note to ask her about it.

'Wow,' Clementine said, as they both stared at the building. 'What should we do? Confront her straight away about the golf club membership? Look at this place, she's probably got a security team to chase us with!'

'Maybe we should just wait and see what's going on,' Margery said. She drove a little down the driveway, passing a familiar looking parked car and parked her own behind the wall that ran from the garden so that it wasn't so conspicuous. They climbed out, and Margery couldn't help but admire the frontage as they stared at the house. Clementine fidgeted next to her.

'What if we just pretend we're getting people to join the Women's Institute or whatever,' she said, with a fleeting gesture towards the front door. 'Then we can see what she says about Don.'

'Do you think he'll be here?' Margery said, the gift bag swinging from her hand. 'Oh gosh, what should we say if he is?'

'He's got more to be afraid of than us if he is here.' Clementine smiled in the smug manner of someone who had unexpectedly found their missing sock. 'The wrath of his wife, for one!'

Margery thought about trying to convince her to stay put, but she supposed that if they did go and confront Vivian it would all be over then. She followed Clementine to the front door. They rang the doorbell and they waited and waited and waited.

'Well, no one's in, are they?' Clementine said. She leaned over and put her hands against the window at the top of the door and looked in, peering so closely she almost touched it with her nose. 'But there is a car here, isn't there? I suppose they could have two cars though.'

'Maybe we should try the garden?' Margery suggested. 'It's a big house and a nice afternoon. Maybe they're outside?'

They wandered around the side of the house, and through the back gate – which was unlocked – into a vast, stone walled garden – the lawn stretching as far as the eye could see. There was still no sign of anyone. There was a large summerhouse at the back of the garden and a shed on the other side – it was all very idyllic. Clementine walked to the back door of the house and tried the handle, it opened. She and Margery exchanged a worried look.

'Should we really go in?' Margery asked, taking her foot off the doorstep and feeling herself blink stupidly. Clementine pressed her lips together.

'Well, we're here,' she said finally. 'Let's go in and say hello. If they're here, we'll say Evelyn told us to say hello. See what she says!'

'Is that a good idea?' Margery asked. 'She might not believe us. She could call the police to report us for trespassing.'

'I don't know. We'll have to cross that bridge when it comes to it,' Clementine said.

'I suppose we can just give her the present,' Margery said, looking down at the gift bag she was holding.

Clementine nodded, before opening the door and slipping inside the house. Margery took one final look at the long green lawn and then followed her onto the cool flagstone floor of the utility room. They crept through the utility room, past the washing machine and clothes horse and into the kitchen which was empty of life if you didn't count the dead flies on the windowsill.

'Hello?' Margery called. There was no returning call.

Clementine went over to the fridge and opened it nosily, revealing a shelf of rotten fruit and mouldy vegetables inside. They had melted into a goo that covered every shelf. The glass bottle of milk on the inside of the fridge door had curdled and separated, a yellow viscous liquid with bits of curd whirling around at the top and a chunky ooze at the bottom. She slammed the fridge shut again and turned to Margery, her face pulled into one of pure disgust. The doctor's appointment letters and Summerview School newsletters attached to the door with magnets threatened to fall off with the force.

The newsletter with the playground renewal news was placed on top of the older one. And Margery noticed the poster she kept seeing – the one about the missing PE teacher – was next to it, also held on by magnets. The woman's face stared out from the photograph.

'Come on,' Clementine said. They made their way out into the dark hallway.

'What was going on with that fridge? All the rotten food,' Clementine said. 'What's that all about?'

'I don't know.' Margery shook her head. 'But where is Vivian? You don't think something's happened to her?' She looked around the hallway as though expecting to see the owner sitting somewhere nearby. 'She's got the school newsletter there, Clem. Do you think she was something to do with the school?'

'Hmmm.' Clementine rubbed her chin. 'Yes, I do, actually. Was she a school governor? I really recognise her name from somewhere more than just Evelyn and whatever bizarre club they were in.'

'Oh.' Margery wracked her brain for the name again. There had just been so many school governors over the years – too many to remember. 'Maybe?'

'Do you think these photos are her?' Clementine pointed to the framed photographs lining the bottom of the landing, the woman in all of them going through all the stages of life before finally appearing as the elderly woman in the newer frames. The man standing next to her had disappeared out of the newer photographs too, Margery thought sadly, wondering if that meant what she naturally assumed it would.

'Vivian!' Clementine called through the house. 'Vivian Black!'

They waited for an answer, but none came.

'I don't like this one bit,' Margery said. 'She can't possibly be here if her fridge is in that state.'

'She would have noticed the post.' Clementine pointed to the pile on the doormat in front of the front door. In all the commotion Margery hadn't even noticed it at all. She walked across the room and picked up a letter on the top of the pile, they were all addressed to Mrs Black.

'Clem, what if something's happened to her?' Margery said, looking down the vast hallway to the tall staircase, and eyeing the smooth floor as she did so. 'From those photographs she's quite elderly, and this house isn't particularly age-proof. What if she's fallen in the shower or the bath and hasn't been able to get back out?'

The thought was horrific. The idea was just too awful. That the woman could have died all alone in her huge house with the nearest neighbour down a long dirt track, or worse, fallen and hurt herself and then died after days and days of suffering. Clementine was clearly thinking the same thing, her face had turned a shade of white Margery hadn't seen since they had ridden the waltzers at Ittonvale Country Fair.

'We'll go and have a look,' Clementine said, looking towards the staircase grimly. 'No one can have been here for days, can they?'

'No, there's a lot of post here,' Margery said. 'It does seem strange.'

They crept up the stairs – one step at a time – until they arrived at a large landing. The walls were decorated with a tasteful array of oil paintings, some of which appeared to depict a young Vivian, along with her husband and their children. There was one larger painting of Vivian as she was more likely to look now – much older, with a Pekinese dog on her lap.

'You do this floor and I'll do upstairs,' Clementine said, heading up the next flight of stairs and disappearing as she rushed up it as fast as she could.

Margery nodded and turned the first door handle on her right, opening it to reveal a study. There was no one inside; just a smooth polished desk and leather chair that Mr Barrow would have died to possess alongside the usual office furniture. The desk had been emptied entirely, its contents strewn all over it, the drawers of the desk hanging open.

Margery looked around in surprise. Nothing else in the house looked like it had been touched. Surely Vivian couldn't have been burgled. Everything seemed normal. Possibly Vivian had been looking for something and emptied the desk and its drawers to find it.

Careful not to touch anything Margery examined the rest of the room in curiosity. The walls of the study were full of old photographs of teams and sporting events. Margery wondered if Vivian or a former husband were keen athletes – the display cabinet full of dusty trophies certainly said someone was. Margery realised where she had recognised Vivian's name from. On the wall behind the desk was another gala photograph, like the one she had seen at the golf course. This one was much older though, from at least a decade before judging by everyone's hair-styles. The same gold lettering was underneath the photograph, running below it on the mount. The text read 'Golden Circle Summer Party 1975', and then listed everyone's names – of which there were many.

Don was there, Margery saw after scanning the list of names, but Evelyn was not. She wondered how old Evelyn would have been in 1975. Perhaps she had been too young. The photograph had been taken in a private house, Margery realised, judging by the fireplace to the side of the group which had family photographs above it on the mantle. Perhaps in one of the rooms they had passed downstairs. She scanned the names underneath the picture and realised that Richard Monroe the auditor was in it, though she hadn't recognised him when she looked the first time. She looked again, and found him next to Don again. He had been hidden partially by how tall Don was.

There were a lot of photographs of Don in the office, a surprising amount really, all showing him at different ages. The youngest Margery could see was in a frame: Don was wearing a chauffeur outfit and standing with his arms folded in front of a sleek black car, the make and model of which eluded Margery, but she knew it would have been what her brother called 'a nice motor'. Billy Black looked out of the frame from his place on the back seat of the car, smiling through the open window.

She left the study and tried the next door, which opened onto a cosy living room that was just as empty of life but much neater than the study had been. She crossed through it to the door of the balcony that ran along the backside of the house and looked out at the garden again. There was a sit-on lawn mower waiting on the grass. She was sure that it hadn't been there before, but maybe she had missed it as they entered the house. She watched for a few moments longer, before returning to the hallway and trying the next rooms. They were all guest rooms with ensuite bathrooms attached, and all empty. Judging by how dusty they were they had not been used for a long time. Margery wondered if Vivian had any family. Surely, if she did, they must stop by and visit her sometimes?

She stood in the hallway for a moment and waited, listening for any noise. The sound of creaking made her jump before she realised it was Clementine coming back down the stairs.

'Come and have a look at this,' Clementine said. Margery followed to another room at the top of the stairs. It was obviously the woman's bedroom. Margery had a bad feeling wash over her at their intrusion into such a personal space. All her things were laid out on the furniture. Her make up and perfume were on the dressing table next to the carefully placed hairbrush, which was next to a neatly stacked pile of hairpins. On her bedside table lay a pair of reading glasses, a glass that had only a drop of water left at the bottom, and a brown tablet bottle that only had a few pills remaining. There was another perfume bottle there too, of the same type as that in the gift bag. A blue glass bottle. Margery wondered whether she should just leave the bag right there on the bedside table, but thought it might seem a bit uncouth when Vivian returned home and realised someone had been in her private space.

'She's definitely not here, then,' Margery said. 'You checked the bathroom?'

'All of them,' Clementine said. 'How many bath-rooms does one woman need? There's about ten on this floor.' Margery chuckled at that. Clementine continued, pointing to the far side of the bed. 'Look at this, it's weird.'

Margery looked. At the side of the bed was a set of suitcases. Not the sort of dreary, battered old suitcases on wheels that Margery and Clementine would use if they were going away, but a full set of luggage. Obviously expensive, but functional, in leather and cream. She bent down to take a closer look and realised that each bag was full.

'Gosh, this is strange,' Margery said. 'It sort of looks like she packed for a holiday but didn't bother taking her things.'

'She must have forgotten to empty the fridge, too.' Clementine folded her arms.

'Do you suppose she had someone who was supposed to do that, and they forgot?' Margery asked, thinking of the probability that you'd leave on the day before a food waste bin day. 'Maybe she left it full for someone looking after the house to eat.'

'Maybe.' Clementine scratched her head. 'Well, she's not here, is she?'

'No,' Margery said.

Clementine sat down on the stool at the ornate dressing table in front of the large bay window.

'What is it?' Margery asked her. 'You're thinking something.'

'Yes,' Clementine said. 'But it's mad, as usual.'

'We're both mad.' Margery smiled at her weakly. 'You may as well have out with it.'

'Has she run off somewhere?' Clementine said. 'It does seem like she left very quickly. And there's no car outside on the driveway. What if she's gone somewhere to hide? And didn't even get a chance to take her bags?'

'You don't think…?'

Clementine nodded. 'What if she has something to do with that playground body?'

'Well, that is a bit mad. We don't even know this person.'

'I know, I know,' Clementine said agreeably. 'But maybe we should look through the school staff folders at work. What if she's in there somewhere? I'm sure she's the governor who retired a few years ago.'

'What do you mean?' Margery said. 'What difference would her being a governor make?'

'That body had to have been there since they laid the tarmac the first time,' Clementine explained. 'Only someone close to the school could have managed to get it put under there before they lay it.'

'I think you might be jumping to conclusions,' Margery said. 'We can't just go about accusing elderly people of murder.'

'I'm just saying it's strange, Margery,' Clementine said, shaking her head.

'The study is a bit of a mess,' Margery said. 'Do you think she couldn't find her passport or something?'

'Maybe,' Clementine agreed. 'I wonder how we can find out.'

'Mr Fitzgerald seems to know everyone's comings and goings. Maybe it's in his weird book,' Margery suggested.

There was a noise from outside and Margery got up to look through the bedroom window. Outside going around and around the lawn on the sit on mower was Don Redburn.

'Clem!' Margery called, Clementine rushed over and looked too.

'Gosh,' she said, scratching her head. 'Now I really don't know what to make of this. Why is he doing her garden for her if she's fallen out with his wife?'

'I keep finding photographs of them together,' Margery said. 'At some sort of group meeting. The Golden Circle Evelyn told us about. They must be old friends.'

'He's probably just been coming here to do the garden when she thought he was at golf,' Clementine said triumphantly. 'Mystery solved!'

'Why wouldn't he just tell Evelyn, though?' Margery said, watching as Don finished the lawn and then began to dig up the empty flower bed lining the green grass. 'And why did Vivian stop paying for his golf membership?'

'To get back in Vivian's good books for some reason?' Clementine suggested, answering the first question if not the second, and rubbing her chin. 'Her car isn't outside, so she must have gone somewhere.'

She must have, Margery thought. But where Vivian could have gone and why remained elusive.

Chapter Twelve

They left the house through the front door, sliding out past the piled-up letters. Margery felt horrible about their intrusion, and she knew by Clementine's silence that she must have regrets of her own about it. They crept back to the car and Margery drove them away from the house before Don could return to his car and spot them, chucking the gift bag of perfume on the back seat.

'Do you really think we can rule out an affair?' Margery asked Clementine, who was looking at the countryside through the passenger side window, her hand resting on her face. Clementine turned to look at her.

'With Vivian, who isn't even home when he's there? Yes. With anyone else, I'm not sure,' she said. 'Maybe we should still go and talk to Evelyn's neighbour? Or his old coworker?'

'Shall we just keep them in mind?' Margery said. 'I don't know if we've got time for the coworker. It's nearly half past five; surely the agency will be shut now.'

'Yes,' Clementine said. 'Why don't we go and have a chat with Evelyn first? We won't be able to ask around the school about her until Monday now, and it's the do over of the Gala Tuesday afternoon, isn't it? There's not much time to ask her.'

'Shall we just call her?' Margery asked, thinking about the look on Evelyn's face when they had arrived earlier.

She felt strange about intruding twice in one day; they hadn't exactly solved Evelyn's problem yet.

Firstly, they would have to prove that there was no actual affair going on. She thought about Richard in the photographs they'd seen, and wondered how well Evelyn really knew him. Maybe she would be able to tell them something about Richard that would help the headmaster win him over during the ongoing audit. Nothing else seemed to be working on that front.

Clementine took out her phone and called Evelyn's number, the Bluetooth car speaker rattling as it rang out. She picked up on the second ring.

'Any news?' she gasped down the line.

'Sort of,' Clementine said with a grimace. 'Did you know that your husband mows Vivian Black's lawn?'

There was a pause over the line for a moment. The silence was stony.

'No… Well, he used to, but he told me he wasn't now,' Evelyn spluttered. 'How do you know that?'

'We saw him at her house today,' Margery explained. 'Don't worry; he didn't see us, he was doing her gardening.'

'So much for his loyalty to me,' Evelyn said, letting out a heavy huff of air. 'Well, did you speak to her? What did she have to say for herself?'

'She wasn't there,' Clementine said. 'It was a bit strange actually…'

Before Clementine could tell Evelyn the strange disarray of the house, Evelyn interrupted her.

'She'll have gone to her second home, then. Typical of her to get my husband to do things for her when she's not even there,' Evelyn snapped. 'She must have a real hold on him.'

'Well, she isn't quite getting him to do that,' Margery said, trying to sound soothing. 'No one has even checked the post and the fridge is full of old food.'

'She'll have forgotten to sort that before she goes again,' Evelyn sneered down the line. 'I usually pop in and keep an eye on the place. I'm not going to do that this time.'

'Do you usually do that?' Margery asked. The conversation seemed to have taken a strange turn, and she wasn't sure she was still following it.

'Yes,' Evelyn snapped again. 'But lately, I haven't.'

'All right,' Clementine said, her face just as confused as Margery thought her own might be. 'But you used to? Obviously you and Vivian were close, and she can't be that angry at you. We saw you in a few photographs there that were on display. If you weren't friends, I doubt she'd have them out.'

'Look,' Evelyn said; Margery could tell how annoyed she was even over the phone. 'Come over, and I'll explain a few things to you about Vivian Black.'

With that, she hung up, leaving Margery and Clementine in a moment of stunned silence.

They returned to Evelyn's house. Margery had begun to feel quite tired, wishing they could give this up and go home to relax. It really had been quite a long day. Before either of them could knock on the front door, it flew open.

'Just come in,' Evelyn said. Instead of leading them back into the conservatory she took them to the kitchen, where she had laid several pieces of correspondence on the table. They sat down opposite Evelyn.

'What's going on?' Clementine asked.

Evelyn thrust a postcard from the table towards Margery, who took it and turned it over, revealing a brief note on the back and a lovely holiday scene on the front. Margery skimmed it.

The card was addressed to Evelyn, and seemed to be all about the person's holiday in small writing. 'All the best, Love Viv', was signed at the bottom, in a trembling elderly scrawl of fountain pen ink. The handwriting was awkward, each sentence was capitalised, and the words didn't flow well.

Evelyn glared at the postcard. Margery couldn't fathom what could be so upsetting about it at all.

'You don't carry around a postcard from your wife's best friend in the pocket of your golf trousers without it meaning something more nefarious is going on,' Evelyn said, her voice cutting through the quiet conservatory.

'Is that where you found it?' Clementine asked, reading the postcard over Margery's shoulder. 'Have you asked him about it?'

'Of course, ages ago when he started disappearing,' Evelyn said. 'He said he'd found it lying around upstairs and took it to put in the bureau with all the others and just forgot. He said he'd put it in his pocket without thinking about it.'

'I don't mean to be rude,' Clementine said, 'but that doesn't seem like a lie. Surely that could very easily have happened?'

'Well, yes,' Evelyn said, her cheeks darkening as she reached over and snatched the card back out of Margery's fingers.

'You haven't spoken to her about it?' Margery asked.

'We aren't talking,' Evelyn hissed. 'We fell out after Christmas.'

'Why did you fall out?' Clementine asked.

Evelyn ignored the question, her eyes sliding down to the rest of the letters on the table.

'Anyway,' she sniffed, placing the postcard face down on the table again, hiding the contents away. 'I'm sure she's having much too much a good time at the bingo. I'll give her a call in the autumn. She'll come crawling back then.'

'I don't really understand why you've called us here to tell us that,' Margery said. 'Do you think Vivian is who Don is having an affair with?'

Evelyn chuckled darkly. 'I didn't, but seeing as he's mowing her lawn or whatever when he knows I'm not talking to her... well, who knows what's going on there!'

'Does Don have a key to her house?' Clementine asked. Evelyn shook her head.

'No,' she said. 'Well, yes... but it's hidden away. We haven't needed to use it.'

She got up and marched to the kitchen window where a spider plant sat in a pot, resting on a cork base. She lifted the pot and took out a key, holding it up to show them. She put it back and then returned to the table.

'And neither do I. I should have given it back to her when she...' Evelyn seemed to remember that she hadn't told them quite why she was no longer talking to Vivian. '...when I decided to no longer talk to her. Not that that's stopped her from sending me the stupid postcards once a week. How did you get into the house?'

'She left the back door open,' Margery said, wondering what Vivian's side of the story would be, especially as she was still sending correspondence. It would be interesting to talk to her and hear it. Perhaps the fall out was entirely one sided. Or perhaps Vivian was enjoying knowing that the postcards would wind her old friend up.

'Gosh, well,' Evelyn said, raising her eyebrows. 'She must be really losing it without me.'

'We locked the door behind us,' Clementine said. 'So, no one else should be able to break in. It was strange. Maybe you ought to go round and sort the letters and the fridge? It'll only get worse once the weather gets nicer.'

'No,' Evelyn said, but she looked conflicted. 'I won't give her the satisfaction. Let her deal with it when she gets back.'

'Where is she?' Margery asked.

'At her other house, I'd imagine,' Evelyn explained with a sigh. 'She has a second home in Devon.'

'Does she drive?' Margery asked. 'We didn't see another car at the house. Only Don's.'

'She does, but she shouldn't. Not with all the tablets and things she's on, I kept telling her to give her licence up,' Evelyn said. 'Why?'

Margery and Clementine shared a look. Margery knew that Clementine would want to poke at the information she was sure they had uncovered, and though she wasn't so convinced, Margery decided to try and pry the information out of Evelyn.

'Maybe we should just go to the other home and confirm a few things,' Margery said, willing Evelyn to answer some of their questions. 'Don mowing the lawn doesn't tell us much.'

'No, I suppose it doesn't,' Evelyn said, her voice rising haughtily. 'I'll text you the address.'

'Does she usually go to her second home this time of year?' Clementine asked. 'Or is this unusual?'

'Everything that woman does is unusual,' Evelyn spat, but then her face turned pensive. 'She usually stays for the swimming gala before she goes down there at Easter. But only if it's at Ittonvale School. I don't know if she knows about the rematch. It's a bit unusual for her to go this early. She keeps sending me stupid postcards, though, so she must be enjoying herself.'

Evelyn got up to fetch one of the postcards, flinging it down on the table in front of them.

Maybe Clementine's suspicions that Vivian had something to do with the playground body were right, Margery thought. She suddenly thought about the school newsletter pinned on Vivian's fridge door. Could she have realised that the body was about to make a reappearance and made a run for it?

'How do you know her?' Margery heard herself ask as her brain thought it all through, picking up the postcard and looking at it. It was a very normal beach scene and the message on the back was a standard holiday greeting, signed by Vivian Black.

'She was my swimming teacher at Ittonvale School,' Evelyn smiled, the warmth returning to her face as she remembered. 'I was quite good. We won the IttonStow gala every year I was in the team, and I made captain my final year.'

Margery and Clementine were impressed by that; the IttonStow gala being at the very peak of sporting achievements in the area. It had been known to cancel rugby matches if the gala happened to fall on the same day. Karen and Sharon hadn't stopped talking about how unfortunate it was that it had been rescheduled. Karen thought they should have cancelled this year's, as now it wouldn't be held on the same weekend and the winner wouldn't get to have the trophy for exactly fifty-two weeks. Margery didn't suppose that mattered as much now that the trophy had disappeared.

'Did Vivian have a lot to do with the IttonStow gala, then?' Clementine asked, her eyes wide with curiosity. 'I've never really thought about its origins.'

'She started the gala,' Evelyn said proudly. 'It used to always be held at Ittonvale. Before Dewstow leisure centre was built of course.'

'But she was always a governor for Summerview School,' Evelyn said. 'Her children went there. She stayed on the board even after they'd left. She only retired last year. Unfortunately, she hasn't thought much about what's been going on at Summerview in recent years.'

She gave Margery and Clementine a poignant look and Margery grimaced. It certainly hadn't been smooth sailing for the school, recently. Margery knew that the board of governors had certainly argued at length about what to do about the murders and trouble that seemed to have plagued the town.

'Are you sure you couldn't just ask Don why he was helping out in her garden?' Margery said, but the look on Evelyn's face stopped her from asking any more questions.

'I could, but I just don't think it'll help,' Evelyn said, leaning back in her chair. 'I'm sure he's probably doing it in hopes of getting his golf membership restarted. It's not just about the money.' She gestured towards the living room wall as if to show their wealth. 'Vivian is influential there. If she's told them he's not to play anymore, then he won't be allowed on site.'

'Why would she do that?' Clementine asked and Evelyn's face soured again.

'Because she's bitter about our fight, I suppose. I'm just angry that Don didn't tell me about Vivian paying for the golf membership before.' She shrugged like that was all there was to it, but Margery wondered if that really was all.

They left the house and Margery found herself hoping that they wouldn't have to visit again for a long time. Don had arrived home at some point in their time inside, his car was sat on the driveway again. Margery had a sudden worrying thought that he might have heard some of their conversation, but she shook it away. Clementine didn't hesitate. Slipping the GPS fob off her keyring and pulling a ream of sticky Blu Tak from inside her bag, she stuck it to the inside of the wheel arch of the car. Then they left as quickly as they could.

Margery thought that the GPS fob was too little, too late. Only time would tell how pointless it would be.

Chapter Thirteen

Monday morning dawned with a clang as always. Margery felt that they could have used another weekend to get over the one they'd just had. The audit was still not going well either, if the headmaster's grim look across the playground that morning meant anything. Margery and Clementine had seen him on the way into work, his eyes fixed on the remaining tarmac as he stood there, deep in thought.

Rose seemed just as stressed. She barely made it into the canteen for lunchtime anymore. Instead Seren would take her a packed lunch and drop it off in her office. Cutting the crusts off her sandwiches, peeling her satsumas and arranging the crisps neatly on a plate for her.

Try as they might, the Education Centre Nourishment Consultant team had not escaped scrutiny either. Richard had spent the better part of last Thursday with them, asking silly questions about why Margery brought in whole onions instead of pre-diced or why they didn't have an expensive laundry service to wash their kitchen tabards. The constant questions were exhausting, as were their efforts at trying to keep the kitchen running smoothly when it was under constant surveillance from someone with a clipboard. Seren was barely able to keep it all together, and had dropped so many things on the floor that Margery suspected she had been a failed juggler in a past life. Karen and Sharon had spent all day making silly mistakes and using the wrong labels. The pressure was getting to them, just as it had to the other departments.

The last straw had been Sharon trying to take a boiling hot tray of gratin potatoes out of the Rational oven using only a folded-up scouring pad. Margery had to call a meeting and ask them all to please calm down and if they couldn't manage that, to at least try and use the oven cloths they kept for that very purpose. Unfortunately, Richard the auditor had appeared behind her at that very moment and asked her for another meeting to discuss his progress.

It wasn't until they were sat awkwardly in the kitchen dry store that Margery realised some of their planning for the golf club was still written on the dry store whiteboard. Clementine had been ironing out finer details on Friday afternoon when she was supposed to be preparing the custard and hadn't bothered to wipe it off. The dry custard powder bag still sat unopened on the top of the chest freezer and Margery realised that was another thing they had forgotten to make for today's lunchtime.

Richard looked around the dry store disapprovingly, his eyes lingering over the writing on the board. Margery hoped that Clementine's handwriting was awful enough to hide that they had planned to do what they had done. She breathed a sigh of relief when he didn't comment, and instead turned back to consider her under his half-moon glasses.

She felt uncomfortable under his gaze. There was something about him that made her feel awkward and small. It was in the way that you could sometimes tell someone didn't like you, and you knew there was nothing you could do to change it, and that everything you might say would only make it all much worse.

Clementine never had any issue in that sort of situation. Margery grimaced to herself as she thought about how different they were under such circumstances. Clementine would chat away with gleeful abandon to anyone, regardless of if they hated her or not.

Richard coughed lightly, breaking her away from her thoughts. 'So, I can see that you passed your environmental health audit last year and received a five,' he said, rummaging through his clipboard to the correct page. 'But I'm not sure if I have your last internal audit down here?'

'We don't have internal audits,' Margery explained, though she could feel herself beginning to stumble over the words at the intensity of his gaze. 'The headmaster doesn't believe in them.'

She found herself regretting the comment as soon as she had made it, watching the auditor's bushy eyebrows rise up. 'What I mean to say,' she tried to correct herself, 'is that we're employed by the school so we don't get audited like outside contract caterers would do.'

'All right,' he said, jotting something down on his clipboard. 'So, what do you do instead? How do you make sure everything is up to date and correct? How do you follow updated policies?'

'We follow the school and government guidelines,' Margery said. 'And I use Safer Food Better Business.'

Richard nodded and wrote that down too. 'Well, I've certainly seen from your paperwork that you run quite a tight ship,' he said, putting the lid back on his pen and putting the clipboard on his lap. Margery wondered where this was going. 'I wonder if you could tell me more about the other departments?'

'Which ones?' Margery asked in surprise.

'You must see a lot of things,' he said. 'You're at the centre of the school – nearly everyone uses the canteen every day.'

'Yes.'

'Well,' he began and then paused, thinking it over. 'You didn't see much of the playground? When it was being refinished, I mean?'

'I don't understand…'

'You didn't see anything out of the ordinary before that body was found?'

'No,' Margery stuttered, 'of course not. Why would you ask that?'

'No, no of course not, forget I said anything,' Richard said, looking at the dry store door. 'Let's have a look at your cleaning rotas, shall we?'

The conversation moved on, but the weird air that had surrounded it continued until Richard seemed to realise that Margery wasn't going to tell him any more school gossip, and really needed to get back to work before one of the dinner lady team accidentally set themselves on fire.

'This all seems above board for the moment,' he said, making a few more notes on his clipboard. 'But I feel like I must warn you that things can change quite rapidly. It would be in your best interests to keep it all exactly as you have it, or better, if you can.'

'What do you mean?' Margery asked, her heart sinking at the stern look on his face.

'Well, any extracurricular stunts like the one I witnessed at the weekend,' Richard began. Margery gasped.

'You were at the—'

'At the golf course on Saturday?' he said. 'Yes I was, and I wasn't expecting to see such a spectacle, quite honestly.'

Margery didn't know what to say to that, feeling her mouth opening and closing stupidly and her cheeks flush as the shame washed over her in a flood. She suddenly remembered seeing Richard in the photograph in the ballroom of the golf club. If he was still a member then of course he would be out on a pleasant Saturday morning enjoying a round of golf. They had caused as big a scene as he said, there had been so many witnesses.

'I've audited a lot of canteen kitchens,' he told her when she didn't respond. 'And the ones that don't manage to keep to standard both in and out of the school end up changing, and probably not in a way you'd like. For example,' he gestured to the monthly menu planner which was pinned on the wall next to the shelving unit of herbs and spices, 'I've seen some schools forced to replace their fresh menu with bought in frozen prepacked meals that can simply be heated all at once in the oven, saving preparation time and worries over things like allergens and waste. The meals themselves are a little more expensive than the individual ingredients of course, but then you save so much money on staff wages that it works out a little cheaper. No pensions or holiday hours to pay—'

'But the staff—'

'You'd lose your entire team.' He nodded. 'They'd keep one or two of you on of course, to fill the vending machines and serve the food, but there really wouldn't be a need for all of you. So, keep it up Mrs Butcher-Baker and perhaps keep the disastrous out of work team meetings in the past. I'll be watching.'

He excused himself and left quickly, taking his paperwork, and leaving Margery feeling dreadful. Surely the kitchen itself wasn't that bad? One small out of work slip couldn't bring it all down, could it? Of course there was the odd loose tile, and she had never been able to get Ceri-Ann to wear her hairnet fully covering her head – she doubted she ever would – but everything else was in order. Margery hoped so, anyway. She couldn't imagine how it could slip so badly that they would all lose their jobs. Perhaps it was less of a warning and more of a threat. She vowed to stop even the slightest of extracurricular day-to-day dalliance. The alternative was unthinkable.

She returned to the kitchen just as lunch hour was beginning. The queue was already sailing all around the room and out through the canteen doorway. Excitedly animated Year Sevens chatted away, while bored-looking upper years waited impatiently for their turn at the hot counter, scrolling on their phones. Margery had only just managed to pull on a pair of plastic gloves and grab the nearest serving tongs before she was interrupted once again. To her dismay, the co-hosts of the *That's So Spooky* podcast were waiting at the counter, grinning at her.

'Can I get you a piece of lasagne?' she asked, hoping that if she got them through the line quickly enough, they wouldn't have time to ask her or any of the other dinner ladies to come on the podcast again.

'Ooh yes please, Miss!' Amelia said, as enthusiastically as if Margery had offered her a rucksack containing a billion pounds.

Margery scooped up a serving onto a plate and handed it over the counter to her, where she put it on her tray with the can of sugar-free cola and the bag of pickled onion monster munch.

'Miss, you and the other Mrs Butcher-Baker have to come on the podcast now,' Oliver said as Margery prepared his portion of pasta. 'We've done you a couples name and everything. We call you Marentine on there.'

'Marentine? Why've you called us that?' Clementine scoffed from behind her. 'We never go sailing, and even if we did, we wouldn't follow maritime law, we'd be pirates, wouldn't we Margery?'

'No, it's a mix of your names!' Oliver protested.

But Clementine scoffed again, even louder this time. 'Our couple name would be Cargery, obviously.'

Margery didn't really know what to say to that, but before she could reply, Amelia continued the conversation for her. 'We need you to talk about the conspiracy, Miss,' she said in earnest. 'It's well important. We go on and on about it all the time, but no one takes us seriously. People would believe you.'

'What conspiracy?' Clementine asked and Margery rolled her eyes internally, just knowing that this was potentially going to become one of Clementine's many work shirking excursions.

'The swimming gala trophy of course!' Amelia tutted. 'Mr Barrow made out like it's been missing for like a few days, but we know it's been longer than that.'

'How would you know that?' Gloria asked from the hot counter, where she had been doling out portions of cottage pie and peas. Margery sighed to herself again, any moment now and the entire dinner lady team would be involved, and they really had enough on their plate. The queue wasn't going down at all with all the questioning.

'My mum's the head cleaner here, but she also does Ittonvale School,' Amelia explained. 'She said some old woman took it home with her last year to have it polished and she never brought it back.'

'And no one's seen it since,' Oliver said in his best podcast presenters voice, looking like a smug frog.

'Well, that's ridiculous,' Margery said. 'It was at the gala the other day, wasn't it?'

As soon as she had said the words out loud, she wondered if they were really true. She tried to wrack her memory for a glimpse of the trophy, but it eluded her. Maybe it really hadn't been there. Clementine certainly didn't seem to think it had been. But for it to have been missing for a year and for no one to say anything seemed very odd indeed. Another oddity was the mention of Ittonvale School, so soon after the recent conversation with Mr Fitzgerald about the missing Ittonvale teacher. Maybe there was something more to it all than they had previously decided.

'Do you have any other information than that?' Clementine asked. 'Only we've been on a few wild goose chases before.'

Literally, Margery thought. Why so many of Clementine's plots involved them being chased by angry birds, she would never know.

'No, but that doesn't mean it isn't true,' Amelia said, with a sarcastic eye roll. 'And obviously we're doing loads of research on it.'

'The truth will prevail!' Oliver cried, thrusting his hand in the air and nearly knocking over Amelia's dinner tray.

Margery decided that they shouldn't dismiss it in hand, but the words of two Year Elevens couldn't really be taken too seriously. They moved on towards the till to pay, and the queue continued to surge forwards so quickly that Margery didn't have time to think about it for much longer.

Chapter Fourteen

Margery and Clementine found themselves a day later in Rose's big range rover surrounded by even more orange segments than the week before.

It had been a terrible rush to get both lunchtime out of the way and the sandwiches and soup for the swimming gala all packed and ready to go. Dewstow leisure centre had managed to clear the mess of orange pulp from the pool and unclog the filters, but it was now fully booked with aqua aerobics and Year Seven swimming lessons. There was no time left in the new term to schedule another swimming gala, and no other option but a dreary Tuesday afternoon. Although Rose had whispered that Mr Barrow had tried to bribe Brian the leisure centre receptionist with a brand-new iPhone.

As soon as lunch was winding down Margery had left Gloria in charge and rushed out with Clementine and Seren. Leaving Sharon, Karen and Ceri-Ann to tidy up.

For someone who was only supposed to work part time anyway, Ceri-Ann was doing a terrible job of working less, especially at thirty-six weeks pregnant. Margery wondered how she was managing to keep up with her college work too. It was her final year, so surely, she would have exams. Perhaps she would be lucky enough to reschedule some of them, or maybe restart the year in

September. She shouldn't have really been there the day before.

'Remember, Seren,' Clementine said gently, patting Seren on the arm, 'we're a team. So we'll lift the oranges together.'

'I don't think I should lift them at all,' Seren replied, wide eyed, 'I haven't even been able to eat a satsuma since... and they used to be my favourite.'

'You just concentrate on the sandwiches, Seren,' Margery said, in what she hoped was a soothing voice. 'We'll organise the oranges and sausage rolls.'

'Yeah, don't try to help us orange anything!' Clementine said, nudging Seren in the ribs and beaming at her. Margery could see Rose rolling her eyes dramatically from the driving seat in the rear-view mirror. It gave her terrible déjà vu that she could only put down to narrowly escaping the horrendous golf club incident a few days before. She had told Clementine what Richard had said as soon as they were alone together, and her thoughts about behaving more sensibly when they were not at work. After all, they were still employees of the school, it wouldn't do to give Summerview any worse a reputation than it already had. What with the murders and auditing it was facing. Naturally Clementine hadn't agreed at all. Clementine had scoffed and reassured her that it was an empty threat. Never-the-less, Margery remained uncertain. Richard had seemed to mean it, and Clementine hadn't seen the look of annoyance on his face.

'I'm amazed they're letting you into Ittonvale School, Rose, after your fight with Mrs Blossom,' Clementine said, noticing Rose's expression.

Rose scoffed loudly from the driver's seat. 'Don't even get me started. If Elizabeth Hallow wants to ban me, let's see her try. She couldn't boil an egg, let alone run a school. She's got twice the budget as we do and still standards are slipping. And she's always poking her nose into Summerview School business – she's got such a long neck you could probably wave at her from the window of a three-storey building.'

They finally made it into Ittonvale School car park. Stopping in the layby meant for the student buses, they all clambered out, heavily waylaid by the numerous cool boxes and bags of sandwiches and strawberries. Margery tried not to let her exhaustion show on her face. By now, they would usually be nearly done in the kitchen and getting ready for home time. That seemed a very long way away. Rose tutted at the petals littering the ground from the flowers lining the car park, gesturing at them as if that was proof of Mrs Hallow's poor management.

It was a lovely day, Margery thought, as she stepped off the steps of the minibus and onto the pavement. Just as well: Ittonvale's outdoor pool would probably be freezing as it was. It wasn't supposed to be opening until the end of April at the very least, but the indoor pool they usually used was being refurbished and Mrs Hallow had made an exception for the gala, Margery was sure at Rose and Mrs Blossom's request. They'd be lucky if any of the children didn't catch hypothermia when the sun went behind the clouds again, although Ittonvale School was hiring out wetsuits for the occasion.

They were met at the school by a young man in well-worn overalls. He had the sort of angelic cherub face that Margery had only ever seen on statues. Ittonvale School's caretaker, Aaron, was the sort of no-nonsense person you'd want to fit doors for you or put up a lovely non-wonky set of shelving, but he was not a big talker.

The trip around the back of the school to the outdoor pool was a long and silent one, apart from the mutterings of Seren and Clementine as they carefully transported the oranges. They'd arrived much too early in Margery's opinion, leaving plenty of time to set everything up but at the cost of having to hang around for a long time before the event, which wasn't until four. The swimming pool cover hadn't even been taken off yet. It sat stretched across it tightly like the tarpaulin of a tent. The pool was half covered by an aluminium and polycarbonate arch that reminded Margery of her mother's old greenhouse, protecting it from the elements while still allowing it to be open air.

'Keeping the heat in for the kids and that, Mum said,' Aaron said when he noticed Margery's surprised face. 'It's got a heater, but that cover is solar powered too. Should be an alright temperature when the students get here. Don't want any of them turning into ice cubes.' Margery wondered briefly who Aaron's mother was, but the thoughts were washed away by their arrival at the pool area.

Someone – Margery assumed it was Aaron – had already set up a series of plastic trestle tables along the outside of the concrete building that contained the school changing rooms. They piled the trays on the tables, deciding that they wouldn't get anything out until at least one student had arrived, for risk of the sandwiches going stale, or the squash attracting flies. They'd have to move them anyway to get the soup kettle and chafing dishes to all fit on. The sun continued to shine, and Margery couldn't help but smile to herself. The warmth melting her worries away.

'We're really too early,' Clementine said while they looked around the empty pool area. Margery longed to go and sit on the grass behind the concrete path around it and lounge in the sunshine.

'Well, we'll need to get the chafing dishes out and the gas burners for them lit straight away once we've carried them up here if we're going to keep the food hot,' Margery explained. 'I hope we bought enough fuel for them. I really don't want to serve anyone a cold sausage roll. Gosh, I suppose this is good practice for your wedding Seren.'

'I'll go and check out the kitchens with Rose,' Seren said, dropping the last of the oranges on the table next to the cool box. 'She said they were supposed to leave it open for us to use the oven once their Education Centre Nourishment Consultants were gone. Maybe the kitchen manager will still be there so I can ask how all their equipment works.'

She scuttled back out and down the path the way they had arrived. Aaron pottered around the poolside, sweeping with a large broom, though any dirt on the spot-less pavement would only have been visible with a micro-scope. Ittonvale School grounds were in much better shape than Dewstow school. Aaron obviously worked very hard on the meticulously shaped and pruned bushes that Margery could see in front of the tennis court. The tennis court itself was a marvel, with its perfect flooring. Dewstow, on the other hand, had a combination netball, football, tennis court with paint lines for goals that were so faded they were barely visible and a net with so many holes in it that the tennis balls just bounced through.

On the horizon she could see Mrs Hallow, huffing and puffing her way up the hill.

'Why is this still closed Aaron?' Mrs Hallow yelled before she had even arrived at the gate to the pool, unclipping it with difficulty using her long-manicured nails. Once inside the pool area, she continued her tirade at the poor caretaker, who was trying without success to explain about the pool temperature.

'Well, get it open now, will you?' Mrs Hallow snapped at him before turning, and seeing that the Dewstow staff were in earshot. Her features rearranged into a forced smile with too many teeth. It did not meet her eyes. She gave Aaron a look that told him how she really felt. He rushed over to the opposite end of the pool and pressed a button.

The motor of the automatic pool cover whirred as it began to wind itself back, the plastic gliding over the sleek surface of the water and revealing the blue tiles below. Waves slid gently over the surface, as calm as the sea on a nice day. Steam rose from the surface and fanned upwards as the cool water met the warm spring air, an age-old fight between hot and cold.

For a moment after Mrs Hallow screamed, Margery had thought she must have been acting out some sort of dramatic joke, perhaps trying to cover up how she'd behaved towards Aaron. It wasn't until she took a step further towards the pool and saw the cause of her upset that she understood, staring down into the depths, speechless with horror. At the very bottom of the pool, resting on the clean blue tiles, was a pile of vaguely human shaped clothing.

Unable to help herself, and ignoring Clementine's hand on her arm Margery stepped forwards again and peered into the water for a better look. She could feel herself blinking stupidly as she stared, feeling sick as she realised that the pile of clothes was in fact a body.

Chapter Fifteen

Mrs Hallow's bloodcurdling scream echoed around the walls of the metal arch, bouncing off the windows and then echoed once again by the shrieks of the gathered staff around the pool. Margery found herself covering her ears instinctively with her hands to block out the sound.

'What... who?' Clementine stammered, trailing off as they all stared down into the depths of the water and watched the body, barely moving at the bottom of it.

'You don't think...?' Mrs Hallow said, turning to Aaron who had gone the sort of white Margery associated with Tipp-Ex and mayonnaise. 'You don't think it could be...?'

Aaron staggered backwards, holding his chest, until his legs met the nearest plastic poolside chair, slumping down into it. He opened his mouth to speak but nothing came out except a stammering wheeze. Clementine pulled her asthma inhaler out of her bag and offered it to him, but he shook his head, waving his hands to show he was okay, he was just in shock. Margery could sympathise.

Mrs Hallow turned her attention back to the pool, taking her mobile phone from her handbag and dialling the emergency service number.

'Do you know whose body that is?' Clementine called after her, but Mrs Hallow put her hand up to silence her before stepping out of the pool area and leaving them to wonder. Margery stepped forwards and stared into the pool again, her sense of horrible curiosity overwhelming her disgust and fright.

Once Mrs Hallow had rung for help, everyone jumped straight into action, determined to protect the children from the sight of the body. It had been a huge effort to stop any students from entering the pool area before the police could arrive and cordon it off. After it had been confirmed the ambulance was on the way, they realised that the person floating at the bottom of the pool was unlikely to swim back up and climb out of it.

To Rose's credit, her deputy head skills had kicked in immediately after Clementine had called to tell her and she had set in motion the plans to stop any students wandering over and seeing the body.

Rose and Seren had left the school kitchen immediately and posted themselves up at the entrance of the car park, warning each car that arrived not to stop at the school, but to keep going around the one-way system and back out. Margery and Clementine hadn't known what to do, but the police wouldn't let them leave, so they sat outside the pool area and watched as Mrs Hallow showed the police force to the area and the squad got to work setting up the crime scene.

Mrs Hallow had been interviewed already and now Margery and Clementine were waiting their turn. The police were still mulling around by the pool, cordoning bits of it off and led by Officer Wilkinson. They had already begun the process of bringing the body up from out of the water. Margery hoped they wouldn't be there for that; she could go her whole life without seeing it again.

'I… I can't even find the words,' Clementine whispered as they watched the police officers' work. 'Another body, in a pool, and at Ittonvale School of all places! I thought Ittonvale was too posh for murder. It's the sort of thing that happens in London, isn't it?'

'We've had a fair few in Dewstow now, haven't we Clem?' Margery reminded her. 'Why would Ittonvale be any different?'

She wondered for a moment if they were slowly becoming desensitised to the violence that had haunted them for the past few years, or if it was just that nobody seemed to recognise the victim. They had seen too many dead bodies over the past years. Two people had even died in front of them – one of whom had been a colleague. It wasn't that this death was any less horrific, but the unknown made it easier to cope with. Similarly with the skeleton in the car park – they were so far removed from it that Margery hadn't really given it too much thought, she had become so distracted with work and Evelyn's husband's affair.

'I know.' Clementine reached over and gave her hand a squeeze.

Margery squeezed back. She didn't know what to do now. They couldn't leave until they had been interviewed, and Rose and Seren had control over the car park, there wasn't much more they could do on that front. Yet she didn't think it was much good to stay either. They would only get in the way.

Margery was starting to think that maybe they should go and at least try to give Rose and Seren a hand, make themselves useful, when she noticed a car rumbling through the car park at the bottom of the hill. The driver didn't bother to park in one of the empty parking spaces.

Instead they flung the car door open. The man who emerged slammed the door shut again before sprinting up the hill towards them.

Officer Wilkinson had also noticed him. Margery watched as he turned his gaze to the running man with interest.

'It is her?' the man panted, his face red with exertion. He bent over, clutching one hand to his chest as if he was trying to will his heart to slow down, while his other fumbled on the arm of the bench.

Margery found herself leaning away from him and his panicked face. He couldn't have been much older than Officer Wilkinson, but his panic made him seem decades younger, like a child that had lost his parent in a super-market.

'Is it her?' he begged again, his eyes wild, 'is it Leanne? God, tell me it's Leanne, please...'

'Who?' Margery asked, feeling stupid, her brain not comprehending his words at all.

'My girlfriend,' he sobbed. 'She's been missing for weeks.'

'Not the missing PE teacher?' Clementine asked.

He nodded. 'Yeah... Where is she? Is it her?'

'They don't know who it is,' Margery told him.

Officer Wilkinson strode over, and they stepped out of the way so he could talk to the man.

'Come with me please,' Officer Wilkinson said. The man followed him away, leaving Margery and Clementine to watch on in sympathy. Clementine's phone beeped again and she took it out of her bag.

'Stupid thing,' she groaned, trying to stop the beeping noise. 'It's probably the GPS keyring telling me it's about to run out of battery.'

'Where is it?' Margery asked. 'Back at Evelyn's?'

'Oh,' Clementine said, her eyes bulging as she looked at her phone. 'It's not the battery at all.'

'No?'

'No.' Clementine flipped the phone over to show her. 'Guess where Don Redburn is?'

'Devon,' Margery gasped. She didn't even have to look down at the phone screen to know that. 'He must be at Vivian's house. What's he doing there?'

'I'm not sure,' Clementine said. 'But it matches up closely to the address Evelyn gave us. Maybe they really are having an affair!'

Margery tried to chuckle along with Clementine, but all the humour had gone out of her.

'We could go after him?' Clementine suggested, putting the phone back in her handbag. 'Catch them together like we were going to before?'

'Maybe,' Margery said, as carefully as she could without Clementine becoming suspicious. She had taken Richard's blunt advice to heart and didn't think it was a good idea, although he would probably never find out. 'But we can't leave here yet, can we?'

They could not. Margery put all thoughts of chasing Don down to Devon away to the back of her mind, and waited for the police to come for them.

–

Margery couldn't get the image of the body under the water out of her head, especially now she'd had time to process it at home for a few hours. She could still see their clothes billowing around in the water; an unmarked grave. How long could the body have been there? And what had happened to them? If it was the missing PE teacher, then maybe she had fallen into the pool and drowned, although that seemed very unlikely. Miss Hawthorne taught swimming lessons at Dewstow leisure centre in the summer holidays.

There had to be some other reason she had been found under the pool cover. Perhaps she had been swimming in the pool and the cover had been closed over her by mistake. But surely someone would have heard her cries and rescued her. Margery hadn't thought to ask about Aaron's hearing, but he hadn't seemed to have a problem when they had met him.

'Anything can kill you,' Clementine had said in her adamant way when they were in bed the night before, 'if you drank enough eyedrops you'd drop dead. It wouldn't mean it was another murder.' But Margery still wasn't sure.

The ongoing mystery of the playground body suddenly seemed even more important than it had been when they'd been insisting they wouldn't get involved. The likelihood of one body turning up like that was unheard of, but two in less than a few weeks was unthinkable. If the body in the pool was Miss Hawthorne, then who had been buried and forgotten under the school playground? The thoughts whirled around her head as they sat on the sofa with the television on low in the background.

'Are you okay sweetheart?' Clementine asked, snapping Margery out of her thoughts.

'Yes,' Margery said. She got up and went into the kitchen. She grabbed the folder from the kitchen table where it had sat awkwardly in the way of the butter dish ever since they had been given it, and brought it back into the living room. She put it down on the coffee table. Clementine looked at her expectantly as she sat back down. She sank into the comfortable old sofa again and opened Mr Fitzgerald's bizarre missing persons folder. Richard's words may have scared her enough not to entertain leaving for another county, but she was sure he wouldn't be able to find them investigating in their own home. Perhaps there was something in the folder that could help the police.

'Do you think that will help?' Clem said, as Margery thumbed through the folder.

'I don't know,' Margery let out the heavy sigh that had been building since they returned home. 'I just don't know what else to do.'

'We don't have to do anything,' Clementine reminded her.

'Yes, we're not really detectives, are we?' Margery said, feeling a relief at saying the words out loud. 'But… oh it's silly, isn't it? Trying to help?'

'Of course not!' Clementine said. 'Obviously people are constantly telling us to stay out of things, like that auditor and the police, but that's just because they don't want us to best them.'

Margery grimaced at the way Officer Wilkinson had spoken to them earlier when he had interviewed them. He'd been cordially polite, but his annoyance at the sight of them was palpable enough that the entire encounter had been terribly awkward.

'I don't think that's—'

'Anyway,' Clementine interrupted, 'we are basically detectives now. We've got a website and everything. That's the bare minimum for being a detective.'

'Oh Clem,' Margery said. 'It's never got us into anything but trouble though, has it? I think at some point we have to concentrate on the things that are important—'

'What's more important than helping people?' Clementine said, her eyes flashing with a sudden hint of fury. 'Nothing, and we've helped so many.'

'We help people every day at work by feeding them,' Margery reminded her. 'Just because it's not very glamorous or exciting, well, that doesn't mean that it isn't important.'

'I'll remind you that it's you that brought those files in here,' Clementine said, gesturing to the open folder on Margery's lap.

'Yes, well,' Margery said, feeling her face turn red. 'I just feel like we should go through these again.' She began to flick through the sheets of paper inside the folder even faster. 'I know it probably won't help, but if the police are missing something, we should report it immediately.'

'Well, they've already found the missing teacher, haven't they?' Clementine said, their disagreement already mostly forgotten. She began to help Margery go through the box of files again earnestly, sometimes oohing to herself at the sight of a familiar name or two.

Chapter Sixteen

Sleep evaded Margery for a while – thoughts of the playground skeleton and the body in the pool whirled around in her head – but eventually her brain stopped fighting against exhaustion. She had fallen into an uncomfortable rest, being woken several times by Pumpkin coming to curl up at the foot of the bed, or Crinkles playing with her toy mouse in the hallway, even though the noises of the cats wouldn't usually bother her.

Mr Fitzgerald's folder hadn't yet turned up anything useful, except that Miss Hawthorne's name was written in it. The date of her disappearance in red ink on the left side and the right column still blank. If that was her poor body in the pool, Margery had reasoned, then it was a horrible way to go. Since she had almost drowned a few years ago while on holiday she had struggled with the thoughts of dying that way. Some days she wasn't even able to put her face fully under the shower head to wash her hair. The thoughts came and went, but lingered always.

The doorbell startled her awake properly, and she raised her head to blearily look at the alarm clock through sleep-filled eyes. It had barely gone half past five. Clementine had already begun to drag herself out of bed. She couldn't have slept well either.

'Don't worry,' she said, tapping Margery on the shoulder in a comforting way, 'I'll go and see who it is.'

Clementine left the room and Margery closed her eyes again at the sound of her footsteps going down the stairs and opening the door.

'What are you doing here?' Clementine asked, the note of surprise in her voice palpable even a floor below.

Margery's eyes snapped open again and she reluctantly got out of bed to see what was going on. Grasping her dressing gown from the back of the bedroom door and pulling it on over her pyjamas, she made her way out into the hallway and down the stairs. Clementine had already invited whoever had rung the bell into the house. Margery followed the sounds of low conversation into the living room.

Ittonvale School's headmistress sat on Clementine's favourite pink crinoline chair, looking as out of place as a frog driving a car. Rose paced the floor in front of the coffee table, her shoes catching slightly on the old, worn carpet.

'Hello,' Margery said. Both Rose and Mrs Hallow snapped their heads up as she appeared and moved into the room.

'Would you like a drink?' Clementine asked them both.

'Coffee,' Mrs Hallow said, 'please.' At the same time Rose said, 'Gin!'

There was a horrible uncomfortable silence as Clementine went into the little kitchen and rattled around in the drawers and cupboards. Margery crossed the room and sat down on the sofa. Mrs Hallow looked as upset as Rose did, not at all the bossy teacher who had been running the gala the other day. Margery supposed that finding a dead body in your own school's pool would do that to you. She realised that over the last few years they had become so used to people arriving at their house in the middle of the night, that she had not even thought to ask the women across from her why they were there. Mrs Hallow cleared her throat, as though she could read Margery's mind. Her eyebrows were so blonde in the low light of the single lamp Clementine had turned on that they barely existed under her hairline.

'Rose told me that I should come and see you about all this.' She waved a hand like that would explain what she meant. Rose finally stopped her pacing and sat down in Margery's mother's antique rocking chair. 'The pool, you know. You were there when we... when we found...'

'Yes,' Margery said, finishing her sentence. 'We were.'

'Who told you to come see us?' Clementine asked. She brought in a cafetière, milk jug and mugs on a tray, and set it down on the coffee table.

'Rose. But I've heard about you before of course. Do you know Martha?' Mrs Hallow asked, looking between them.

'We do,' Margery said, trying to hide the small smile that had appeared on her face. She wondered if they ought to be paying Martha Mugglethwaite a decent percentage of the one hundred pounds Evelyn had given them, for her excellent PR work.

'Well, she said you were already helping a friend and you could help sort this all out too,' Mrs Hallow explained. She reached into her handbag and took out her purse, pulling out several banknotes. 'Here, your payment for my case.'

'We do murders for free,' Clementine said, waving Mrs Hallow's hand away.

'What about the website?' Margery spluttered. 'You've been going on about how we're real detectives!'

144

Clementine scoffed at that, but looked conflicted.

'Take the money, for Christ's sake,' Rose said, jumping up and taking the notes from Mrs Hallow. Before Clementine could protest again she'd stuffed them down the back of the television unit. 'This'll probably cost you more than that in petrol.'

'Tell us what's going on, why aren't the police helping you?' Margery asked Mrs Hallow before Rose and Clementine could begin an argument.

'They are,' Mrs Hallow said, but there was some fury behind it. 'But they're looking in all the wrong places. They took my son in for questioning, for God's sake!'

'Why?' Clementine asked.

'He's our handyman and gardener,' Mrs Hallow said. 'I took him on at Ittonvale a year or so ago, he wasn't going to get a job otherwise. He lives on the school grounds in the greenkeeper's house, you see. It killed two birds with one stone.' Her face fell. 'So to speak.'

Margery thought back to Aaron, the young man who had shown them to the pool area when they had arrived at Ittonvale School. 'Was he in charge of the pool maintenance?'

'Yes,' Mrs Hallow said, nodding vigorously. 'So, you can see what sort of trouble we're in. I'm going to end up having an audit like Summerview and I know how badly that's going for you, I mean...' She suddenly realised from Rose's pointed glare that she was in the wrong audience for conversation about the audit and fell silent.

'What do you want us to do?' Margery said, rubbing her eyes. She found herself feeling how tired she still was. Her eyelids felt like lead weights. Mrs Hallow reached into her bag again and brought out a laptop.

'I don't mean to be rude, but I brought this because I'm assuming you wouldn't have anywhere to play my car dashcam footage,' she said bluntly.

She didn't wait for an answer, even as Clementine opened her mouth to splutter something about the ancient desktop computer sitting dustily in their spare room.

'Was there no CCTV footage of the car park?' Margery asked as Mrs Hallow booted up the laptop and began to flick through her files.

'Nothing good enough to pinpoint anyone,' Mrs Hallow said, 'and too far away to be picked up by the school cameras.'

'And you don't have anything by the pool?' Margery asked, thinking about what must have happened inside the swimming pool building.

'I run a school, not a prison,' Mrs Hallow hissed.

Rose raised her eyebrows, giving her one of her patented deputy head stares and Mrs Hallow turned to the computer again, bristling.

She turned the screen so Margery and Clem could see it, then pressed play on the video.

Ittonvale School car park came into view, and the writing on the top of the scene read the date, which was a few weeks ago now. They could see out of the windscreen of the car from the camera angle. It was early evening judging by the darkness beginning to fall, but they could still make out the car as it travelled through the car park from the beams of its headlights, past Mrs Hallow's car.

'Here,' Mrs Hallow said, flicking through the camera settings till they had a better view of it sailing past. The car parked up in a space opposite.

'Why is your car still there?' Clementine scratched her head. 'You surely don't leave it there overnight?'

'Sometimes I do,' Mrs Hallow said. 'I generally walk to work for the exercise, I only live up the road. I usually bring the car and park it in my space on a Monday morning and then take it home on Friday night because I generally have a lot of bags with me then.'

'All right,' Margery said, scratching her head. She couldn't see where Mrs Hallow was going with this yet.

They watched the car parked in front of Mrs Hallow's for a moment and then a figure emerged from it, slowly shuffling along through the school grounds.

'They go up towards the pool,' Mrs Hallow said, pointing at the screen as the person walked past, slowly but with purpose in their stride, a canvas shopping bag swinging from one arm.

'They never came back,' Mrs Hallow said, her eyes wide.

'What's in the bag?' Clementine said, pointing to where the bag had been.

Mrs Hallow looked haunted, and Margery suddenly had a bad feeling wash over her. It was like seeing smoke billowing towards you unexpectedly on a calm summer's walk in the woods.

'It was a trophy,' Mrs Hallow said, her voice going up a pitch. 'The IttonStow cup.'

'The IttonStow cup?' Margery whispered. Mrs Hallow nodded.

'The trophy has been missing for months now,' she said. 'Of course, we only recently reported it missing so as to not cause a panic in either town.'

Rose glared at her from the corner at the revelation, though she didn't say anything. Margery remembered Amelia and Oliver's insistence that the trophy had been missing since last year and was sure that they would be overjoyed when the news came to light that they had been correct.

'Can you go back to the car?' Margery said. 'Have the police found the owner yet?'

'They're certainly looking for it. I think they were able to do a search for the owner, but obviously no one would tell me anything,' she explained.

'What do you mean?' Clementine asked. She was answered immediately by the screen changing again, back to the parked car, but on a much darker night. Mrs Hallow sucked in a deep breath before explaining the change in scenery.

'This was the night before last,' Mrs Hallow breathed. 'The night before we found the body.'

Someone else was walking through the car park, their face deliberately covered by the hood of their large rain-coat. The time on the video was just past three in the morning. They reached the car and opened it with the keys, getting inside and driving away.

'So, someone else took the car somewhere?' Margery said. 'After whoever it was had died? And they had their keys!'

'Yes,' Mrs Hallow whispered. 'Exactly, so they must know the person quite well.'

'Don't the police think it was Miss Hawthorne's boyfriend?' Margery asked, 'Surely that's the most obvious person to have the keys?'

'They haven't confirmed if it's her, yet, but it looks very likely, doesn't it?' Mrs Hallow looked haunted. 'And of course, that wasn't her car. She used to have a hatchback. So either she came into possession of a different car, or someone lent her it.' She took another deep breath. 'I hate to say it, though, but the timelines do add up. She went missing a few weeks before all this happened. But the police don't seem to think it was Liam. They did ask him some questions, but they let him go.'

Margery felt her eyebrows raising of their own accord. She had thought that Miss Hawthorne's boyfriend would have been the number one suspect for her disappearance anyway, even before her body was found. She wondered what the police knew. They must know something to have let him walk free while the groundskeeper was kept in.

'You realise that this looks bad for your son?' Clementine said. 'Surely he was supposed to check the pool more often. Why didn't he find the body before?'

Rose nodded so hard that it was almost violent. 'I agree! That would never happen at Summerview School, people are constantly in and out of Dewstow leisure centre's pool. The water barely has time to settle down overnight before there's someone else splashing about in it.'

'I remember the day we arrived at Summerview for the badminton tournament and the school didn't own a single shuttlecock,' Mrs Hallow snapped. Rose glared at her. Mrs Hallow's eyes turned pleading to Margery. 'We had the maintenance people in last month, as always. We always get it ready to go at the end of February because the Golden Circle sometimes book it for the spring equinox.'

'Have they booked it this year?' Rose asked. 'Aren't they the ones who complained last time that the sunrise wasn't glorious enough?'

'Yes,' Mrs Hallow said, with gritted teeth. 'I've been trying to contact Vivian for ages, but she's just not answering my calls. I think she's annoyed that the gala was rescheduled and she's avoiding me. Well, two can play at that game.'

'Vivian Black?' Clementine asked. Margery wondered what kind of group the Golden Circle really was. The only photographs they'd seen were of parties and Christmas events, they hadn't seen what the group was either way. Margery had assumed it was some sort of social club, but maybe there was more to it.

'Yes,' Mrs Hallow said. 'Do you know her?'

'It's a long story,' Margery said.

Rose was looking at Margery thoughtfully, tapping her long perfect nails against her chin. Mrs Hallow continued, oblivious to the recognition that had passed between them.

'Anyway, you've got to at least have a look into this,' Mrs Hallow said. 'The police are looking for the car, but I want you to look too.'

'And you didn't notice it was there before?' Margery asked.

'No,' Mrs Hallow said, her face falling. 'Lots of people park there overnight, though we try to discourage it. But we can't stop everyone. And anyway, it's a big free car park and it's open to the public. What can we do?'

Margery didn't know. They rewatched the dashcam footage in silence, Clementine making notes and Margery wondering how on earth they would be able to help at all.

They were interrupted by the letter box opening and closing again with a clang, startling all of them. Margery got up and went to the front door, where the *Dewstow Freepress* hung halfway out of the letterbox. The paper usually arrived on a Friday morning, so it was strange to see it on a Monday, but she reached for it anyway. She pulled it out, meaning to take it into the living room and put it down on the coffee table to read that evening or tomorrow, but the headline splashed across the front page caught her eye. '*School Skeleton in DNA Reveal*'.

Chapter Seventeen

A body found under the playground of a local school has been revealed by DNA testing to be of a local man. Eugene Price was found on Monday the fourth of March during Summerview School's playground refurbishment. It is believed that his body has been there for several decades and police are calling for information on the deceased. Investigating officer Mark Wilkinson of Dewstow police force said: 'We are keen to hear from anyone who has any information at this time. Your help, no matter how small, could help us make progress in this case. We are determined to resolve what happened to Mr Price and put his family's mind to rest.'

Officer Wilkinson would not comment on a second body, found yesterday at Ittonvale School, saying, 'Details will be given in time.' Please turn to page three for more information.

–

'Well, at least we know who that body was. And it's good that they found that PE teacher too,' Margery overheard Mrs George say to one of the other English teachers as they stood and stared out of the canteen window, her brain slow and drowsy still after the morning they'd had. 'Now they can get on with hiring a new one.'

Gloria, who had also been listening, turned to Margery and gave her such a look of disgust at Mrs George's comment that Margery almost laughed out loud in surprise. Gloria shook her head and returned to setting up the sandwich fridge, but her jaw remained clenched tightly shut with anger. No one seemed to know who Eugene Price was, and the newspaper hadn't told how exactly he had ended up under the concrete playground yet, other than the autopsy revealing that he had likely died of a headwound. Margery assumed that the police were still trying to work out the finer details, though it seemed impossible to her. The DNA testing on the skeleton must have been a huge undertaking in itself.

'Seren, go and get the brush and sweep those idiots out of here,' Clementine said. Seren went to grab for the broom before realising she was joking. At the same time, Rose swept into the room and the English teachers seemed to remember that they all had much more important places to be. She looked so much different than she had in the early hours of the morning, Margery thought, almost like it had never happened at all.

'Vultures, all of them,' Rose sneered, glaring at the teachers as they disappeared through the canteen double doors. 'What are they even looking at? There's nothing left to see in the playground. They know who the body was now.'

Margery had noticed first thing that morning that the police tape was gone, and the builders were already there, busily pouring concrete over the playground. In a few days it would be like nothing had ever happened, and everyone would move on. Although Margery wondered if Eugene Price's family would be able to. She was sure he had to have some somewhere. Though she thought back to what Nigel had said about the missing persons reports. No one had reported him missing at the time, after all. Maybe there was no one left to look for him.

'Can I speak with you in your office, please, Margery?' Rose said, lowering her voice. Margery caught her eye in surprise, briefly wondering if they had accidentally served her a stale sandwich, but Rose just looked concerned.

Margery nodded and followed Rose through the kitchen and down the hallway to her office in the dry store. As soon as they entered the room, Rose shut the door behind them. Margery looked up in alarm. She had thought Rose might want to discuss the audit or similar, but the frantic look in the other woman's eyes told her immediately that this was much more serious.

'I found something the other day,' Rose hissed, pulling an A4 envelope out of the folder she had been carrying under her arm. 'And I took it because it seemed useful, but I haven't been able to put my finger on why until now.'

'Okay,' Margery said, wondering where on earth this conversation was about to go and trying not to look at Rose like she was trying to give her a letter inviting her to a surprise colonoscopy. Rose thrust the envelope to Margery and then glanced back at the door to check that they wouldn't be interrupted. Blearily Margery opened the envelope and stared at the contents inside.

'What's this?' she asked, a little afraid to find out. It seemed a long time since she had poked around in anyone else's business, even though she knew they had been at a complete stranger's house without their knowledge the other day.

'I saw your face when Mrs Hallow told me about Vivian Black and the Golden Circle,' Rose explained, a look of triumph crossing her features. 'And I just knew you'd been investigating the skeleton.'

'We haven't,' Margery said, looking down at the paper in her hands. 'But… is this…?'

'Yes, it's the original sign-off for the school playground in 1975!' Rose said, her voice rising excitedly before she could help herself. 'Look who signed it off.'

'Is that Vivian's signature?' Margery read the tiny writing and accompanying scrawl. 'Gosh, how old is this woman? We thought she might be having the affair with Don Redburn, but she's got to be at least eighty.'

'I wouldn't have thought so,' Rose said, shaking her head and pointing out the full name further up the document. 'Well, stranger things have happened, haven't they?'

'I suppose so,' Margery agreed. 'Did you find anything else?'

'Here,' Rose pulled a photograph from another envelope in her bag. How she had organised it to be able to find anything again, Margery would never know. It was not like Rose, who was usually a well put together and meticulous teacher, who had been promoted to deputy headmistress heavily based on her talent at organising. She handed it to Margery, who immediately noticed the Summerview School logo at the bottom. It was a staged and seated group photo of the schoolteachers and staff, the same year as the playground renovation. It looked very similar to the class photos the Year Sevens and Elevens had taken every year.

Former kitchen manager, Caroline had desperately tried to get the dinner lady team to be part of a photograph one year, but the photographer had refused to let them sit for it. Caroline had threatened that they would come back the next year dressed as students, but had died before they could enact her plan.

Margery occasionally wondered how it would have gone and it made her smile, imagining seventy-five-year-old Caroline and the rest of the much-too-old dinner lady team arriving in school sweatshirts.

Caroline was in the Summerview photo, Margery realised with surprise, looking so shockingly young that it would have taken Margery's breath away if she hadn't seen a photograph of her in her youth before. Caroline had been there from the beginning, she remembered now. She hadn't begun as the catering manager, which tracked with the humble dinner lady tabard she wore, sitting alongside the rest of the kitchen team on the right. The man on her left wearing the chef hat must have been her boss. Mr Fitzgerald, who somehow looked much the same, stood on the other side of the photograph with the rest of the governors. The only difference was that his long beard was still dark and not white.

'There's Vivian and her husband Billy,' Rose said, pointing them out in the top row. 'And lots of other people I don't know. But their names are all on the back.'

Margery flipped the photograph over and saw that was indeed the case. Printed on the back of the cardboard casing in the same gold lettering and fancy font as the front was a left-to-right description of each person.

When Margery turned the photograph back over, Rose pointed out another man in the front row. 'That's Professor Harold Whitford. He was the first headmaster of Summerview School.'

'Wow,' Margery said. 'I don't know anyone there. Apart from Caroline of course! Hmmm… hang on…'

She looked back at the list of names on the rear, and ran her index finger down to the name she was looking at. 'Eugene Price.'

'Yes!' Rose said, nodding so hard her hair bobbed up and down. 'The man they found under the playground.'

'There's a Price family in Dewstow, still, isn't there?' Margery said. 'Gosh, I wonder if Vivian knew him.'

She glanced at the clock and realised that if they were going to be ready for lunchtime, she needed to get back to work. Rose seemed to realise the same.

'Where did you get these?' Margery demanded to know. 'Clementine's convinced Vivian's done a moon-light flit because she knew the skeleton was going to be dug up.'

'Well, then I agree with her,' Rose said. 'Storeroom on the top floor at work. The one you nearly suffocated and died in.'

Margery winced at the memory of trying to escape the small room without her phone while a murderer got away.

'Sorry,' Rose said, grimacing at her apologetically. 'I was looking for the periodic table display that used to be up there so I could replace Mr Beaker's science classroom display before the auditor gets there. For some reason he thought an entire wall about how prions could cause an apocalypse and bring about the downfall of mankind was appropriate, and then he wanted to replace it with one about antibiotic resistance...' She waved her hands in dismissal. 'Anyway, I found a lot of the older files and thought I'd look back. But there's loads of them, you need to go and have a look. Preferably today, you might well find something that proves this Vivian woman killed whoever Eugene Price was.'

'The thing is,' Margery said, suddenly feeling very tired. 'We can't. The police and the auditor have already warned us off of it all.'

'Well, when has that ever stopped you or Clementine?' Rose asked, her face dropping in astonishment.

'Can you not tell the police about it?' Margery asked, feeling as weak as her voice.

'And have the auditor find out about it?' Rose said, shaking her head. 'No. I don't think I have to tell you Margery, it's no great secret that the audit is not going well at all.'

Margery sighed, she agreed that there really was no way to get the police involved without Richard finding out. 'I suppose we don't have any better options. But the thing is Rose, just because Vivian signed off on the playground doesn't mean she had anything to do with his death.'

Rose looked relieved that she hadn't continued to say no.

'I don't know much about the woman,' Rose tried to explain. 'She was still on Ittonvale School's PTA until fairly recently, but she had this group... Elizabeth would know much more than me obviously, but she had this group called the Golden Circle.'

'We've heard of it,' Margery said, remembering the photographs she had seen. 'What was it?'

'What is it, you mean,' Rose said, leaning back on the chest freezer and crossing her arms. 'It's her and her husband's social club, made up entirely of people they cherry-picked to join them.'

'That sounds a bit odd,' Margery said.

'A lot of them were her best students, or people he met doing business,' Rose explained.

'Were you part of the group?' Margery asked. 'Was Mr Barrow?'

'Oh God no,' Rose spluttered. 'I haven't been here long enough, growing up in the countryside and obviously I've been all over the shop with my acting talents…' Margery nodded along in what she hoped was an agreeable fashion. 'And James, well… he's always been a bit plain, bless him. He wouldn't have caught either of their eyes I don't think.'

'Do you know anyone who's part of it?' Margery asked, thinking about the photographs of the Golden Circle meetings with Richard. She wondered if she ought to tell Rose about it, but decided in the end that if Rose didn't know much about it anyway, then it would make no difference.

'No,' Rose said, 'not really. I did a while ago, but a lot of people have moved away since. I think it's died off a bit anyway, now that Vivian's husband is dead, but still… I thought it was worth mentioning to you.'

'Well, thank you,' Margery said. 'Though I think it might be a very long shot.'

'Maybe not,' Rose said. 'But it's something. And unless you find that missing car I can't see any more leads.'

'I bet the police already know where the car is,' Margery said, feeling her brow wrinkling at the thought. 'And who owns it.'

'Well, we can't know that,' Rose said. 'And we won't, unless you have some sort of insider information I don't know about.'

Margery thought about Nigel and his offer to help during their meeting at the golf course, but still said nothing. It all seemed so long ago, and she now was even more certain that his grand idea to break into the police station was a terrible one.

They crept through the halls after their shift had finished, their shoes squeaking on the old linoleum. They had waited until everyone else had left to begin their quest – it seemed much less illegal than sneaking up there during the middle of the lunch hour or when they were supposed to be working. If anyone caught them, they could innocently explain that they had stayed late to fetch something from the storeroom for the kitchen. The dinner ladies certainly stored their fair share of things in there, and so it wouldn't seem an unusual occurrence. Margery had wondered if they ought to delay the visit to the storeroom until tomorrow before the school's opening hours, but Clementine had reminded her that the police were more than likely still snooping around. If they saw Margery and Clementine removing anything or even entering the storeroom in the first place, there would be questions. Questions they couldn't answer.

Margery didn't know what she expected to find. Hopefully something even more damning than Vivian's signature on the playground's plan, though in the haze of tiredness she felt, she couldn't think of anything much worse. They had decided to look for council minutes and school records from the year the playground had been refinished. She wondered if they ought to drive down to Vivian's holiday house and ask her a few questions – they still had her address. More concerningly though, they knew Don had been visiting her and they still didn't know exactly why. Still, she knew that they had probably evaded suspicion from the police and the auditor by not going.

'What do you think we'll find?' Margery asked Clementine, who was doing her best to tiptoe through the halls in her clunky kitchen clogs.

'Well, the storeroom is notoriously full of junk, isn't it?' Clementine said as they reached the storeroom door. 'Probably an original copy of the Magna Carta and thousands of Christmas and birthday cards Mr Barrow doesn't want to throw away just in case he needs them one day.'

Margery chuckled as she turned the door handle and they entered the room. Clementine flicked the light switch and the bulb clacked on, filling the room with a horrible florescent glow.

'I forgot what a mess it is up here,' Clementine said, gesturing at the piles of things with a grimace.

Margery joined her in going through box after box of files. Rose had told her they were right at the back of the room, but there was so many of them that Margery really didn't know where to start. She began by opening the nearest one and flicking through the long-abandoned records. As she watched the dust fly from the pages as she turned them, she wondered why they had all been kept for so long. Surely the school must have moved everything to digital storage by now. There couldn't be much use for such old records. They pulled apart boxes and opened the filing cabinet at the back of the room. Margery was about to give up hope of ever finding anything and was going to suggest they gave up, when Clementine gave a whoop from where her head was half inside the filing cabinet.

'Ooh, look here!' Clementine said, showing Margery what she had found. 'Meeting minutes from when Vivian was a governor here, exactly what we hoped for!'

She passed Margery the box folder, which was labelled, 'School Minutes and Events 1970–1975'.

'Here she is with the swim team,' Margery said, showing Clementine the photograph of Vivian stood next to the assembled sports team, who were all in modest bathing suits and goggles. She turned it over and read the names, turning it back around again in surprise once she recognised one. 'Clem, is this… is that Evelyn?'

She pointed her finger at a girl in the second row, who was wearing Evelyn's annoyed expression, as though it was a mask of the Evelyn they knew now.

'Yes, I think so,' Clementine said, taking the photograph for a better look. 'She did say she was her swimming teacher.'

'Well, Eugene Price could be a relative,' Margery tried to find the words, 'look at her name.'

Clementine turned the photograph over and read the text, where she saw the name, 'Evelyn Price'.

'You don't think that Evelyn knows what's going on?' Margery said and watched in real time as the lightbulb turned on inside Clementine's brain. 'She was close with Vivian. Who is Eugene to her? A brother? A cousin?'

'Oh my! Yes, it's quite possible,' Clementine said. 'We need to talk to her.'

'Let's take this all with us,' Margery said, finally remembering that the clock was ticking down till everyone else had left and it would be suspicious for them to be there. 'We'll put them in the car and take them home.'

'Alright,' Clementine nodded.

'And then we'll go and see Evelyn tonight and ask her what she knows,' Margery said. 'And see if she's all right. I'd imagine the news of a relative being found like that must be horrific.'

They packed all the folders up into the boxes they had brought with them and then moved to the door. They turned the light off again and moved to leave, but as soon as Clementine opened the door, she closed it again, turning to hiss at Margery, 'It's Richard!'

'What?' Margery whispered back.

They stared through the gap in the door and watched as he walked past them. This afternoon he was walking with purpose, seemingly on his way somewhere, but without the clipboard he seemed to carry everywhere with him. The fact he didn't have it made Margery nervous somehow, though she couldn't quite put her finger on why.

'Let's escape before he comes back this way,' Clementine said, already turning the door handle.

'But...' Margery began, but she followed Clementine out into the hallway anyway, weighed down by the box under her arm.

They snuck back down the corridor, but not sneakily enough. Richard spun around and caught them.

'Hello, both,' he called out, causing them both to freeze. When they turned to face him, he said, 'On your way home?'

'Yes,' Margery stammered. Clementine nodded behind her.

'Lovely,' Richard said, shifting his weight from foot to foot. 'I'm just off to look over the science department.'

'I thought you were doing the inspections with the headmaster?' Clementine asked him, her eyes narrowing.

'Yes...' Richard said, looking between them. 'I am, of course! I just... um... wanted to get a little head start before tomorrow.' He looked down at the boxes in their arms. 'What have you got there?'

'Nothing much,' Clementine said at the same time as Margery said, 'Stocktake records.'

'Hmmm,' he hummed in a way that told Margery he didn't believe a word they'd said. 'Well, I suppose we'd all better be on our way.'

He walked off the way he had been going leaving Margery and Clementine to scuttle off in the opposite direction.

'What was that about?' Clementine said, as they walked. Margery shook her head, the box in her hands suddenly feeling like a dead weight.

Chapter Eighteen

Despite the slight hiccup of Richard interrupting them, they did exactly as they had planned to do: going straight home, dropping the boxes off before driving immediately to the Redburns' house. For all the good that would do, Margery thought worriedly. At least Richard had not seemed to notice what they had been holding, and if he had then he hadn't felt the need to comment. Margery was sure after their meeting the other day that he would almost certainly say if he thought they were doing something amiss. Margery hoped that he assumed they were carrying kitchen equipment in the boxes.

Clementine had voiced several theories as to who Eugene Price could be to Evelyn as she drove them there, none of which Margery felt would hold much water. She had avoided reminding Clementine about Nigel's offer to sneak them into the police station. It really wouldn't be a good idea, even if they did want to know what had happened. She had a horrible feeling that Vivian's sign-off of the playground and Evelyn's deceased relative, might also be related. Clementine's feet-first jump into assuming Vivian had killed him, or at least covered his death up, might be about to be revealed as the truth.

As soon as they arrived at Evelyn's, Clementine went straight over to Don's car and fumbled around under the wheel arch.

'What are you doing?' Margery hissed.

'Getting my fob,' Clementine hissed back. 'I'm sure I put it... ah, here it is!'

She pulled out the GPS fob and held it up triumphantly. Margery glanced over at the house to see if the Redburns had noticed anything. Luckily the car was half hidden by the hedge that ran along the driveway.

'Put it away, Clem,' Margery whispered. Clementine did no such thing. Instead, she replaced the battery and then the fob, sticking it back under the arch with the industrial strength teacher's Blu Tack.

'I'm amazed that managed to stay on there all this time,' she said, standing up again and wiping her dirty hands on her black trousers. 'They should use this as an advert for it.'

'Have you lost your mind?' Margery snapped. 'Why have you changed the battery? Take it off. We're not investigating anymore.'

'Evelyn hired us to find out about the affair,' Clementine explained. 'We took her money, and we haven't finished the job. I feel like we owe her that.'

Margery weighed this up in her mind. While Clementine was theoretically correct, it did not make it the correct thing to do in reality. However, she reasoned to herself, it would be good to know if Don was still visiting Vivian. If only to find out where she was.

If she had something to do with Eugene Price's untimely demise and burial under the school playground, then knowing where she was might come in handy, but the ethics of how they were going to find her were all wrong, as per usual. But she couldn't see another way around it.

'Fine,' she snapped. 'But the minute it runs out of battery again, that's it. It's over.'

They left the car, walked to the front door and rang the bell. Mrs Redburn answered a minute later, and it was clear that she had been crying.

'What do you want?' she asked them, Margery didn't quite know what to say.

'We came to give our condolences,' Clementine said.

Evelyn looked for a moment as though she wanted to do nothing more than shut the door in her face with all her might, hoping it hit Clementine on the way, but instead she stepped back from the doorway to let them in. They followed her inside – saying hello to Don, who had left the kitchen to see who had arrived – and into the living room, where she gestured for them to sit on the other side of the three-piece suite.

'Are you all right?' Clementine asked when they had sat down. 'We're very sorry for your loss Evelyn, we didn't realise that Eugene was your family member.'

Evelyn shook her away with her hands, slumping back into the sofa. Don came into the room with a pot of tea and several cups on a tray. He put it down in the middle of the coffee table and then sat down next to Evelyn, taking her hand and giving it a squeeze.

'Poor Gene,' she sobbed. 'He didn't deserve that.'

No, he didn't, Margery thought. Don poured his wife a cup of tea and added milk from the jug with his free hand. She took it from him with shaking fingers and put it straight back down in front of her. She shook his hand away, and curled her own arms around herself. Don moved away, giving her space on the sofa.

'We're terribly sorry for your loss,' Margery said, even though Clementine had just said the same thing.

After her own mother had died, Margery had hated the trite platitudes people would come out with to describe how awful they felt for her and how terribly sad it all was. In some ways she would have rather been left alone. It was weird to think about now that she was edging closer and closer to the finish line of the race she had begun when she had been born. Still, if she'd known how she'd have felt without her mother she would have tried to keep more parts of her when she was alive, held on to the letters and postcards she had sent, made a recording of her answerphone message to listen to occasionally. She could barely remember what her voice sounded like now. She tried not to think about that too much.

Evelyn sat up and wiped her eyes, taking the cup now she was ready and taking a sip, wincing as she did so. 'No sugar?' she said to Don, who jumped up, flustered and took the cup with him, leaving the women alone.

'In some ways it's a relief,' Evelyn said. 'We finally know where he is, and we can bury him properly.'

'Has he been gone a long time?' Margery asked. Evelyn nodded.

'Decades,' she explained. 'But he always wrote, until a few years ago, from all over the place – wherever he was on his travels. Letters at first, and then we went to email not that long before he stopped writing altogether.'

She got up and went to the antique writing desk in the corner of the lounge. It had obviously not been used for its intended purpose for a long time, but Evelyn pulled out a bunch of letters held together with an elastic band.

'I used to keep the stamps from them years ago when I was little,' she said, unwrapping the bundle and laying them out in front of her. 'He always travelled. Well, I thought he did. Turns out I was probably wrong about that. I just…'

Don arrived back in the room and saw what they were looking at. He put the tea down in front of her and then scurried off again. Evelyn picked up the nearest letter and opened it, her eyes filling with tears again.

'The police said he's probably been there for decades,' she sobbed. 'So, he can't have gone to any of the places he said he did. I used to get all sorts of letters from New Zealand, Australia, even Singapore once. I thought he led such a fantastic life, but the police said he's been dead for decades. Someone else has been writing them all!'

'Didn't the police take the letters for evidence?' Margery asked.

'I haven't told them about the letters,' Evelyn said, her face darkening. 'I didn't want them to take them, to take him away from me, even more than they already have. I know that seems like a mad mistake now. I think I was in a bit of denial that none of the lovely things he wrote about were true. He's been dead the entire time, he didn't even get to ever leave the village, let alone see the world. I'm going to drop them at the station tomorrow.' She began to sob again. 'If it can help to explain Gene's death.' She took a tissue from the box on the table and wiped her eyes.

'I always thought it was strange he never married, or visited,' Evelyn continued, her brow furrowing at the memories. 'He wasn't much of a homebody, I knew that. But we were very close. I always felt that he'd sort of abandoned me with Mother. She wasn't very nice, you see? And I was a lot younger than him. He was twenty-one or twenty-two when he left, and I was only fifteen. But he sent her letters too, well… someone did, until she died. I tried to invite him to the funeral, but of course

I didn't have his address…' She shook her head, her eyes wide and haunted by the long con that had been played on her.

Margery almost gasped out loud at the very idea. Someone had written his loving sister letters pretending to be him, for decades. Why? Who on earth could do such a thing? Was it an elaborate practical joke that had got out of hand? Surely no one with a conscience could do that on purpose. Evelyn continued.

'And he had a girlfriend at the time, Sandra Rowles, and he just broke up with her by letter! Obviously, it makes sense it wasn't really him now. He was devoted to her…'

She trailed off, looking down at the letters again. 'I tried to invite him to our wedding. He was good friends with Don, but I like I said, I couldn't get a forwarding address for him… always on the move. I did ask him by email once, but he said he preferred to stay travelling and he had work on cruise ships, so he was always somewhere else. It all makes sense now.'

'Does it?' Margery found herself saying out loud, regretting it immediately when Evelyn's face fell again.

'No, it doesn't, does it?' she said in a gasping howl. 'Why would anyone kill him? How stupid am I for believing that all these years?'

They fell into silence, neither Margery nor Clementine wanted to break the moment with pitying words that would mean nothing to the grieving woman sat opposite them. Margery didn't think she was stupid at all. Margery suddenly longed for Don to come back and comfort his wife.

A sudden thought crossed her mind. Where had he been the last few weeks when he was supposed to be at golf? Where was Vivian? And what had she been doing?

'Was Eugene part of the Golden Circle?' Margery asked, surprising herself. Evelyn wiped her eyes and sniffed. 'We saw a picture of him at Summerview School.'

'Yes,' she said. 'But we all were. Me and Don. Vivian picked me to join once Ittonvale won the swimming finals.'

'That's how I knew Eugene,' Don said, coming back into the room and sitting down next to Evelyn once again. His sudden arrival startled Margery, who hadn't realised that he could hear them. 'We met a few years before me and Evelyn.'

'Gosh,' Margery said, she didn't really know what else to say now.

'He was a lovely man,' Don nodded. Evelyn put her hand on his leg and looked up at him with tear-filled eyes.

'The police might be able to find whoever did those emails from the IP address,' Clementine said. Margery looked at her in surprise.

'Who's been telling you about IP addresses?' she asked.

'The children,' Clementine said smugly.

'Hopefully they will, I'm going to send them everything I have. But I'll tell you this now though,' Evelyn said, her expression steeled with an anger Margery had never seen before. 'If I ever find out who did this to him, I'll kill them.'

–

They left the house even more confused than they had been when they entered it and got straight into the car.

Margery drove out of the driveway and then pulled into a nearby layby, their car tucked so close to the hedge that if Clementine had opened her window, she would have been sitting inside it.

'What on earth?' Margery said, turning to Clementine, who didn't seem perturbed that they had suddenly stopped. 'Somebody has been forging Eugene's letters for years, and no one reported him missing?'

'If they hadn't dug the playground up, it would never have been found out,' Clementine said, moving her fringe out of her eyes. 'That really doesn't bear thinking about.'

'Do you think whoever knew about it, knew that the playground was coming up?' Margery said, thinking about the Summerview School newsletter attached to Vivian's fridge. 'Say, a former school governor who still kept in touch with school affairs?'

'She did it, didn't she?' Clementine said, her eyes glassy as she thought about this theory. 'It makes so much sense.'

'But why?' Margery said. 'And how?'

'We've got to go to Devon,' Clementine said adamantly. 'It's the only way to find out. Evelyn sent me her address, didn't she?'

Margery nodded grimly and waited while Clementine set up the GPS for the long drive that was ahead of them.

Chapter Nineteen

It had been a while since she had driven so far – not since their miserable summer holiday to the little town of St Martins-on-the-water. She hoped that they'd get there before the light faded, she hadn't driven in the dark for a long time. Probably not since winter when the days were shorter, and definitely not in the left lane of a motorway. Her hands clutched the steering wheel tightly as they were passed by yet another lorry, the little car shaking as it rumbled past them with ease. Clementine had offered to drive, but Margery knew she wasn't as good with directions, and anyway, Clementine's driving experience was minimal. That was even before large motorways were brought into the equation.

'Should we tell Nigel what we've been up to?' Clementine asked, drumming her hands on the passenger side dashboard as the countryside flew by in the window.

'Why?' Margery said.

'He'll know something we don't, of course,' Clementine explained. 'Mary will have told him loads of things that the public aren't supposed to know. It could help us. Come on, I'll call him now. The only reason he hasn't been telling us things is because we keep insisting we don't want to know about any of it. We can't really say that anymore!'

'Sometimes I wish you'd forget your phone a little more often, Clem,' Margery joked. Clementine stuck her tongue out at her before dialling Nigel's phone number with an unnecessary flourish.

He answered on the third ring with a grumpy, 'Hello?' The sound travelled through the car speakers, crackling around Margery and Clementine. Clementine turned the volume up, anyway, and the sound rose with a horrible hiss.

'Nigel, it's us,' Clementine said into the phone in her hand. 'We've got a lot to tell you.'

'Mrs Butcher-Baker,' Nigel said. 'Alright, let me get a pen and paper, I've got a feeling I'm going to need it.'

Once he was ready, Clementine didn't waste a second, instead jumping straight into the beginning of the story and telling him everything. About Mr Fitzgerald's folder, about Vivian's house, about the photographs of Vivian at the school and her signature on the playground fitting. About how they were sure she was something to do with it.

'Obviously though,' Clementine finished her rant, 'we don't want to tell the police yet, because, well… we've been wrong before.'

'You have,' Nigel said cheerily over the line, but Margery could imagine that he was remembering how much work they had caused him the autumn before. It was amazing that they had managed to get away with that one – accusing the wrong person, suspecting two or three other people, and then finally helping the police to track down the real murderer. It was probably one of the reasons why Officer Wilkinson was not their biggest fan.

'Hmmm,' Nigel said, 'let me see what I can find out for you. I can't promise to find out everything, but Mary will know something. She's on a night shift at the moment, just left. They've got a lot on, with that swimming pool body and the playground body being named.'

In all the chaos surrounding the discovery of Eugene's identity, Margery had forgotten entirely about the body in the pool. She didn't know how; she could only blame exhaustion. She wondered if the police had found the car from the playground yet, and if they knew who had been driving it. Someone had to have known that Miss Hawthorne was at the pool that evening, and had left her to it while she drowned.

Nigel rang off. Margery breathed a sigh of relief when they came off the motorway and were brought back onto little country roads, the car bouncing along quite happily again. They were nearing a town, coasting easily down the hill towards it. Under the streetlights the road glowed orange and the town across from them at the bottom of the hill was just twinkling lights.

'It's just up here on the right,' Clementine said. She had been uncharacteristically quiet since they ended the phone call with Nigel, only speaking to give Margery directions. She supposed that Clementine was as worried as she was. They were about to confront a possible murderer, which was always frightening in Margery's experience.

The house loomed on the right, as Clementine had said it would. It was not a small abode by anyone's standards and Margery wondered briefly what on earth the Redburns and Mr and Mrs Black had done for careers to afford such a colossal thing. Surely they hadn't been bought on Vivian's swimming teacher salary. She slowed the car down and put the indicator on, before driving through the open gates. It seemed strange that they would be open, but when they pulled into the driveway she realised why. There were several cars already on it, lining the front of the garage. The back of the house was set into a slope, with a balcony that obviously led to some sort of loft conversion. A man came to stare at them over the balcony as they climbed out of the car gingerly, a glass of wine in hand.

'Can I help you?' he yelled. Margery could barely see his face at the distance.

'Does Vivian Black live here?' Clementine shouted, just loud enough to be heard.

'Yes,' he yelled. 'Wait there!'

They stood awkwardly outside the front of the house, which was overwhelmingly beautiful – more country estate than the little holiday home Evelyn had described. The sun was setting, and Margery knew that if she went to the end of the driveway and looked down, she'd surely be able to see down towards the bay and across the town. It must have been absolutely breath-taking by daylight. The man finally opened the door and strode out towards them. He was probably only in his early thirties, but he had the air of someone important, even while dressed casually in a polo shirt and chino shorts. He crunched across the gravel in his boat shoes and greeted them, brushing his mid-length hair back from his face where it fell into a perfect coif.

'Did you ask about Vivian Black?' he asked. They nodded. 'She's my grandmother.'

'Oh gosh, so you are...?' Margery said, though she wasn't sure where she was going with this.

'I'm William. Jeffery's son,' he smiled at this, placing a hand on his chest as he spoke.

'Named after your grandfather?' Margery said, realising that Billy must be a nickname for William.

'That's it,' he smiled. 'What can I do for you?'

'We wanted to have a chat with Vivian,' Clementine said, waving her hands about. 'We're... er...'

'We're old friends,' Margery said. 'From her days at Ittonvale.'

'Gosh, did she teach you swimming lessons too?' William asked. 'Well, she's not here at the moment, but come in anyway. We'll try and call her for you.'

'Oh,' Margery said, unable to think of a way out of going into the house. 'Of course.'

They followed him in through the front door and Margery admired the house from the inside as he led them down the hallway. She peered around at the walls as they followed; there were as many family portraits as there had been in her Dewpond home. There were signs on the walls as well, one of which led to 'The Pool Room'. Margery wondered how big the rest of the house was, and if Vivian had an indoor swimming pool. What she had thought was the front of the house was actually the back. Once William had led them through into the comfortable sitting room, she realised that she could see the water through the wall to ceiling windows.

'Drink?' William offered. They each accepted a glass of water and then he sat down in the chair opposite them. He took his phone out of his pocket and called Vivian's number, waiting till it rang and rang and then rang off.

'She's terrible at using her phone,' he said apologetically. 'You'd probably be better off going to her house in Ittonvale.'

'We just came from there,' Margery said, 'she isn't home.'

William paused to think about it. 'Then she's probably at Evelyn Redburn's house. Do you know her?'

'Yes, we do,' Margery said. Much better than you know, she thought.

'Well, if she's not here or at home, she's there,' William said, sitting back in the chair with his foot resting on the opposite leg comfortably. 'She's not due here for a few weeks, anyway. She said as much in her letter.'

'Her letter?' Margery asked. 'Can we see it?'

William raised an eyebrow at the strange request but got up and went into another room, returning a few minutes later with the letter. Margery took it and began to read, Clementine reading over her shoulder. It was dated the beginning of February and written in swirling loops of fountain pen on pristine paper.

My dear boy,

Of course you must simply take the house, for as long as you need! I would never begrudge you to stay, however I feel it necessary to tell you that I do not possess the internet and have absolutely no intention of ever travelling down that road again, so to speak. Not now that your grandfather is not here to work the router for me. That might make your work harder from the house, but of course if you are merely travelling there for leisure then it is yours for the taking!

If you need me, I will be here at Scout Hall in Dewpond, or at my dearest Evelyn's home until after the usual Spring Equinox dawn pool swim. You can contact me here or there, and please know that I am thinking about you always.

I have something to speak about the next time we see each other, and I hope we will all be together again soon, but I expect I will not be down at

Summerhouse for a few weeks yet. I don't mean to spook or alarm you, but the fact of the matter is that one day I will no longer be here, and I mean to set some things right before I go off to whatever is next. The past is not always a pleasant place, but I find solace and comfort in knowing that my children and grandchildren are swimming along quite nicely. Please excuse the pun, dear!

As crude as it is, this will mean planning what happens next financially. Your grandfather and I were very lucky, and your great grandfather was even luckier, God bless his soul. This family has long been blessed with extraordinary fortune, which has led to extraordinary opportunities. I have lived well, as did your grandfather when he was still with us, but I have not squandered our fortune idly. We used our funds well and invested well, and they have grown larger than I ever could have dreamed. It is my wish that yourself and the rest of the family will have the opportunity to do the same, and you can provide for my wonderful great grandchildren and your wife as I have done for you.

More than all that, do not squander any time. I hope you will remain blessed in your life and marriage.

Your loving Grandmother

X

'Does she always write like this?' Clementine asked as she finished reading. 'This is quite heavy, isn't it?'

'Wow, you really haven't seen her for years!' William chuckled. 'She's been warning me she's about to die since I was a child. Very dramatic my grandmother, although

I think maybe she's planning on organising her will from that last letter. She's been saying she's going to for ages. Since Grandad died, in fact.'

The letter stuck Margery as a bit strange. There was also no mention of a fall out with Evelyn, and Margery remembered Miss Hallow saying that Vivian hadn't arranged the Spring Equinox pool swim yet. The equinox was only a week or so away, surely Vivian would have had to arrange it by now. Going solely by the information given in the letter, Vivian should still be at her house in Dewpond or with Evelyn and they knew for certain that she was not at either. Margery couldn't help but wonder why it seemed so different to the postcards Vivian had apparently sent to Evelyn. Were they less formal because Evelyn was a close friend? Or was there some other reason? Something they hadn't managed to stumble upon yet? Margery's brain told her that it was the second. Clementine's theory was beginning to make the most sense of all, perhaps Vivian had found out about the playground being refitted and ran for it.

'When was the last time you spoke to her?' Margery asked. 'In person, or on the phone?'

William shrugged, but then sat back and thought about it. 'Probably last month? Maybe before that. It's hard to keep track. She never answers the phone and I'm based in London now. I rarely go up to Ittonvale. I'm only here now because I have a meeting with an associate in Exeter tomorrow and it's a good excuse to spend the weekend away. My wife is going to bring the kids down afterschool on Friday.'

'Then why would she make the journey here?' Clementine asked, pointing to the letter. 'What's all this about the past being unpleasant?'

'I'm not really sure,' William said. 'She's been getting a lot more open about things since Grandad went, I assume it's something to do with that.'

Margery didn't know what to say. It seemed even more likely that Vivian was hiding now. Where else could she be? Perhaps they should tell the police what they were convinced of, surely the police would have even more information than they could ever imagine. Perhaps they were already on their way over. Hopefully Nigel would be able to tell them something else. William showed them out, wishing them well as they left and leaving Margery and Clementine standing outside, wondering where on earth Vivian could be.

–

If Vivian wasn't at her house, wasn't at Evelyn and Don's house, and wasn't here, then where was she?

Margery drummed her hands softly on her knees as she thought about it, half-waiting for Clementine to return from paying for the petrol and half-dozing off in a daydream.

Where was Vivian? Surely you didn't just disappear like that. Not when you were supposed to visit family and have all sorts of other plans. She supposed that Vivian's letter had told William to expect her in a few weeks at the minimum, and she was certainly wealthy enough to be able to afford a few nights away in a hotel. Maybe she wasn't even in the country. Perhaps, after her fall out with Evelyn there was not much left to hang around in Ittonvale for. And maybe she hadn't been ready to be surrounded by people.

But if all that was so, then why had Don been in Devon recently? Was he helping to hide her? There were too many coincidences for him to just be helping with her gardening. Perhaps he had been in Devon to collect things for her to help with her escape, clothes or her passport. But why would he help her?

'Can you please not use your phone near the pumps!' a voice came over the tannoy system from the petrol station's main building, as Clementine rushed out of it and began to hurry towards the car again, phone in hand.

'Sorry!' Clementine yelled, but instead of putting it away she wrenched the car door open, jumped in the passenger seat and turned the screen towards Margery so she could see what it showed. She had the cat camera app on, which they usually only used to make sure that Crinkles had returned safely from her night out playing in Dawn Simmonds' garden, and to see which of the neighbours' cats they were inadvertently feeding.

'The cat camera is going mad Margery,' Clementine said, tapping the screen. 'What are they up to?' Then she gasped, her face falling, as she watched the phone screen. 'Someone's in our house!'

Chapter Twenty

Margery sped away from the petrol station, the car rattling as they careened back up the hill towards the motorway and once on it, she drove as fast as she dared. The car struggled as it approached the top speed. Margery thanked the heavens it was getting late, and the traffic was much lighter than it had been on the journey down.

'They're still there, Margery!' Clementine shrieked. 'What if they take our CDs... or the cats?'

Clementine had already rung Nigel, who had promised to call Symon and get him to go straight to the house.

Margery hoped with all her might that he would get there in time to apprehend whoever it was.

'Look at their shoes prancing about on our new Ikea rug!' Clementine cried, trying to show Margery the phone screen, where a pair of shiny leather loafers were indeed walking across their kitchen floor.

'We'll just have to hope the police catch them Clem,' Margery said through gritted teeth, her knuckles white on the steering wheel. She put her foot down further and hoped they wouldn't get stopped by the police for speeding before they could get back.

When they got to the house, there was a police car still in front of it. Symon was waiting for them, along with Officer Wilkinson.

Officer Wilkinson didn't look pleased. He seemed angry even. Margery was becoming accustomed to this being his usual expression.

Clementine barely waited for Margery to stop the car on the driveway before unclipping her seatbelt and climbing out, slamming the door behind her.

'Did you catch them?' she asked, as she did so.

Margery followed her to where the police officers were standing outside the house.

Symon shook his head. 'Sorry, they got away before we got here,' he said, looking crestfallen. 'I've rung for a locksmith to come and change your locks.'

'What did they take?' Margery asked, as Clementine paced along the boundary of their driveway and the patch of grass that formed their front garden.

'Not my Charles and Diana commemorative wedding spoon?' Clementine cried.

'You'll have to go through the house and make a note of anything missing,' Officer Wilkinson said, raising his eyebrows. He sounded bored, like he felt this was a waste of time when he could be out digging up mysterious skeletons and dredging bodies out of swimming pools. 'But your electrical items are all still here – your TV and that. It doesn't look like much has been moved.'

'Really?' Margery took a step into the house and peered through the small hallway into the living room. The television was still there, along with the CD and DVD players, and all her ornaments.

'You can't go in there yet,' Clementine said. 'The police will need to fingerprint it all, won't you?'

She turned to Officer Wilkinson who shook his head. 'We'll give you a crime reference number for your home insurance, but to me it really doesn't look like anything's been touched,' he said, in a cold manner that made Margery finally understand that he didn't really care.

Margery looked back into the room and couldn't help but agree with him. All their belongings were there, except... she realised what was missing and felt her jaw drop.

She gave Clementine a look, hoping that if she had noticed as well, she would not say anything out loud. The missing persons folder that Mr Fitzgerald had given them was gone. It had been sat where she had left it on the coffee table. Now there wasn't even a scrap of it to show for its presence. The boxes of paperwork from the school storeroom was also gone. This couldn't be good for either Margery and Clementine or Mr Fitzgerald. Mr Fitzgerald was surely not supposed to be making his mad records of missing people, and they were not supposed to be investigating anything at all. The policeman in front of them really didn't need to know anything about it. If news got out then they would surely also be in trouble with Richard the auditor, and that couldn't do any good either.

Still, she thought, if Vivian had something to do with the playground skeleton, they really ought to tell him. But a few disorganised facts were not enough to establish her guilt. She decided in her head that what they really needed to do was go and see her, as soon as possible. If she wasn't at her second home, then she must still be hiding in Dewpond. They wouldn't be able to go tonight, who knows how long it would be before the locksmith arrived, and they couldn't go tomorrow daytime, they had work. But there would be time after the school day had finished to zip to Vivian's and see what was going on there.

'We'll need to review your camera footage,' Officer Wilkinson said, gesturing for them to follow him inside the house. Clementine went inside, and Margery was about to follow when she caught the eye of their neighbour, Dawn Simmonds. Dawn was pretending to sweep her driveway with what was obviously the mop from her kitchen. Dawn always seemed to be around whenever anything of interest happened in the street, Margery thought in amusement. Dawn must have spent most of the day looking out of her living room window.

Ignoring her, Margery turned back to their house and followed the others inside. Clementine had made Officer Symon a cup of tea and he sat at the kitchen table, while Clementine leaned back against the kitchen counter with her arms folded tightly across her chest. Officer Wilkinson had already disappeared. Probably off solving murders or cracking codes, Margery thought bitterly.

It felt very peculiar to be returning to her house when a stranger had been inside it not even a few hours before. The thought made her shiver; there was something vile and intrusive about the experience. Someone else had walked through their house, had looked around at their belongings. Had stolen something from their coffee table.

Symon was finishing taking Clementine's statement, scribbling on a form he had on the table in front of him.

'Hello Symon,' Margery said. He smiled at her kindly as she sat down in the chair opposite him. 'How are you? Sorry to have called you out. You must be busy enough without any of this nonsense.'

'I'm very well, thank you, Mrs Butcher-Baker,' Symon said, signing the bottom of the form and sitting back again. He was much more confident than he had been when they'd first met a few years ago. Margery supposed that's what time and age did to a person, but she was sure that his ream of experiences in the force over the last few years had probably helped immensely. 'Don't worry, I've been busy getting the nursery ready, so this is a nice distraction from flat pack furniture and trying to work out how baby car seats work.'

'What's wrong with you and Ceri-Ann?' Clementine asked. 'She's due in about six minutes and the nursery isn't finished and she's off waddling about at work refusing to stop and now you're here with us refusing to fingerprint for shoe prints instead of being with her, watching her every second of the day in case she's in labour.'

'I know,' Symon said, looking slightly sheepish for a moment. 'It was ready, though. But then she decided that she needed to pull all the carpets up upstairs, and she's been sanding and painting the floors.' He held his hands up in defence at the look Clementine gave him. 'I can't get her to stop. I would if I could, but you know what she's like. How's the inspection going anyway?'

Margery thought back to the auditor confronting them in the school corridor. 'Fine.'

'I heard it's been a bit of a nightmare from what Ceri-Ann said,' Symon said. 'At least that body thing is sorted now. Well, sort of.'

'What do you mean?' Margery asked, suddenly all ears. 'The skeleton?'

'Well, yeah, that. But the one in the pool as well,' Symon said, looking between them, his face flushing red as if he had realised he shouldn't have said anything. 'Oh, well. I'm not supposed to say anything yet. You'll have to forget I said that.'

'We'll do no such thing ever,' Clementine said. 'So the body's confirmed to belong to Miss Hawthorne?'

'What?' Symon asked, blinking at her. 'What makes you say that?'

'She's been missing a while,' Margery said, thinking of the posters around town of Ittonvale's missing PE teacher.

'It's not Miss Hawthorne,' Symon said. 'I can't really say more than that at the moment.'

If it wasn't Miss Hawthorne in the pool, then who could it be? Margery sat back in her chair with a heavy thump. It was awful enough when they had thought the missing teacher was in the pool.

'Who was it?' Margery asked.

'An older woman,' Symon said. 'I can't remember her full name. It's not my case, you see. Miss Hawthorne was my case, actually. I asked a little while ago to be transferred to the fraud team. That's what I've been working on.'

'Fraud? What did she do?' Clementine asked. Margery found herself digging into the table top with her finger tips.

'Well, she was the ringleader of a pyramid scheme that's been recruiting in the area, mostly women. Lots of people lost their life savings,' Symon explained. 'Thing is, she thought that if she disappeared to Scotland that we wouldn't find her. She was staying on her uncle's farm. Took us ages and loads of work with Police Scotland, but we got her in the end. She didn't tell her poor boyfriend – he'd been arranging search parties to look for her.'

'But the woman in the pool...' Margery stumbled over her words unsure of what she wanted to say, thinking of the body they had seen in the water and not quite believing what was happening. 'What a horrible way to go. Who do you think killed her? Why did she have the school swimming gala trophy in her bag?'

Symon looked over to the kitchen door to make sure they were still alone, that Officer Wilkinson wouldn't suddenly appear and tell them all off.

'I can't say much, to be honest I don't know everything,' he said. 'But it wasn't even the real trophy. It was a plastic one, from the pound shop.' He craned his neck back to the door once more. 'Sorry, I really shouldn't say any more in case Mark comes back.'

Margery and Clementine shared a worried look and Margery found herself wishing that they had taken better care of Mr Fitzgerald's files.

The trophy wasn't real.

She let the words whir around her head as she processed them. The trophy being fake raised even more questions, why had the dead person had it, and where was the real trophy? She found herself looking around the kitchen and noticing all the individual things in it as though for the first time, seeing everything in a different light. Her eyes fell on the garage door key on the hook by the back door – she was sure it had been facing the other way around on the nail the last time she had used it. Maybe Clementine had gone out to check it hadn't been broken into while she had been distracted by Dawn.

–

They lay in bed, both unable to sleep, which was a rare occurrence as far as Clementine was concerned. She was usually out like a light before Margery had even put her book on the nightstand and turned off the lamp.

Margery watched the ceiling, counting the cracks in the paint.

'Clem,' she whispered into the darkness. 'Are you awake?'

'Of course,' Clementine rolled over to look at her; the mattress squeaked as she adjusted her weight.

'Who do you think took the boxes?' Margery asked, finally saying what had been haunting her since the night before. 'Do you think it was someone we know?'

The silence was heavy as Clementine mulled it over.

'I really don't know,' she said, finally. 'Why do you think that?'

'I just keep thinking about Richard catching us taking them from the storeroom. He didn't seem very happy when he saw us when we were taking them,' Margery said, remembering the look on his face as they had bumped into him.

Clementine reached over for Margery's hand, taking it and squeezing it on top of the duvet cover.

'I think we should talk to Dawn,' she said.

'Dawn?' Margery said quizzically.

'She was outside her house earlier, pretending to paint her garage door or whatever she was doing when the police were here,' Clementine said. 'And she's always out there, planting things or whatever it is she's doing in that recreation of the Eden project she calls a garden. It's peak planting things time, isn't it? Ready for summer. What if she heard something in the least?'

Clementine could well be right, Margery thought. It was a long shot, but it also might just help unravel some of the mystery. They fell silent again for a moment. Margery closed her eyes, ripping them open again when Clementine gasped like she was drowning and bolted upright, jolting the bed.

'You know Symon said the body in the pool was an older person?' Clementine grasped for Margery's arm in the dark.

'Yes?' Margery said, turning to face her.

'I would put money on it being Vivian Black.'

Chapter Twenty-One

Even if Richard had done nothing but simply carry out his audit it seemed to finally be getting to the headmaster. Richard and his team had been at the school for weeks now, but had shown no signs of leaving any time soon. Even on the march to the canteen on their way into work, Margery had seen Richard measuring the distance between two art displays, one featuring *Saturn Devouring his Son* and the other *The Temptation of St Anthony*. The Easter holiday was only a week away, and Margery could see many of the teachers counting down the seconds till they would be free.

Mr Barrow prowling the halls looking for faults before Richard could find them was beginning to become a nightmare. Worse still, the revelation that the body might be Vivian Black had sent Margery's brain into overdrive, making it very difficult to stay on her A-game at work. Neither Margery nor Clementine really knew what to do with that information at all.

'We'll just have to go back to Vivian's and find out something else to prove she has something to do with the body, and then find something to prove that she was also murdered,' Clementine said, as she chopped the peeled potatoes into halves and put them in the large saucepan of water until they were cooked tomorrow.

After their restless night worrying about what to do the night before, waiting for Nigel to call them back, returning to Vivian's really felt like the last thing Margery wanted to do. In her opinion, they ought to have been hunkering down and staying out of trouble until the end of the audit. Margery was terrified that the kitchen standards would slip enough that Richard would visit them again, but so far, they had remained safe.

Clementine's phone had remained silent and useless as a tealight to warm your hands during a winter storm, although she had been checking it over and over since the night before. It was almost lunchtime now. They hadn't managed to catch Dawn on their way to work, and the questions Margery had for her reeled around her head.

'But what would the police even find if they went there?' Margery said. 'Not much more than we saw and why would they take us seriously? We haven't even told them anything. And you're forgetting that she's probably dead.'

'You don't think the Redburns have anything to do with this?' Clementine said. 'It was a relative of Evelyn's who died all those years ago, and, well… the plot thickens even more!'

The plot had thickened indeed. Thickened and then burnt horribly like an unattended pan of bechamel sauce, Margery thought. Only this time she wouldn't be able to boil the burn off with washing-up liquid.

'Yeah, don't you reckon that Mrs Redburn knows more than she's letting on?' Karen asked. Margery turned to look at her for explanation, but she barely looked up from the bowl of cream she was whipping for tomorrow's trifle. 'She was Vivian's best friend, wasn't she? And she knew Vivian was a governor, she's probably known about it for years. Biding her time till she can get her back for killing her brother.'

'I think you should be most worried about Don,' Sharon said, topping the sponge base in the gastro trays with boiling hot water and jelly crystals. 'He's been going over to her house for no reason anyone can understand. Why?'

'We'll just have to go to their house and see them again,' Clementine said.

'I don't think that's a good idea,' Margery said, releasing the heavy breath that had been weighing her down.

'If I were you, I'd be getting another camera for your house that isn't sat at floor level for the cats,' Gloria said. 'At least then you'd have a shred of evidence to give to the police.'

'I wish they'd just take our word for it,' Clementine said. 'I have a very strong hunch about it all.'

Her tabard pocket began to ring. Clementine gasped before she delved into it to pull her phone out, fumbling it. 'Margery, it's Nigel!'

She dropped the phone and it clattered onto the floor and disappeared under the workbench. Clementine cursed as she bent down to grasp for it.

'Oh no,' Ceri-Ann said, interrupting their conversation by dropping the peeler on the worktop and putting the hand on her stomach instead, 'these pains are just getting worse. I'm so uncomfortable, it's mega annoying mate.'

'What pains?' Gloria asked narrowing her eyes at her.

'Ah you know, just like… early labour ones,' Ceri-Ann groaned, picking up another potato to peel. 'Braxton Hicks or whatever. But I suppose these do feel a bit worse now… a lot stronger than they were.'

'What on earth do you mean?' Gloria took the potato from her and put it back in the sack. 'Are you telling us you're in labour and you didn't think to mention it?'

'I've probably got ages, mate,' Ceri-Ann said, trying to grasp for the potato again. 'Chantelle said she didn't even realise she'd been in labour till the baby was already basically out. She had him on the way to the hospital on the bus.'

Gloria looked horrified at that, dropping the knife she had been using to chop vegetables and grabbing Ceri-Ann by the wrist. 'You've got to go now!'

'I'm not even in labour mate,' Ceri-Ann batted Gloria's hand away.

'Ooh I bet the size app can tell us if you're in labour!' Clementine announced, waving her phone, which looked none the worse for its journey underneath the worktop. 'Let's have a look… ooh Ceri, the baby is the size of… a Ryan-Air carry-on luggage bag today!'

'Well, that can't be right.' Karen shook her head. 'When me and Sharon went to Spain, we could only fit a single trainer in each bag. We had to share a pair and take it in turns to do our morning run.'

'I'm fine,' Ceri-Ann said, waving her arms around in a manner of someone who had never seen the dictionary definition of fine. 'I've been a centimetre dilated for a week. It's all fine!'

'One centimetre?' Gloria cried. 'That doesn't sound fine.'

'The midwife did a sweep and they said I didn't need to come in unless I'm in active labour.' Ceri-Ann began peeling another potato, but then dropped the peeler again. 'Ooh here's the pain again.'

'Should we measure your contractions?' Seren asked, leaving the prep table at the back where she was making sandwiches in the corner and coming over to the main kitchen. 'I'm sure I saw that on an episode of *Call the Midwife* or something.'

'Oh yeah, we can use my new sports watch!' Sharon beamed at her. 'Good idea, Seren.'

'I don't trust that watch,' Karen said. 'Not since it made that mistake of saying I hadn't actually broken my parkrun record.'

'The watch never lies,' Sharon said ominously, tapping its face on her wrist.

'We'll use the kitchen clock,' Margery said, trying to stop the argument before it could begin.

'It's not even a contraction mate,' Ceri-Ann said, but she turned to the clock expectantly.

They waited for Ceri-Ann's signal and then all turned to stare at the clock, for what felt like hours. A minute ticked by and then another few seconds.

'See, that's it,' Ceri-Ann said, with an easy wave of her hand. 'It's all good.'

'You're in active labour.' Gloria gripped her by the arm again, Ceri-Ann batted her away gently. 'Come on, we're going to hospital.'

'Remember your promise to call the baby Clement,' Clementine said over the tussle.

'I'm not going.' Ceri-Ann shook her head, trying to escape from Gloria's grasp. 'I've decided not to have it. Remember that private 3D scan we had? The baby just looks like mini-Symon. I told him, "Where's my ring mate? Because it's just going to look exactly like you and we're going to give it your last name anyway", it's like a group project I've done all the work on. I can't cope with it.'

'It'll be okay,' Gloria said, soothingly. 'You like Symon's face.'

'Yeah,' Ceri-Ann said with a sigh. She took her phone out of her tabard pocket. 'I'll call him and let him know we're going to the hospital.'

She dialled his number and held the phone to her ear. They looked at her expectantly until she put it back down again.

'He didn't answer,' she said sheepishly. 'He's been really busy, though.'

'I'll kill him,' Gloria said. 'The baby's due any minute and he's got his phone off.'

'It's not off, it's just…' Ceri-Ann began to say, but her voice rattled off when she realised that she didn't have an argument. She called the number again and they all waited.

Rose appeared through the kitchen doorway, leaning on it in a relaxed manner that felt jarring with the mood inside the canteen kitchen.

'Someone's phone's ringing in your staff room,' she said. She took a bite of the apple in her hand, crunching it between her teeth and then looking around at their startled faces.

'Oh no,' Ceri-Ann said, her eyes widening. 'He left his phone at home this morning. Oh, I texted him to tell him I had it! I'm such an idiot!'

They all gasped in horror.

'Oh no! How'll I get there?' Ceri-Ann said, her hands flying up to her face. 'He's supposed to come and get me. Oh my god, he doesn't even know I'm here.'

'What?' Gloria said. 'Where does he think—?'

'He thinks I'm still at home resting,' Ceri-Ann interrupted her. 'Don't look at me like that!'

'I'll take you,' Margery said, taking off her tabard and heading to the staff room to get her keys. 'I've got the car.'

She was the only one who did. Everyone else either walked to work or caught the bus. She quickly grabbed her things and went back into the kitchen. Clementine was wringing her hands anxiously as Ceri-Ann tried to call Symon again, and then realised her mistake. Gloria glared at the phone.

'Come on,' Margery said, taking Ceri-Ann by the other arm. 'Gloria, you'd better come too. Clementine, you're... actually, Karen, you be in charge.'

'Hey!' Clementine protested as Karen smiled smugly.

'It's chicken and leek pie day,' Margery said. 'And I need you to help Seren with the mashed potatoes. Let Karen run the front and Sharon can do the till after she's finished making the Jamaican ginger cake. Hopefully I'll be back by then though.'

Clementine's phone beeped and she swiped the screen to reveal the message.

'Christ, Margery,' she said, her eyes widening as she read. 'Nigel says we have to ring him as soon as we can, he's got some huge news about the case! He says we need to meet him again.'

Margery suddenly felt conflicted in a way she never had before. Usually, they could separate their detective lives and their work life. The two rarely met, unless you counted the many times things had nearly gone wrong while at the school, of course. But this time felt even more personal than usual. For a moment she considered calling Nigel back and finding out what he wanted, leaving Ceri-Ann and Gloria to make their own way to the hospital.

But then the look of panic in Ceri-Ann's face dragged her back to her senses with a thump.

'Well, you ring him then, when you get a chance,' Margery said, making the decision before there could even be a discussion. There were some things in life that had to be priorities, and this was one of them. Clementine nodded, her face serious for once.

'What's going on?' Rose had entered the room properly with her apple core, looking around at them all in concern.

'Ceri-Ann's in labour. We're going to hospital,' Margery said at the same time Gloria shrieked, 'Ceri-Ann took Symon's phone by mistake and now we can't call him.'

Rose raised her eyebrows. 'All right then. You go to the hospital, and I'll find him for you.'

They rushed to the car and Ceri-Ann and Gloria both climbed into the back, Gloria taking extra care to help Ceri-Ann with her seatbelt, as Margery started the car. She looked into the wingmirror at Ceri-Ann's panicked face and felt a rush of maternal concern.

'How are you doing, Ceri?' Margery asked as she manoeuvred the car gently onto the main road, heading away from Dewstow to the border of Ittonvale. Ceri-Ann had been looking out of the window and ignoring Gloria's soothing mutterings, but she turned to meet Margery's eyes in the mirror.

'It's really happening, isn't it?' she asked. Margery nodded.

'It's just that I'm not sure if I'm ready,' Ceri-Ann explained. 'I'm worried that I won't be any good at it.'

'Of course you will be,' Gloria said, her eyes widening at Ceri-Ann's confession. 'The thing is, no one knows what they're doing when they have children. When we left the hospital with Luis, I was terrified. But he's eight now and I haven't accidentally broken him.'

'Yeah,' Ceri-Ann said. 'And you'll help me, won't you? If I need advice?'

'Of course,' Gloria said soothingly. Ceri-Ann nodded, seemingly calmed for the moment.

'And you'll all be godparents?' she asked, looking between Gloria and Margery. 'All of you dinner ladies? I think we'll need all the hands we can get.'

'Of course,' Gloria said again.

'Clementine might try and convince the baby his name is Clement,' Margery said. Ceri-Ann laughed.

'All right then,' Ceri-Ann said. 'Let's do this.'

Margery smiled at her in the mirror again. They weren't far away now. She pulled away from the traffic lights and entered the hospital car park.

'What's all this stuff in your car Margery?' Gloria asked, holding up the gift bag meant for Vivian. 'Whose birthday is it?'

'Oh, no one's,' Margery said, realising that she had forgotten all about the perfume bottle. They really ought to return it as soon as they could.

—

Margery unlocked the front door and went inside. She took off her coat and then let her head fall back against the wall of the hallway and sighed, closing her eyes tightly together. It truly was amazing, she thought, the miracle of birth. For all Ceri-Ann's doubts she really was going to be an excellent parent. She had no doubt Symon would be, too. The baby would grow up surrounded by love and support. It meant a lot in times like this where things were very up and down, especially for the people of the town, who seemed to be dropping like flies with all the murders and other events of the last few years.

She put her coat away on the hook and entered the living room. Clementine was waiting for her on the sofa, smiling happily. A pot of tea in front of her.

'How was it?' Clementine asked. 'You look tired.'

'Not as tired as Ceri-Ann, probably.' Margery smiled.

'No,' Clementine said. Margery sat down next to her. 'Everything alright though?'

Margery nodded and took Clementine's hand, resting her head on her shoulder. They sat like that for a while, enjoying the silence and stillness.

'I spoke to Nigel in the end,' Clementine said. Margery looked up at her face.

'What did he say?'

'He said that the car being driven on the dashcam footage was Billy Black's, and the body was Vivian's.'

'Oh gosh, it really was Vivian?' Margery gasped. Clementine nodded.

'Yes, so obviously they aren't looking for her husband,' Clementine explained, with a grimace.

'No,' Margery said. It wouldn't be hard to find the dead man. Billy Black was probably buried in Ittonvale or Dewstow graveyard.

'But they are still looking for the car,' Clementine said. 'And they have a suspect in mind.'

'Who?'

'He couldn't say, I don't think he knows,' Clementine said. She picked up her phone from the coffee table and unlocked it. 'But I think it might be Don. Here...'

She passed Margery the phone so she could look at the screen. The GPS monitor had died and was probably lost forever now, but the last known location was…

'Vivian's house. Wait, do you think he's been going to Devon and posting Evelyn the postcards? I'm sure the one she gave us had a Devon postmark. She couldn't possibly be sending them herself if she's dead.'

'Yes!' Clementine exclaimed. 'And I think he's the one who drove the car out of the school car park.'

'What should we do?' Margery asked. Clementine thought about it for a moment, before her eyes widened as she came to a conclusion.

'Mr Fitzgerald must have got those files from some-where,' she said. 'He'll know where the rest of them are.'

'Would they really help us?'

'Well, no, maybe not. But didn't he used to keep a record of townspeople's number plates and where they parked their vehicles?'

'Someone needs to stop Mr Fitzgerald from making his weird records.' Margery shook her head. 'I don't know where he finds the time.'

'I think he's a time traveller.' Clementine tapped her chin thoughtfully with her index finger. 'It would explain the capes.'

'We could go and talk to him, but then what?' Margery began to twirl her fingers together, her hands moving anxiously.

'Then we'll try and find out who took the ones he gave us in the first place,' Clementine said. Margery nodded. There didn't seem to be much else for it.

Margery flinched as the phone bleeped again in her hand, lighting up the screen.

'Oh, Clem!' she said, feeling the smile creeping back onto her face. 'Look!'

Clementine bent to read the message Symon had written on the kitchen team's WhatsApp group and beamed, too.

Chapter Twenty-Two

When they arrived at Mr Fitzgerald's curiosity shop it was already closed for the night, but that was no matter – he was still inside and must have seen them through the glass of the shop window, because he opened the front door for them immediately.

The bell above the door tinkled as they entered the shop floor, where trinkets and assorted nonsense littered every surface. Margery smiled at the photo frame hanging above the counter which showed former kitchen manager Caroline meeting a prime minister. Mr Fitzgerald had tried to sell a few of the items he had taken from her house after she died and had obviously not been able to shift most of them.

Whenever she came here, Margery's eyes always took a moment to get used to the sheer number of things in the room; a Fabergé egg rested precariously on top of a bowl of plastic oranges, an oil painting of Queen Elizabeth the Second hung above a clock featuring an EastEnders actress with pint glasses for hands. Mr Fitzgerald welcomed them in and then sat back on the stool behind the shop counter, pulling Jason onto his lap again.

'What can I do for you on this fine Dewstow evening?' he said, although Margery couldn't help but notice that he didn't seem quite as jovial as he usually did. His hands were stained from ink, as though he had been writing an enormous amount of letters, and then the pen had exploded. 'It's late for you to be here.'

'It is,' Margery said. 'Ceri-Ann had the baby.'

Mr Fitzgerald jumped up from his seat and clapped his hands together. Jason fell off his lap with a yelp and landed on the floor, unharmed, but more than a little put out. 'Fantastic news! Gosh, I have just the thing...'

He went into the back room behind him and rummaged around for long enough that Margery began to wonder if he'd forgotten them entirely, but then he brought out three coupe glasses and a dusty unlabelled bottle.

'I had some Babycham, which I thought might be appropriate... but the bottles are forty years old and I'm not sure any of us would survive drinking it,' he said, chuckling to himself as he poured them each a portion much too generous for Margery's liking. Drinking one of Mr Fitzgerald's homemade concoctions was never on her to do list, but she felt obligated to partake at the sight of his eager face, and given the nature of the toast. She took a tiny sip, realising as she did so that it was elderflower wine and then returned the smile, though she felt like it was forced, sticking to her face and straining to stay there.

'What is it?' Mr Fitzgerald asked. 'What did they call them?'

'It's a boy.' Clementine grinned. She had already finished her drink and put the coupe down on the sideboard containing a bronze bust of a Roman emperor. 'Nicholas Krzysztof Taylor.'

'Lovely,' Mr Fitzgerald smiled again, 'I'm sure Ceri-Ann will be a fine parent. Enterprising at the very least.' He looked down at Jason who was sat looking up at him, and was wearing the diamante collar Ceri-Ann had sold

Mr Fitzgerald a few years ago. Mr Fitzgerald's face fell as he looked up again.

'Why do I have the feeling that you didn't come here just to tell me this good news, or buy a jigsaw puzzle?' he asked, his pale blue eyes seemingly searching Margery's soul. 'Everything seems to revolve around a case for you both now.'

'You're the one who gave us the file of missing persons,' Clementine said, much too defensively.

'Yes, I suppose I did,' Mr Fitzgerald said with a regretful sigh. He put his glass down on the counter and then rubbed the bridge of his nose with his fingertips.

'Somebody stole them,' Margery said, seeing no need to beat around the bush. 'We don't know who.'

Mr Fitzgerald's eyes widened. 'Oh dear – not my missing persons record? Gosh, I didn't even make a spare.'

They both nodded. He returned to the stool and sat down heavily, reaching to pick Jason up and sit him on his lap again.

'Do you need some of the information in it?' he asked finally. 'I might have some of it backed up, gosh... but not from this year though. But you know, the police have found who the skeleton was. A terrible business. I remember when Eugene disappeared, he was a lovely young man by all accounts. His mother used to come into the shop all the time and tell me what he'd been up to on his travels. We all thought he must be having the time of his life. It certainly must have been murder knowing all we know now. He can't have gone anywhere far at all.'

'We're investigating another case,' Margery admitted. Clementine, she realised, was uncharacteristically quiet next to her. 'To do with the swimming pool body, not the skeleton in the playground.'

'I see,' Mr Fitzgerald said. 'Well, that's certainly another nasty one.'

'We were on a case for his sister, Eugene, we mean,' Clementine explained. 'She hired us to find out if her husband is havig an affair, but well... this seems more important now.'

'Oh right,' Mr Fitzgerald said. 'And is he having an affair?'

'We don't know,' Margery told him.

They told him everything. How the missing person record and the school files had been stolen from their living room. How Evelyn had continued to receive Eugene's letters, their suspicions of Donald and his comings and goings to Devon even after Vivian had died. The horror of Vivian's death and how they had found out. How the car that belonged to Vivian's dead husband had been driven out of the car park. Mr Fitzgerald had gasped and covered his mouth in horror when they had told him the body belonged to Vivian. He had known her very well, having worked with her for decades on the school council.

'Maybe there's more than meets the eye here,' Mr Fitzgerald said finally, after soaking it all in. 'But Vivian... I just don't believe she would have killed Eugene. I really can't think of a single reason she could have had to. She had her favourites of course, even in her group, but I can't say she felt particularly strongly about him either way. She never mentioned him, all these years.'

Well, of course she hadn't, Margery thought, it wouldn't have done to draw attention to him if she had something to do with his death.

'But she signed off the playground building,' Margery said.

'Did she?' Mr Fitzgerald suddenly looked very tired. 'Gosh, yes. Maybe she did. It's all so long ago I can't really remember.'

'What about her husband?' Clementine asked. 'You knew him. Could he have killed Eugene?'

Mr Fitzgerald thought about it for what felt like a very long time. 'I don't know,' he finally said and Margery could tell he was telling the truth. 'Look, the files... well, I can't really help you with that. I don't have any backups, like I said. But there is something I could do to help. You say you saw Ittonvale School car park on the headmistress's dash camera?'

'Yes.' Margery nodded.

'But it wasn't good enough footage to see who drove the car away?'

'No.'

Mr Fitzgerald looked conflicted. Margery had seen a lot of expressions pass over his face over the decades they had known him, but this was different. Something crossed over it and Margery watched his brow furrow and then relax.

'Come with me.'

He didn't wait to see if they would follow him, but instead went behind the shop counter, opening a door that led to a staircase which twisted up inside the building. Clementine went after him first and Margery followed, treading carefully on the narrow staircase. It was an old building, and the stone steps were worn with age in the middle, so many people having used them over the decades. Margery wondered how Mr Fitzgerald had never fallen down them to his death. She would be too afraid to go up and down them every day if they lived in the building, would probably end up trapped on the ground floor.

Mr Fitzgerald, however, sauntered up them easily and into the tiny hallway above. Margery and Clementine stood awkwardly on the stairs waiting behind him. Margery clung to the wall with her fingertips. He took out a keychain from his trouser pocket and opened up one of the doors, leading them into a room. There was nothing extraordinary about the room at all. It was as full of things as downstairs, and must have been the shop's storeroom judging by the shelves of old unpriced books, and boxes of dusty broken lamps and old shoes. Mr Fitzgerald skipped right through the mess and pulled at the bookcase that lined the back wall. Margery gasped audibly as it swung forwards revealing a windowless room.

'What?' Clementine puffed as Mr Fitzgerald turned to look at them, grinning sheepishly.

'Please don't mention this to anyone on the council,' he said. 'Or the school in general, or anyone really. The police would have a field day.'

He led them into the room and Margery saw why he didn't want anyone else to know about it. There was not much behind the bookcase, just a desk and a chair with a computer sat on top of it and behind that a wall of screens all showing CCTV of Dewstow.

'You've had this the entire time?' Margery breathed.

'No,' Mr Fitzgerald said, waving his hands at her with his eyes wide. 'Good lord, no! This is just where I used to record my podcast on the impending apocalypse and financial crash.' He pointed to the large tape recorder still at the side of the small room. 'But after my shop was vandalised last year, I realised that the town had a severe lack of cameras.'

'This absolutely can't be legal,' Clementine said, looking around and shaking her head.

'Well, no,' Mr Fitzgerald said, wringing his hands together. 'But I thought it might be useful one day. Sometimes useful trumps legal.'

'How much CCTV footage do you have?' Margery peered at the screens. Each showed a different view of the town.

'Enough,' Mr Fitzgerald said guiltily, rubbing the back of his neck with a hand.

'Enough?' Clementine scoffed, gesturing at the nearest screen which showed a clear view down the high street. 'This is mad!'

'Yes,' he said. 'Well, I may have gone a little bit overboard.'

'A bit!' Clementine said, shaking her head.

'Have you seen anything useful though?' Margery asked, before Mr Fitzgerald could change his mind about showing them his secrets. 'From the night before Vivian Black was found?'

'I might have something,' Mr Fitzgerald said. 'Not enough maybe, and certainly nothing from Ittonvale... I only have cameras in Dewstow, of course.' He spoke about the cameras easily, like they weren't a new mad addition to his shop. 'But I have the driver in the car. It's a Mini, isn't it?'

'Yes,' Margery said.

'Well,' Mr Fitzgerald leaned over and tapped at the computer keyboard. One of the screens above the desk changed to show the road by the Bell and Hope pub. The mini zoomed by. Mr Fitzgerald slowed the tape so they could see the numberplate clearly.

'That's the first time I saw it,' he said. 'But then I saw it again, hang on.'

After a tremendous amount of clicking, he managed to switch the camera view. The mini disappeared up Dew Pond Hill and off into the night.

'Is that it?' Clementine asked.

'Yes,' Mr Fitzgerald said. 'For now. I'm still trying to work out where it went.'

'That's the way to Vivian's house, isn't it?' Margery said, trying to remember which way they'd gone. 'And to Don and Evelyn's.'

'And to many other places,' Clementine said.

'I keep thinking of those letters Vivian sent to Evelyn,' Margery said. 'Even after she was dead. Surely Evelyn must have some idea who really sent them.'

'I think Don must have,' Clementine said, in the matter-of-fact manner she always used when she was sure she was right. 'Mystery solved.'

It did make sense, Margery thought, but the idea was still missing the reason why. Why would he kill her and then cover it up? There had to be something more to it all if that was the case.

'But did he forge them or did Vivian actually write them?' Margery asked.

'I know her handwriting,' Mr Fitzgerald said.

Margery took the postcard Evelyn had given her out of her handbag and showed it to him. He hummed as he read it.

Dearest Eve,
  Hav4ng quite the time at Summerhouse! 7
hope you're both enjoying the sprl1ng wea1her.
  Lots of love,
  Viv

'It's either a very good forgery, or the real thing,' Mr Fitzgerald said. 'I'd know her writing anywhere after all those forms I watched her sign over the years.'

'Her writing's truly dreadful,' Clementine scoffed over Margery's shoulder, leaning back on the computer table with her arms crossed. 'Who writes their I's like that?'

'Those are numbers, aren't they?' Mr Fitzgerald said from where he had been reading over her shoulder too. 'Look, there's a seven there.'

Clementine took the postcard, held it very close to her face and then turned to look at him in surprise. 'You're right!'

'But what does it mean?' Margery asked.

They returned to staring at the postcard, no one knowing the answer.

Chapter Twenty-Three

It was late by the time that they arrived home. They sat in the car for a moment on the driveway, digesting all that had happened in the last few weeks. Margery folded her arms across her chest tightly, worried about what they had missed, although she had to wonder if they were really helping at all.

The police would arrest someone soon for Vivian's murder, she was sure of it. And she trusted that whoever they did arrest would be the culprit. Officer Wilkinson seemed very much on the case, as it were. She couldn't imagine he would allow for any mistakes.

What concerned her more was Mr Fitzgerald's illicit CCTV. What if the man had something useful recorded but hadn't noticed? The police would never see the footage or have any idea it could even exist. Were they complicit now that Mr Fitzgerald had showed them what he had?

When they finally got out of the car, Margery noticed Dawn Simmonds, their across-road neighbour waiting for her outside her house and waving at them manically.

'Oh God,' Clementine said. 'Not today, Dawn, thank you. Quick Margery, let's get inside.'

'I'll go and see what she wants,' Margery said with a sigh. 'I'm sure she's just going to tell us something dreadful Crinkles has done in her garden again.'

'Remember when she brought that mouse into Dawn's house?' Clementine hissed. 'And Dawn took it to the vet and then made us pay for her petrol and parking? No, let's get inside.'

Clementine rushed to their front door and opened it, disappearing inside with what Margery thought was far too smooth a motion for someone her age.

She sighed, wondering if she should just disappear into the house as well. Social niceties stopped her from running away from Dawn, who was still beckoning her over. Crinkles' mother, Sprinkles, sat in the bay front window of the house glaring at her. Margery walked over to the house, crossing the road and suddenly remembering that they had meant to speak to Dawn anyway, after the police had visited and their house had been broken into. In all the horror of the last few days she had completely forgotten. Clementine must have as well.

'Hello, Dawn,' Margery said, though her voice sounded as tired as she felt. 'How are you, on this fine Dewstow evening?'

'Much better than you I expect,' Dawn said, dropping any pretence of cleaning, leaning the broom against her garden wall. 'The police came to ask me if I'd seen anything the other day. Told me all about it.'

'Did you see anything?' Margery asked. Dawn hesitated, before nodding.

'I did,' she said, 'but you can't go telling the police.'

'Why not?' Margery said in alarm. 'If you saw someone break into our house, then you should definitely tell the police.'

'I don't want to get into trouble,' Dawn said, looking alarmed, like she'd only just realised what she'd done. 'That's why I didn't tell them anything.'

'Who was it, Dawn?' Margery asked. 'Did you see how they got in?'

Dawn glared at her, probably remembering the fateful day that Margery and Clementine had crashed their car through her hedge.

'I shouldn't tell you.' She huffed as if fighting with herself. 'Will you tell the police?'

Margery paused and thought about it. The only things that had been taken were the boxes of files from the school and Mr Fitzgerald's bizarre missing persons list, which were not things they would normally have in their possession anyway. And it didn't really look like either of those items was going to help them much with their investigation into Evelyn and Don. Any use they would have had was long gone. And anyway, falling out with Dawn wouldn't help get them anything back.

'No,' she said.

'Well,' Dawn said, leaning in to whisper conspiratorially. 'He came over to mine asking about you after he saw me in the garden.'

'All right,' Margery said, shaking her head. 'But I don't understand how they got from that to climbing through our window.'

'I know,' Dawn bristled, 'but he didn't climb through the window.'

'Then how did he get in?' Margery asked.

How the intruder had entered their home had been bothering both Margery and Clem an enormous amount ever since it happened, making them feel uneasy in their own home. She had never felt like that before. She had always felt perfectly safe in their little house with all their things and the cats. Whoever the intruder had been, they

215

had stripped them of that feeling for the time being. She wondered if they would ever feel completely safe again.

Pushing such thoughts from her mind, she noticed that Dawn's face had gone an unusual shade of red, only usually reserved for post-boxes, and Margery realised that Dawn had known the person.

'Who were they Dawn? How do you know them?' Margery asked.

Dawn's face fell. 'I barely know him,' Dawn spluttered. 'Gosh, I didn't realise he'd stolen something, he came from over there, and told me you were friends with his wife, and I thought I recognised him.'

She pointed down where the cul-de-sac joined the street and split off in turn to more of the housing estate. Margery suddenly had a sneaking suspicion why Dawn hadn't wanted to talk to the police, and why there hadn't been any broken glass or front doors.

'You let him in, didn't you?' Margery said. Dawn's pointing finger stilled, and her shoulders fell like an under-proved loaf in the oven.

'Oh Margery, please don't be angry,' Dawn begged. 'I didn't know, he said he knew you. I didn't realise he'd taken anything. He saw me in my garden and asked if I could let him in to wait for you… and I still have your spare key.'

'Dawn.' Margery shook her head, lost for words. 'We'll probably need that back now.'

'I understand,' Dawn said, her head drooping.

Margery wondered how on earth she would explain this to Clementine, who had still not forgiven Dawn for the day she had helpfully moved their food waste bin for them. Unfortunately, she had pulled it off the pavement and onto the road where another neighbour had run it over while they drove to their own driveway. Curiosity got the better of her.

'What did he look like?' she asked Dawn. 'This man?'

'He was quite tall, greyish hair,' Dawn said. 'His car was quite old. A bit strange really.'

That sounded like Don Redburn, Margery thought, as a cold chill danced down her back and raised the hair on her arms. What could he have been doing in their house? She wondered where he had taken the school files and what he had made of them. Surely he couldn't have known about them?

She suddenly had the alarming notion that maybe Donald knew more about what was happening than anyone could have imagined. What had he thought when he saw the files? He could have had the suspicion that they were working on the case. Could he have killed Eugene? All their suspicions were adding up now, into an unexpected sum.

Don was looking more and more guilty as the days went on.

'When you say you thought you recognised him, what do you mean?' Margery asked.

'I used to go to club meetings with my husband. I wasn't a member, but I'd go for the events that family were invited to.'

Margery had the sneaking suspicion she knew exactly what Dawn was talking about.

'Golden Circle events?' Margery asked. Dawn's eyes lit up in acknowledgement.

'Yes!' she said. 'Great fun they were, but I stopped being invited after my husband died, you know, which was a bit rude really. Some woman turned up at his funeral and gave me a cheque to help pay for it though, so I suppose that was something.'

Margery found herself reaching into her bag and bringing out the photograph of the Golden Circle Mr Fitzgerald had given them before they left his shop. She unfolded it and handed it to Dawn, who wiped her hands on her apron before taking it with her stiff, arthritic hands. She looked at it and then back up at Margery, a quizzical expression crossing her face.

'I wasn't there that year,' she said as her eyes slid across the photograph. She tapped a finger to it over a face. 'It was one of these lot, I'm sure of it. He was some big shot at that club. One of the founder's favourites from what Harry used to say.'

Margery stared at where Dawn was pointing at the group of men – Don Redburn was stood in the middle, with Richard Monroe next to him.

Dawn nodded grimly, leaning heavily on the brush.

'Did you see him leave after?' Margery asked, feeling everything she knew melting into the ether. 'Which way did he go?'

'He walked off towards the high street,' Dawn said. 'I remember because he complimented me on my hedge sculpture on his way past the garden.'

They said their goodbyes. Margery left Dawn and went home, feeling dazed. She breathed a sigh of relief as she entered the front door, closing it behind her and making sure the key was turned in the brand-new lock, resting her hand against the door for a moment, thinking.

'Clem,' Margery called out as she walked through the hallway and into the living room. She felt for a moment as though the blood was rushing back to her brain. 'How has Vivian been sending those postcards to Evelyn? If they aren't forged and she's been dead all this time.'

Clementine didn't answer and Margery thought for a moment that she hadn't heard her. When she finally stood up straight and pushed open the living room door fully, she saw that Clementine was staring into the space above the television in front of her, thinking hard, her brow so furrowed it looked almost painful.

'Someone sent her letters from her dead brother for years,' Margery said out loud, though she knew she didn't really need to remind her. 'And now they're doing the same with Vivian. And... Don has been visiting Devon a lot recently, hasn't he?'

'That's all true...' Clementine began.

'I think Don killed Vivian. And now he's trying to cover it up by pretending she's still alive,' Margery explained. 'I think he's been sending letters to the family, too.'

'And they've all fallen for it, I agree,' Clementine breathed. 'But how did he kill her?'

'I don't know yet,' Margery said. 'But I think the post-cards might hold some answers.'

'So do I,' Clementine agreed.

'You know...' Margery said, squinting at the television as she thought about it. 'The swimming gala trophy... if it's been missing as long as the students think it has, then maybe there's something to that as well.'

Clementine's eyes widened. 'Yes, there certainly might be, she was found with a copy of it, wasn't she?'

'She was,' Margery said. Though she couldn't work out how they would find that information out. It stretched on – a mystery as far as the eye could see.

Chapter Twenty-Four

No matter how badly they wanted to rush over to Evelyn's and confront Don with their suspicions, they couldn't. Clementine had argued that they should just arrive at the house as early as they could that morning, but Margery reminded her that if they were wrong then that could potentially backfire on them as well. It would be better to go about their normal lives and finish the workday before they spoke to Evelyn.

They didn't want to get into trouble with the head-master. Not with the audit still in full flow, and not after Margery had already missed most of a day of work. It would not do to cause Richard to hammer down the kitchen team like he had threatened to. Margery had reasoned that if they went to Evelyn's after work, they could pretend they were just visiting a friend if something went wrong. For once, Margery had won and they had trudged into work like they usually did, even more thankful than usual that it was nearly the start of the Easter holiday break. The rest of the team had arrived in a gaggle of excitement, full of joy for Ceri-Ann's news and breaking the gloom that had fallen over Margery and Clem.

'It's just so lovely,' Karen said, while Sharon shed a tear. Margery hoped she wouldn't make the sandwiches soggy with all her crying. 'Little Nicholas. I bet he'll grow up to be just like Ceri-Ann's hubby.'

Margery was glad that Clementine was in another part of the kitchen – the abbreviation of the word husband would have made her flinch.

Margery decided to excuse herself and get on with some of the paperwork and ordering she hoped to complete before the break. If it wasn't done in time, then they'd have to come in during the holiday and she knew that no one wanted that. Hopefully they would get all the weekly deep-cleaning jobs done so they could be out in good time on Friday afternoon. She already had Clementine and Seren sorting through the dry store, checking the date labels and cleaning the shelves, while Gloria, Sharon and Karen got on with cooking lunchtime's food.

Wednesday had always been roast dinner day at Summerview, though Margery had never known why and had always been too afraid to ask. She had once changed the menu to something else as an experiment and there had nearly been a riot when the students and teaching staff realised that there weren't any roast potatoes or gravy. Caroline used to buy in six boxes of frozen Yorkshire puddings at a time and hoard them in the walk-in freezer, but Margery had insisted that they make them from scratch after she had taken over. Sometimes she wondered if that was a time-consuming mistake on her part.

Somehow in all the chaos of yesterday, the remaining team left on site had managed to get most of the preparation done for the day. The vegetables had been peeled and stored in water, the Yorkshire batter mix was made, the crumble and custard were ready to be heated up. All that was left to do was to actually cook everything. Margery wondered if the kitchen really needed her at all. Perhaps once they retired it would all just run itself, having been turned into a well-oiled machine over the last few years.

She entered the dry storeroom and found to her surprise that Clementine and Seren had actually settled into a comfortable cleaning rhythm and were making good progress. Clementine was checking dates and discarding anything that wouldn't last the two-week holiday and Seren was dutifully cleaning with the sanitising spray and cloth. They had even pulled the shelving out to sweep behind it without being asked to, which made Margery's heart swell with pride.

'Seren and I have been talking,' Clementine said, looking the dictionary definition of smug as always. To her credit, Seren looked just as baffled as Margery felt.

Margery realised that Clemetine had probably been ranting to Seren about Vivian the entire time they had been in the storeroom.

'We think someone here must know more about the real trophy than they're letting on.'

'I'm sure that's true,' Margery said with a nod, getting her clipboard down from its hook on the wall. 'But who?'

'Miss Morgan?' Clementine said, forgetting she was supposed to be tidying the shelves and leaning on the nearest one.

'No,' Margery said. She couldn't imagine Miss Morgan knowing anything about it, not judging by her reaction during the assembly.

'I think the leisure centre would know,' Seren said. 'They would have been the ones who stored it ready for the big day. And they sort out the cleanings. They might know who took it this year.'

'That's a really good point,' Clementine said, clapping Seren on the back. 'Vivian can't have had it, could she? Or wouldn't she have had the real trophy with her in the pool, and not a fake?'

There seemed to be something to that. Why did Vivian have the fake trophy in the first place? Amelia and Oliver had seemed convinced an older woman had taken it, but that could have been anyone.

'Right then,' Margery said, putting the clipboard back and sighing internally about the work that wasn't about to get done. 'I'll help the others get lunch ready and then we'll go and find out.'

—

It didn't take long to set up the hot cupboard and bains-marie for service. Margery and Clementine had an entire half hour to spare before they needed to be back. They practically ran to the leisure centre, as fast as their feet would let them, their kitchen safety clogs catching on the rough carpet. The school hallways were long and always seemed dark to Margery, but they finally reached the interconnecting doors that led to the steps down into Dewstow leisure centre.

'What are we going to ask them?' Margery panted as they rushed down, ignoring the glowing lure of the row of vending machines with its prepackaged delights.

'Where's the trophy!' Clementine said. 'Or something to that end I suppose.'

Brian the leisure centre receptionist had already heard them arriving and looked ready to leave and never return rather than talk to them for even a minute. He turned back to his phone screen behind the desk, as though if he ignored them then they would disappear.

'Brain!' Clementine cried. He glared at her mistake with his name, as always. 'Why are you here – why aren't you helping your uncle at his solicitors?'

'I work here three times a week,' Brian said with a sigh, finally looking up from his phone. 'As you well know Mrs Butcher-Baker. And before you even start, I can't and won't tell you anything private involving swimming memberships.'

'We don't want to know any of that,' Clementine scoffed. 'We just want to know all your secret information about the IttonStow gala cup.'

'Why do you think I know a thing about the IttonStow cup?' Brian said, with a withering roll of his eyes.

'There's a folder behind you that says something about it,' Margery reminded him, pointing to the shelf behind him on the wall. The label on the box folder only said 'Gala Information', but surely there had to be something in it that could help them.

'That's just for arranging the races,' Brian explained. 'I wasn't lying, I don't know much about it. It's always arranged by the teachers and then we send the lifeguards to support.'

'Can you think of anything that could help us?' Margery asked. 'We wouldn't ask if it wasn't so important.'

'I heard about that body with the cup,' Brian said, his eyes widening. 'Isn't that where it is? At the bottom of Ittonvale School swimming pool?'

'It was a fake,' Clementine told him. Brian didn't look surprised at all.

'You already knew that,' Margery said. 'The police have been here, haven't they?'

Brian nodded. 'Yeah, and I told them exactly what I told you. I've no idea where the trophy is.'

'We heard that someone took it to clean it,' Clementine said, almost demanding an answer.

'She did,' Brian said. 'That's what I told the police, she took it and never gave it back.'

'Who?' Margery asked.

'I couldn't possibly tell you that,' he said. Clementine scoffed.

'Well, you've told us enough, why not tell us that?' she said.

'Was the person who took it an elderly woman?' Margery asked, feeling her voice rise in desperation. 'Was her name Vivian Black?'

The look on Brian's face told her it was. He tucked a strand of hair behind his ear and then sighed haughtily.

'If you tell anyone about this then I'll deny it all,' he said. He reached for his phone, flicking across the screen with his finger. 'A lady came and arranged to take it recently… to clean it.' His brow furrowed. 'Well, not that recently, like the end of last year? Something like that. But you're right she never returned it.' He held up the phone to show them the text messages from a name Margery recognised, organising to come and pick the trophy up.

'Evelyn Redburn took the trophy?' Margery gasped. 'But why?'

Of course – when Amelia and Oliver had talked about an older woman, they must have meant Evelyn. Margery supposed that anyone over the age of thirty was practically a historical monument to someone still at school.

'She did most years,' he said. 'On behalf of the school councils. I've never really given it much thought to be honest. But that's all I know, so you can leave me alone now.'

They did leave him alone, barely saying goodbye in their shock rushing back up the stairs and into the school corridor again.

'Evelyn took the trophy,' Clementine said out loud as they marched back to the kitchen, the hallways passing by in a blur.

'Vivian died with a fake one,' Margery gasped. Clementine stopped dead and turned to her, her mouth slack.

'Where's the trophy then?' she asked. 'You don't think that Evelyn still has it? What is she doing with it?'

Margery didn't know, but she suddenly wondered if they ought to have gone straight to the Redburn house that morning.

Chapter Twenty-Five

They parked outside the Redburn house, and went to the front door. Clementine knocked briskly. Then they stood back and waited.

Margery hoped that they were not too late, but they hadn't been able to leave work any earlier without it being noticeable to the auditor, who was still making his rounds. Margery wondered if she should have gone back to the police as soon as she had heard Dawn's accusation, but something in her head told her it would have made no difference.

It would, she thought, all have been much simpler if Don had been having an affair. This would all be over now, and they'd be on their way home from work, instead of standing awkwardly outside his house about to accuse his wife of having stolen a school trophy. She hoped that once they left today they would never have to visit ever again, but she knew that was futile. For one thing, she hadn't seen the trophy in Evelyn's house on their previous visits. If it was here, she was hiding it.

Finally, the door opened, and Evelyn peeked out her head, not fully committing to opening the door for them, but not slamming it in their faces either.

'Come in,' she hissed. Margery and Clementine didn't need to be told twice.

They followed her into the living room where Evelyn wrung her hands together anxiously. She didn't look well, Margery thought. Evelyn had always had a worried look about her, but this was something else. Her eyes were drawn, and her skin was shockingly pale. Her fingers playing with her wedding ring, which had been attached to her finger for so long that the gold and diamond bands had almost become part of her skin. They didn't sit down, and neither did Evelyn.

'Evelyn what...?' Margery began but Evelyn interrupted her.

'Don.' She drew in a sharp intake of breath at the mention of his name. 'He's not having an affair, is he?'

Margery shook her head, feeling frozen, unable to do much more. Evelyn's face crumpled.

'Why do you say that?' Clementine asked, her voice a whisper.

Evelyn moved to the bureau like she had done a few days before, this time bringing with her a pile of postcards. She handed them to Margery, who held the one on top up to look at it. It was a beach scene, with 'Beautiful Salcombe' written underneath it. She flipped it over and read the message scrawled on it, which was a seemingly normal note wishing the recipient a good weekend and lots of love.

'Her son rang me and told me you'd been to the house, asking not so subtle questions.' She gave them a look that said she had been expecting that they might turn up at her house at some point. 'He asked when the last time I'd spoken to her was,' Evelyn said, her voice a broken sob. 'And I said, not for a long while now. In person anyway. I said, she can't be dead, don't be so stupid, she wrote me a postcard. It had come that morning! But then I read the postcard again and I told him about the letter she wrote me, but then I thought… those letters from Gene, they were fake… and Vivian…' She pointed at the postcard in Margery's hand desperately as though they must be able to see the problem with it too.

'She never would have written "lots of love",' Evelyn scoffed. 'She always put something funny, like, hope the seagulls don't catch me with my ice cream or forgot to pack my bikini for the trip.' She took a deep breath and then continued. 'And the more I thought about that, the stranger I thought it was, so I went to ask Don about it, but he was in the garden.' She waved her hands as she spoke, becoming more and more animated. 'He was in the garden and he'd lit the bonfire and…' She put her hand over her mouth for a moment like she was trying to unconsciously stop herself from saying whatever it was. 'I thought he was just getting the garden ready for summer. But he was burning all of Gene's letters.'

'What?' Margery asked, as, beside her, Clementine gasped. 'Why?'

'That's just it, he wouldn't tell me a proper reason, he said he'd just thought it was better to put it all behind us,' Evelyn said. 'And now I think that he must have something to do with all this.' She waved a hand as though to try and convey what a hideous mess it all was. 'Do you think he killed Vivian? Or worse, did he kill Gene? Why? Why would he kill him? I didn't even think he knew him before then – we didn't meet till a year after Gene left and we've been friends with Vivian forever; he's known her longer than I have.'

'Where is Don?' Clementine asked. 'Have you spoken to him? What's he got to say for himself?'

'He's in his shed,' Evelyn snapped, putting her hand over her mouth. 'I don't know what he's done. Oh god, did he kill her? How could he kill her!'

Evelyn slumped down on the sofa and put her head in her hands.

'Why did you fall out with Vivian?' Margery asked. 'Is that the last time you saw her in person?'

'No,' Evelyn said, her face flushing as she looked up. She looked ashamed, Margery realised, like she'd been led along a path and only just realised. 'The last time I saw her in person, we had a perfectly lovely day. We went to the garden centre to see if they had any Christmas decorations in the January sale. It was a perfectly normal day out for us. I dropped her home.'

'And then?'

'And then I had a letter from her,' Evelyn said, gesturing to the bureau behind her with her hands. 'That said she needed some time apart from me and I was suffocating her.'

Evelyn looked haunted by the words. Margery wondered if they were always something she had feared hearing anyway, and the realisation of them had hurt her in ways she hadn't expected.

'I know that sometimes you don't keep up friendships with everyone in your life,' she said. 'Sometimes they just stop working, or you move on, or they move on, or you're at different parts of your life than they are. After we found out we couldn't have children, I couldn't tell you the amount of people who eventually cut us out when they realised that we weren't in the same place as they were. We were going on holiday or to restaurants while they worried about babysitters and primary schools.'

Margery felt a twinge of empathy at that. She and Clementine had never had children either of course, and they certainly had a number of close friends who'd faded away into the ether of childrearing. She hadn't felt it was anyone's fault at the time, and she still didn't now, but sometimes the loss of a close friendship could be as acute as a breakup or a divorce. Though, she supposed, at least when it was a friendship that ended, it came with a lot less paperwork. But there was still a horror in it, a reminder that you couldn't always really know anybody, even the ones closest to you could one day leave and never return into your life. No matter how many letters you wrote, or voicemail messages you left. Or birthday cards you sent to their children.

Evelyn shook her head. 'But I never thought that would happen with Vivian. She was always there for me, and I thought I was a good friend to her too, despite our age difference.'

'Do you still have the letter?' Clementine asked. Evelyn nodded. She went over to the bureau she had hoarded Gene's letters and Vivian's postcards in again and took out another piece of paper, handing it to Margery, who was still struggling to hold the pile of postcards.

The letter was still in the envelope, and addressed formally to Mrs Evelyn Redburn in fountain pen. The stamp was postmarked from Ittonvale's Royal Mail sorting office. There was also the newer mark that reminded everyone to use up all their normal stamps before January 2023 next to the old stamp.

'Evelyn, where's the trophy?' Margery asked. Evelyn turned to her in surprise, a look of rage passing over her features.

'At the bottom of a pool with my best friend,' she spat. 'As I'm sure you know!'

'We know you took it away last year to be polished,' Clementine said placidly, sounding remarkably calm against Evelyn's wave of anger.

'Yes, but I gave it back to her,' Evelyn insisted. 'Like I always did, to be inspected before it was returned. We did that every year – she was very particular about it.'

'Are you sure?' Margery asked.

'Yes!' Evelyn cried.

The doorbell rang, the sound clanging through the house and into the living room and causing them all to jump. Evelyn turned towards the bay living room window with wide eyes.

'I forgot to say,' she said, all the anger gone from her voice and the fear returning. 'Before you arrived, I called the police.'

'Did you?' Margery asked, as Clementine turned to stare at the closed curtains of the bay window.

Evelyn's hand wringing increased, till she was practically writhing in front of them. 'You know, Gene's letters stopped... I wasn't going to say anything, but they stopped just after... gosh, please don't think I'm mad, but they stopped just after Billy died.'

'Billy Black?' Clementine said.

'Yes,' Evelyn said, 'I'd never put it together before, but there's got to be something to that, hasn't there?'

There might well be, Margery thought, though her mind couldn't quite put the pieces together yet. But if there was, then surely Don could just have been forging Vivian's postcards? Even if Mr Fitzgerald seemed to think that they were real, and Evelyn had been fooled too. Then again, she hadn't realised that her brother's letters had been fake. Evelyn looked from the window she had been staring out of to the letters and postcards in Margery's hands.

'I don't know what's going on,' she said, 'so I had to call the police. Don's just been too suspicious. They've come to arrest him. You'll have to leave. I don't think it's a good idea you being here when they are.'

'Why not give them the postcards?' Margery said frantically, holding the letters in her hands up. Evelyn shook her head.

'What if I'm wrong?' Evelyn said. 'What if Vivian did actually write them and found a way to send them? He's burnt everything else. Take them.'

'Okay,' Clementine agreed, though Margery didn't know what they were agreeing to.

'Where's your car?' Evelyn asked, as the doorbell rang again. It seemed much louder this time, as though the person had pressed the buzzer with much more force, though Margery knew that couldn't be possible. Evelyn looked towards the living room door and then back at them in determination.

'You'll have to go out of the conservatory door,' she said, gesturing behind them at the double doors. 'And don't let Don see you. I'll distract them for a moment by telling them my suspicions about him.'

The doorbell was replaced by frantic knocking, making the chime of the bell seem almost gentle in comparison.

'Don't come into the hallway, they'll see you through the door,' Evelyn said, gesturing to the conservatory doors. 'Don't go yet, let me distract them.'

Before either of them could as much as peep that they didn't think hiding was a good idea, Evelyn had left the room. They heard her open the door, sharing a frightened look. Clementine took her hand and dragged her behind the sofa. From behind it, Margery could just about see through the half-open living room door as Evelyn opened it and the police poured into the house, led by Officer Wilkinson.

'Mrs Redburn,' he said, and even from across the room Margery could see the look of concern in his eyes.

'Hello Officer,' Evelyn said, stepping forwards to shake his hand bravely. 'Thank you for coming so quickly. Shall we go into the kitchen so I can explain to you what's been going on properly?'

Clementine grabbed Margery's hand again as the officers followed Evelyn out of the hallway. They ran for the conservatory door, not looking back as Clementine fumbled with the lock. It didn't budge and Clementine turned around, her eyes scanning all over the room for another escape. Margery froze for a moment, thinking, and feeling her knees grow weak as she saw Don through the conservatory window, leaving the shed and saun-tering over the grass back to the house, towards the kitchen where Evelyn and the police officers were talking animatedly.

Clementine seemed to have had a lightbulb moment, grasping for Margery's arm again. She pulled her back into the living room. Then she rushed to the door and poked her head out, confirming the way was clear. She motioned frantically for Margery to follow her and then began to sneak through the hallway.

Margery felt dizzy, but she followed Clementine anyway, as they crept through the half-closed kitchen door and deeper into the house. She inched along behind Clementine, using the wall to steady herself as they passed the kitchen. The officers inside were so engrossed by Evelyn's story that none of them noticed.

Margery could hear Evelyn sobbing and suddenly felt a horrible wrenching sense of guilt that almost caused her to double back, enter the kitchen and apologise for each stone they had unturned.

Instead, she followed Clementine out into the room they had seen before when Evelyn had shown them the golf clubs that Don had obviously no more intentions of using. Clementine didn't pause for a moment; she crossed the room and opened the door that Margery had only given a momentary fleeting glance to when they had been here before. It swung open and they rushed through and over to the door that led to freedom.

Chapter Twenty-Six

They had got away from the house, but only by the luck-
iest of chances in the end, creeping through the garage
and out of the side door into the garden. Margery didn't
dare think too much about how they had run down the
driveway past all the police cars, as though thinking about
it too hard would undo their escape and they would be
sat in front of Officer Wilkinson being interrogated about
the letters Margery had been holding under her arm.

The pieces of card and paper were now sat on their
coffee table. Margery had wondered at first if going home
was the right thing to do, as the last time they had a coffee
table full of clues, they had all been stolen. But there hadn't
seemed to be much alternative. Margery wished that they
knew what was happening back at Evelyn's house; if Don
had been arrested.

'What should we do now?' Margery asked, as she put
down the tea tray on the coffee table and joined Clementine on the sofa. She hadn't even turned the television
on yet, so wrapped up was she in the pile of postcards in
front of her on the table.

'I suppose we'd better look through all of these,' Clementine said, rubbing her eyes. The postcards Evelyn had
given them sat in front of her. She looked tired, Margery
thought, and not as enthusiastic as she usually was.

'Have you found anything?' Margery asked her, sitting down on the chair next to the sofa and reaching down to the side table next to it to bring out the tin of emergency Quality Street. She opened it to find only a fluttering of toffee penny wrappers left from the last time Seren had visited. She sighed. Having to buy another emergency tin during an actual emergency was all they needed.

'Hmmm, maybe,' Clementine mused, not concerned with the lack of sugary provisions – which was most unlike her. She was squinting at the postcard in her hands. 'She's got horrible writing, Vivian. It's hard to believe she was a teacher.'

'Do swimming teachers need to have good hand-writing?' Margery asked, picking up one of the postcards to have a closer look too. This one wished the recipient a very fabulous Easter and had a picture of the river that ran past the bottom of Dewstow town. Sometimes, Margery thought, a clue was a clue but sometimes, a postcard was just a postcard. There was nothing special or unique about it that she could see. She picked up the letter Vivian had sent Evelyn – the one that had caused such a fallout – and read a few lines of it. It was certainly rude, but Margery wondered if Vivian had really sent it. There could be no way to know now. She assumed that Don must have sent it to Evelyn, but why would he have wanted them to fall out? There was something much more to all of this.

Clementine shrugged, taking the teapot and pouring the liquid out of it into the mug next to it. Most of it went into the mug, but a few drops dribbled down the side of the teapot and onto the postcard sitting next to it, splashing the ink and blurring it.

'Careful, Margery!' Clementine exclaimed, just as much to herself as to Margery. She flapped the postcard like a flag trying to dry it off. 'Oh dear.'

'Oh, Clem.' Margery took the tissue out of her cardigan sleeve and dabbed at it, only succeeding in nudging the stamp in the corner. The left corner peeled horribly, like wallpaper coming unstuck.

'Margery, this is a police investigation!' Clementine shrieked again. She tried to stick the stamp back down with her finger, making it worse. 'Wait a minute…'

Clementine peeled the stamp off entirely, Margery gasped.

'I think there's some sort of message here,' Clementine said, lifting the stamp with her finger. Underneath it, were tiny letters in Vivian's handwriting. She hadn't written it in ink this time, but biro, and it hadn't smudged when the stamp had been stuck down.

Remember the code.

'What could that possibly mean?' Margery said.

'God, I love a puzzle!' Clementine cried gleefully, dropping the postcard back down on the table, where it sat forlornly as she rummaged in the drawer of the coffee table. She pulled out a notepad. Grasping for the postcard again she began to jot down the message onto the first page of the notepad that wasn't covered in shopping lists and things Clementine was going to complain to the council about.

Margery took another postcard from the line up and scratched gently at the stamp until it came loose. Vivian was lucky the stamps had made the post with the ease they peeled off. Clementine's puzzling would have to wait,

Margery thought with disappointment. This one had no such thing hidden under the stamp. Clementine put her notepad down and determinedly picked up the next. That postcard had a tiny drawing of the Ittonvale School swimming cup underneath its stamp. Margery gasped.

'Why does that one have something, and the one you looked at doesn't?' Clementine scratched her head. Margery thought about it for a moment.

'The dates,' she said. 'I bet that one was sent before. Look…' She pointed to the ring of black ink around the stamp. 'That one is from February.'

'Wishing Evelyn a happy birthday?' Clementine said.

'Yes,' Margery said.

'But her birthday's in July,' Clementine said. 'She told us so at her house the first time we went there, remember?'

'That is strange,' Margery said. 'And why the picture of the swimming gala trophy?'

'Very strange. Hmmm,' Clementine said as she picked up the next postcard and peeled the stamp off. This one had a picture of a swimming pool sign.

'Pool room!' Margery and Clementine cried at once.

'She was Evelyn's swimming coach,' Margery said, a lightbulb going on in her head. 'The trophy was found with her body.'

'But not the original trophy,' Clementine said. 'But Evelyn swears she gave it back to Vivian.'

'Yes!' Margery exclaimed. 'So do you think that Vivian took the real trophy and put it somewhere?'

'Yes, for some reason,' Clementine said. She looked at Margery with a blank gaze for a second and then Margery saw the realisation flood into her eyes. 'Do you think there's some clue with the trophy?'

239

'Yes!' Margery grinned, relief that they were on the right path flooding her brain. 'But surely that isn't in the swimming pool?'

'No,' Clementine said. 'It was stolen ages ago, remember?'

'Then where?'

'Her house,' Clementine said the words out loud, and Margery realised immediately that she must be right.

'Not her house here though,' Margery said scratching her head. 'I didn't see the trophy there.'

'No,' Clementine said. 'I'd bet it's at her holiday home.'

'By her indoor pool,' Margery gasped, remembering the sign on the wall in her hallway. Clementine nodded.

'Maybe it explains how she died?' Clementine suggested. 'Maybe there's some clue to why Don was driving her car around after she went into the pool area and never came back out.'

'Should we go?' Margery said, thinking of how late it would be by the time they got there.

'I really don't know.' Clementine shook her head. They thought about it for a moment in comfortable silence.

'Let's sleep on it?' Margery suggested. 'We still don't know what she means by a code.'

'What about the numbers on the postcard Evelyn gave us before?' Clementine said, rushing to Margery's bag to take it out and reunite it with its sisters. 'Look these letters are numbers, like Mr Fitzgerald said! So, the code might be 4, 7, 1, 1.'

'Do you really think so?' Margery asked, rereading the postcard and realising that Clementine was right. 'Oh wow! Do you think the code has something to do with the trophy?'

Clementine nodded. 'Yes, so I think we should get down there as soon as possible.'

'The perfume,' Margery said, with a sudden flash of realisation. 'The perfume is a number, isn't it? It's still in the car. I'm sure it's called 4711.'

Clementine gasped beside her, 'My Auntie used to wear that scent! Why didn't we think about it before? Gosh, so this is what Vivian meant by those numbers?'

Before they could discuss it any further Clementine's phone rang. The ringtone disturbing the peace as Gwen Stefani's voice boomed out of it and vibrated the table.

'Hello?' Clementine said into the speaker. 'Hang on, let me pop you on the loud phone.'

'Ladies, it's me,' Nigel said as soon as Clementine had put the phone down on the coffee table in front of them.

'Hello Nigel,' Margery said, wondering why on earth Nigel would be calling them at this time of the evening. 'How are...'

'Sorry Mrs Butcher-Baker, but I have to interrupt you for a moment,' Nigel said. He sounded stressed, Margery thought. Usually, he had an easy breezy sort of conversational tone and Margery wasn't sure she liked what was coming.

'Officer Wilkinson is on his way to arrest you. He's just got the warrant,' Nigel said, his matter-of-fact police officer voice returning. Margery and Clementine exchanged a shocked look.

'What?' Clementine spluttered. 'What for?'

'Don and Evelyn Redburn have told them she believes you have something to do with the death of her friend Vivian Black,' Nigel explained.

'What!' Clementine cried as Margery gasped. 'But Evelyn called the police to report her husband as the culprit!'

'I know, but he managed to provide an alibi,' Nigel said, his voice thick with worry. 'I don't know what he told them, but they haven't arrested him.'

'Nigel, Evelyn told us he burnt all the letters she got from whoever was pretending to be Eugene,' Margery said. Clementine threw her hands up in agreement. Nigel paused for a moment.

'It seems strange to me too,' he said finally. 'They must have a reason to believe it's not him. You'll have to tell them when they get there.' He hesitated. Margery could hear him sighing over the line. 'I just thought I'd warn you before they arrived.'

'Does she not believe Don killed Vivian anymore?' Margery asked. 'Why?'

Evelyn had been very clear with her thoughts when they had been in the house, but maybe Don had talked her round. Had somehow convinced her that he was innocent and Margery and Clementine were not.

'Donald told them they think you're the ones who've been forging the letters,' Nigel explained. 'I don't know what proof they think they have, but I expect when the police get to you they'll be able to find something in your home that implicates you.'

'They don't know about our cat camera,' Margery said, the realisation arriving like a late train. 'She doesn't know that we saw someone break in.'

'I bet he's planted something here,' Clementine said, looking around the room nervously. 'That's why nothing was taken.'

'Exactly,' Nigel said. 'It would be easy enough to explain away to the police.'

Margery wished they had more than Dawn's word that someone had broken into their house and she suddenly had a horrible thought that sent a chill down her arms and spine. Dawn had said that she had seen Don walking away from the house past her garden, and he had arrived in an old car.

'Vivian's car is here,' Margery said, the words arriving before the thoughts were fully formed.

'What?' Clementine said at the same time that Nigel gasped on the other end of the line.

Margery didn't even try to explain, instead she rushed to the back door and grasped for the key to the garage that hung on the wall. She had been unsure about it the other day, but now she knew the key had been moved. She threw open the back door and rushed out to the back garden, her fingers shaking as she put the key into the garage door lock and turned. Clementine crashed into her back as she stopped dead in the doorway. They collided, and Clementine grasped for Margery's wrist again, her mouth falling open in shock. The old Mini that had belonged to Billy Black was sitting in their garage.

Margery turned to look at her. Clementine shook her head, her gaze elsewhere and Margery knew exactly what she was thinking. For once, she agreed with her. There was no point in waiting here until the police came to arrest them, they had to get something concrete to prove he had something to do with it and clear their names once and for all.

'Ladies,' Nigel said, making Margery jump. 'Are you still there?'

'Yes, but we won't be when the police arrive,' Margery said, folding her arms across her chest.

Clementine looked up in surprise, and then smiled as she realised what was happening.

'What do you mean?' Nigel asked.

'Nigel,' Clementine said, leaning over to speak directly into the phone's speaker. 'We think there's something else to prove how Vivian died and we're on our way to Vivian's house in Devon.'

'I'm sorry... you... you're what?' Nigel said. 'It sounded like you said you were on your way to Devon to visit the deceased's house?'

'Yes,' Clementine said, 'don't worry. We've been before.'

'You've been there...?' Nigel spluttered. 'I can't tell you how bad an idea I think this is. Evelyn's told them you blackmailed her. She said she gave you one hundred pounds—'

'She hired us as detectives!' Clementine scoffed.

'And you were the one who was poking us for clues a few weeks ago,' Margery said, the fury arriving without warning. 'Now suddenly you don't believe us. You called us a few days ago to tell us things, and today!'

'Yes... well...' Nigel spluttered again, falling silent for a moment. Margery wondered what he was thinking. 'Of course I believe you. All right. Look, I'll call Wilkinson and stall them, you get to Vivian Black's house. But be careful. This could all blow up in your face if you're wrong. I've already tried to talk him round, and he won't hear it.'

'Yes,' Margery breathed. Maybe this was a silly plan. Maybe it was all a huge waste of time and effort, but they had to try. They wouldn't be able to explain away the car sat in their own garage, no one would ever believe them.

'I don't think this will be the end of it,' Nigel said. 'I think Wilkinson is trying to tie it all up too quickly, rookie mistake, you see. Go to her house, see what you can find out. I'll be on the other end of the line.'

Margery looked at the clock on the dashboard. 'We'll leave in a few minutes. If we don't contact you by five…'

'Don't worry,' Nigel said. 'I'll keep an ear out.'

Chapter Twenty-Seven

'I'm really not enjoying the last couple of weeks,' Margery moaned as she clutched the steering wheel tightly, trying to concentrate on the motorway lane in front of her as they were overtaken by another lorry. It was far too much driving for her; she suddenly had a deep wave of sympathy for lorry and delivery drivers. It didn't help that the weather had also betrayed them, and the rain was landing heavily on the car windscreen. The windscreen wipers battled the monsoon pitifully as water from the car in front splashed upwards.

'I'm not either,' Clementine said, with a shrug. 'It's almost as bad as when I sat on my glasses and had to wait two weeks for the new ones to get to the optician.'

Margery smiled at that. Clementine had not had a choice but to wear her prescription sunglasses every time she needed to read anything. It made all jobs involving the till at work very difficult indeed.

She squinted through the rain pattering against the windscreen and the driver's side window, making it nearly impossible to see what was happening in the other motorway lanes. The wipers slammed back and forth against the car. The perfume bottle that Evelyn had wanted to give Vivian sat on Clementine's lap, the name on the label the same as the code they had discovered.

Clementine had already unscrewed the top and looked inside it, but it had revealed nothing but the scent of citrus.

'I'm going to call Nigel and let him know how we're getting on,' Clementine said, getting her phone out of her handbag.

'Do you think that's a good idea?' Margery asked her, flinching as another lorry passed, water flying up behind it. 'He didn't really like the idea in the first place.'

'No,' Clementine said, already dialling the number. 'But let's do it anyway.'

'We do have a track record for that,' Margery said. She took the next exit and Nigel answered the phone as the car rumbled up and onto the country lane, splashing through the muddy path.

'Mrs Butcher-Bakers,' he said, in an exhausted tone. 'How are you getting on?'

'Fine, fine,' Clementine said. 'We just thought we'd let you know we're nearly there.'

'Good, good,' Nigel said with an awkward chuckle. Margery knew immediately that something was wrong.

'They know where we're going, don't they?' Margery asked.

Nigel's silence said it all.

'Yes,' he said finally. 'And they found writing materials and a bundle of postcards at your house in one of your living room drawers.'

If they had already looked through the living room it was only a matter of time before they searched the rest of the house and found the car, Margery thought grimly.

'Christ,' Clementine said. 'This is what we get for never throwing anything away or cleaning anything. It was an accident waiting to happen!'

'They've just left to find you,' Nigel said, his voice urgent. Margery could imagine him pacing up and down the room with the phone pressing tightly to his ear. 'If you can get in and out quickly, you might be able to miss them.'

'All right,' Margery said.

They thanked him and he finally hung up just as Margery was pulling the car in through the front gates. The house was just as large as the last time they had seen it, but it wasn't as pretty, even though the rain had finally stopped. It was too big – looming over the car and making Margery feel tiny in comparison. The gravel of the driveway rattled as she slowly crossed it, pieces hitting the underside of the car and clattering gently back down again. The sky was dark, threatening rain again with every dark cloud.

'What now?' Clementine asked.

Margery shook her head. For all their bravado and the rushing down to the house, she hadn't thought the next stage through. She had been hoping that Clementine would have had some marvellous idea on the way, but the hopeful look on Clementine's face revealed that she had been relying on Margery's brain. Which had run out of ideas days ago.

'I suppose we could just knock?' Margery said. 'See if William is in? We'll say it's an urgent matter about his grandmother. I'm sure he knows about her by now. The police will have called.'

'If the police have called, then he'll know they're after us,' Clementine said nervously.

It was true, but Margery didn't have a retort. Instead of worrying about it anymore, they crossed the driveway and stood on the impressive front porch. The bulb in the hallway was on and light flooded through the stained glass of the door. Clementine rang the bell and they waited. Nothing happened. Clementine reached out and touched the door handle, which turned easily. They shared a worried look.

'What's with all these millionaires leaving their houses unlocked?' Clementine whispered. 'I suppose they wouldn't worry about paying their home insurance premium.'

They had come this far, Margery thought. She took a step into the house. Clementine reached for her arm, but Margery was already stepping onto the tiled hallway floor and entering the building.

'Hello!' she called through the house, her voice sounding echoey and alien to her own ears. 'William, are you here?'

They were met by nothing but the oppressive silence that seemed to ring out in its emptiness, filling Margery's ears with static. She took a deep breath and turned back to Clementine, whose eyes had become very wide as she glanced around the hallway.

'He's not here, is he?' Margery said. 'Should we just go down to the pool room and see what she meant in her postcards?'

'I don't see why not,' Clementine said, pointing at the arrow that had the words on it. 'I bet she's got two Olympic-sized pools in her basement. Gosh, this house is massive Margery. We couldn't live here! I'd never be able to remember where I'd put my glasses.'

Margery fought the urge to smile in the seriousness of the moment. Instead, she marched purposefully down the hallway, peering inside every door just in case some other more immediate clue made itself known. Clementine joined her in the search, tapping the doors with her finger-tips to open them.

'I'm sure I saw a big glass roof last time we were here,' Clementine said as she opened the next door. 'I saw it out of the living room window.'

'You might be right about the basement then,' Margery said, still creeping along. Her brain was stumbling over itself, trying to think of ways that they would explain their presence and not get arrested when the police arrived. How they would explain the evidence that had been planted at their house.

Clementine gestured dramatically at another 'Pool Room' sign on the wall. She opened a doorway, revealing a staircase. She didn't hesitate for a second, taking a tent-ative step down into the darkness. Margery followed, all her smiles from earlier evaporating with nerves. They crept down and around the corner of the stairs and down another, feeling their way along with their fingertips on the old textured wallpaper. Clementine found the light switch with a hurrah and clicked it on, flooding the room with light from the main bulb sitting in the glass ceiling. Margery blinked as her eyes readjusted and found that they were in an entirely different room than she had been imagining.

'Not a swimming pool,' she said to Clementine, who was taking in the splendour of the glass ceiling and wood walls, a smile returning to her face as she did so. Margery couldn't help but join her in looking around.

'No,' Clementine said, turning to Margery in triumph. 'It's a billiards room! Look at that pool table.'

In the centre of the room sat a large billiards table, with the balls already lined up waiting for the next game. On the wall to the right sat an impressive-looking bar and, on the left, hung the pool cues of all sizes. To the back of the room sat a large trophy cabinet full of shiny, but dusty trophies. Clementine was drawn to it immediately.

'What did she draw on the postcard again?' Margery asked. 'The little picture of a trophy?'

'Yes,' Clementine said, peering behind the trophy cabinet. Margery eyed the ones inside it. They were for various things, mostly snooker and darts. It was obvious that her house in Dewpond was where the family had kept their more prestigious Ittonvale-sourced trophies, but this display was for the sports they played while on holiday in the house. Clementine reached around to the back of the cabinet and began to pull out trophies, so coated in dust that it almost made Margery sneeze as Clementine wiped off the front plaques of them and then put them back when they weren't what she was looking for. Margery looked around the room again. High on the left-hand wall hung a reproduction of a painting in a frame – a man swimming leisurely under the water of a swimming pool, while an onlooker observed from the side of the water. Margery was sure she had seen the painting at some point before, but she couldn't recall its name.

Below the painting was a cabinet. She opened the doors at the same time, revealing pool cues hanging on either side – and the trophy sat on the shelf in the middle section. It took her breath away for a moment, the trophy had a splendid shine compared to the dusty ones sat in the trophy cabinet. Clementine whooped as Margery picked it up.

'Here it is,' Margery smiled, handing Clementine the enormous gold trophy.

'Well done, Margery!' Clementine cried as she pointed to the plaque at the top and Margery read, 'Itton/Stow

School Swimming Gala' and underneath that a long list of engraved names and dates of which school had won. It started back in the seventies and the last engraving read 'Ittonvale 2023'. Vivian must have had the trophy since the last gala, just as Evelyn had told them.

'Well, that's one mystery solved, I suppose,' Margery said, as Clementine looked it over.

'Yes,' Clementine said, lifting it up and down. 'But I can't see anything particularly special about it.'

Margery took the trophy back and looked inside the cup at the top of it. There was certainly nothing inside it. All in all, it was quite a normal school artifact. There was nothing much of note to it at all, other than that it had been missing for an entire year and a person had been found at the bottom of a swimming pool with its replica.

'Are we sure it's this trophy she means?' she asked, turning it over in her hands with difficulty due to its weight. 'Do you think there's something inside it?'

'You could try and twist it,' Clementine said, reaching to take it. 'Here, let me have a go.'

'There's a combination lock at the bottom,' Margery said, nearly dropping the trophy in surprise, 'look… for four numbers!'

Clementine whooped in surprise and then began to input the numbers, Margery waiting patiently for it to open.

She turned the lock with her fingers gently, murmuring '4, 7, 1, 1,'. They listened for a click or something similar, but nothing happened. Clementine took the trophy and shook it, but it stayed the same. 'Hmmm,' she said, 'maybe I put it in wrong.'

She tried again with the same result, scrabbling at the bottom of the trophy to try and get it to reveal its secrets.

'Maybe she changed the code?' Margery said.

'Maybe,' Clementine said, putting it down on the pool table so she could inspect it without her arms aching. 'Are we sure that's the right numbers?'

'They're what she wrote down,' Margery said. 'And it's the perfume.'

'Let's try again then,' Clementine said, hefting it upright with a sigh. Margery stepped forwards to help her. 'Ooh let's try 1975!'

'Why?' Margery asked, baffled.

'I bet that's the year she got married.' Clementine smiled smugly.

'I doubt it,' Margery said, shaking her head, but letting Clementine input the numbers anyway. 'She was well into her eighties – they were married much longer than that, weren't they? I bet they married in the sixties.'

The lock didn't open for those numbers either. Clementine tutted while Margery glared at the trophy in defeat.

'Are there any other numbered perfumes?' Clementine asked, glaring at the trophy in frustration. '6821, or something?'

There was a noise behind them, and they both paused, the trophy held up in mid-air in both their hands. Margery let it go and Clementine's arm dropped to her side, still holding it as footsteps continued down the stairs, each stair creaking as whoever it was made their way down. Margery sucked in a breath expecting to see Officer Wilkinson's angry face as he entered the room. Instead, she found her mouth dropping in surprise.

'What are you doing here?' Don asked, coming into view in the doorway. He ducked through and entered the basement, looking around in surprise at the room. 'Wow!

I didn't know any of this was here. Vivian kept this quiet. She never showed us this room when we stayed over.'

'Why are you here?' Margery asked him before she could stop herself. She couldn't work it out. Was he here for them? Or was it a coincidence?

'Your wife said she was going to have you arrested,' Clementine told him. Don's face didn't reveal anything. Margery couldn't tell if he cared about it or not.

Don didn't say anything, he looked over at the pool cues and reached for one, sliding it off its stand on the wall. He rolled it over in his hands and then considered the table.

'No, she didn't,' he said. 'She's been trying to have you arrested.'

'She really wasn't. Not until you got involved,' Clementine said. 'We've been trying to help her.'

'Haven't you heard?' Don said. 'You've been blackmailing Evelyn and forging Vivian's letters. I have it all squared away with Dewstow police.'

'Did you force Vivian to kill herself?' Clementine cried. Don's head snapped up from where he'd been looking down at the pool cue.

There was a thump upstairs and a muffled cry as though the person who was screaming had something over their mouth. Don moved to block the doorway, looking up the stairs for a moment as footsteps began to come down them.

'What was that?' Clementine asked. Margery could hear the nerves in her voice.

The stairs creaked as the unseen person stepped down them lightly. Upstairs, the banging continued. Margery gasped as the unexpected person entered the pool room.

'I think it's time we all had a little chat,' Richard – the school inspector – said, his mouth pulled in a grim line. He went to stand by the bar, folding his arms tightly across his chest. His jaw set as he studied them. He looked different without his usual clipboard and Margery found herself blinking at him stupidly.

Don swung the door closed with a thump behind her, and Margery and Clementine turned to each other, exchanging looks of terror.

Chapter Twenty-Eight

'What are you doing here?' Margery heard herself ask out loud, even though she knew deep down in her gut exactly why Richard was standing in front of her, eyeing her smugly.

'I'm as surprised to see you,' he said, smiling a playful grin. 'I really do hope this won't affect our working relationship.'

'They'll throw the audit out now!' Clementine sneered, pointing a finger at him. 'Now that you're involved in all this.' She made a swirling gesture with her hands, as though to show what a mess it all was.

'The results of the audit are already in, it's out of my hands. Although I must say, I don't think I'd have taken the job on if I'd have known about your little detective agency. It's caused a lot more trouble than it's worth. I should have asked them to send another auditor,' Richard said. He held his own hands up at the admission. 'But I would never ruin my professional reputation with a false audit, regardless of the situation. Summerview School has been given the grade it deserves.'

'Which is?' Clementine asked. Richard just smiled again. It wasn't a nasty smile, Margery thought, but there was no warmth to it.

'I couldn't possibly say,' he said. 'But of course, school audits are like house surveys. Sometimes it's all fine, and sometimes you find asbestos in the roof. You'll have to wait and see.'

That didn't sound good to Margery, but before they could dwell on it anymore. Don tapped the bottom of the pool cue on the floor to get Richard's attention.

'What are we going to do with them?' Don asked. Richard grimaced.

'The same as I did with William I suppose,' he said.

Margery's blood ran cold at the suggestion. 'Wait,' she said, stalling as she tried to think of something, anything, that could help them. 'Tell us how you killed Vivian.'

'We didn't,' Don said, his eyes widening in an alarm that Margery could tell was genuine. 'She killed herself.'

'Did you coerce her into it though?' Clementine said. 'We know you drove her car home from Ittonvale School.'

Margery wondered briefly which was worse. What had Don said to her in the last few moments she was alive?

'I didn't drive the car,' Don scoffed.

'But it was at your house?' Margery said, more as a question than a statement.

Don huffed. 'He drove it to ours and made me put it in the garage.' He stabbed a finger towards Richard. 'Quite against my will.'

'Did Evelyn really not know about it?' Clementine asked him. Don suddenly looked very uncomfortable.

'I told her that Vivian wanted me to do it up,' he said, 'and that I'd get it back to her in the next few days.'

'And she really never asked about it again?'

'No. I didn't kill her,' Don said, 'and neither did Evelyn or Richard. That's all that matters.'

'But you're both here?' Clementine asked, gesturing between them. 'Why? And what was that noise?'

'Yes, what did you do to William?' Margery demanded to know. She took a step towards the door and Don stood in front of it again, making her jump back. Richard and Don shared a look. 'What have you done to him?'

'Why are you here?' Clementine said again, even louder this time.

'We're tying up loose ends,' Richard explained mildly. 'Which is why it's perfect that you're here.'

'I'm looking for something,' Don interrupted him. 'Something to get us all off the hook.'

'What could you possibly be looking for here?' Clementine demanded to know.

Margery wondered if they were looking for the same thing as they were. The trophy sat on the floor behind Clementine and Margery moved so she was blocking it from view too.

'I don't know yet,' Don said, adjusting the pool cue in his hands. 'But there will be something here. Trust me, Vivian left enough evidence to damn us both, I just have to find it.'

'Because Vivian and her husband killed Evelyn's brother, Eugene?' Margery asked, suddenly realising what this was all about. The clarity flooded her brain, like an unexpectedly warm day in the darkness of January.

Don was silent for a moment. Richard watched him from where he was leaning against the bar, waiting to see what he would say, Margery thought. She was beginning to lose hope that they would be able to get out of this situation alive. Don was telling them much too much.

'Vivian was already dead by the time I went to check on her,' Don snapped. 'She said she wanted to go and visit the pool and then she'd forget all about it all. But she didn't. She went up there, took all her sleeping pills and climbed into the water. By the time I got up there she'd drowned.'

'So, you didn't kill her?' Margery confirmed. 'But you did leave her body in the pool?'

'Yes,' Don said. 'I put the pool cover back over her, and then I decided I'd work out a way to come back and deal with it.'

That was somehow worse than if he had killed her, Margery thought.

'I rang Richard. He was supposed to help me.' He glared at Richard. 'But he just came and moved her car...'

'What else was I supposed to do?' Richard snapped. 'The plan was that we would return when we had got somewhere ready for her to go and could get her out of the pool.'

'But you never found a way?' Clementine asked, though they all knew the answer from the fact Vivian had been discovered there.

'No,' Don said. 'They tightened up security because they had a break in over the February half term. We'd planned to sneak back with my bigger car and somehow load her into the back. Then we were going to bury her in her garden, honestly. I'd dug the grave.'

'That's what you were doing on the day we visited,' Margery gasped. Don raised his eyebrows at that, he hadn't known they had been there.

'Yes,' he said. 'It was all ready, we just never found the time to do it and then it was too late. If I'd kept up with school news, I'd have known about the change of plans for the swimming gala and sped it all up. Richard should have known all about that. But for some reason you didn't think it was important did you, Rich?'

Richard glared at him again. 'Well, none of it would have happened if you hadn't antagonised her, would it?'

Margery and Clementine turned their heads from one man to the other with each shouted insult, like they were watching a particularly interesting tennis match.

Eventually Richard held his hands up in defeat. 'I should have known about the school, of course.' He ran his hands through his short hair. 'But it was all such a mess, and I've been busy with the audit. We were supposed to have a few weeks left, you see? That pool isn't supposed to open till after Easter, probably not even till May.'

'Why did you say Don coerced her?' Clementine asked. 'Did you know what she would do?'

'Yes, of course,' Richard said. 'I suspected that after Billy died, she would care less about hiding his secrets. But then Donald here goes and winds her up about stopping his payoff money, getting her to do stupid things and she kills herself.'

'What did you get her to do?' Margery asked in surprise. She couldn't think of what someone could say to her to get her to want to leave the planet.

'He got her to write postcards for Evelyn. He told her if she stopped paying his money, he'd kill her and no one would ever know because he'd keep sending the postcards,' Richard explained, giving Don a withering look. 'And then she did it herself, and he still had to send them. She really called your bluff.'

'So she did really write them?' Margery asked. Don nodded.

'Can we start from the beginning?' Clementine asked. 'We know that Vivian used to be your swimming coach,' Clementine said to Don. 'And that you were part of her golden group.'

'A lot of people were,' Don said, 'including Evelyn.'

'And me.' Richard smiled the same infuriating smirk.

'Yes, but you also worked for her husband, Don,' Margery reminded him.

'I did,' Don said. 'But I don't see how that…'

'You were his driver,' Clementine said. Margery thought back to the photograph in Vivian's home office. Of Billy Black and Don, who had been wearing the silly peaked hat.

Don seemed to realise that the jig was up. 'I was, for a bit,' he said.

'Did you kill Eugene Price?' Margery asked him.

'No,' Don said.

'So, Vivian and Billy did?'

Don shook his head, looking at Richard.

'Billy thought he did.'

Richard suddenly looked very uncomfortable. His weathered old face was red and Margery was sure she could see the sweat forming on his brow.

'You killed him?' Clementine asked astounded, looking at Richard. He opened and closed his mouth like a fish gasping for air.

'We'd been drinking,' Don began. 'We'd been drinking at the clubhouse.'

'The clubhouse at Dewstow golf course?' Margery asked. Don nodded.

'Yes. I hadn't wanted to go crazy, but the old man wouldn't take no for an answer. He kept plying us with whisky,' he said. Margery was aware of Clementine narrowing her eyes at him. 'I told him, I can't drive you back in this state, so he said he'd drive, but that was just to convince me to get in the car. He couldn't even get his seatbelt on. Richard was convinced he wasn't too bad, so he took the wheel in the end.'

'Alright,' Clementine said. 'So, Richard was driving.'

Don ignored her and continued. Richard folded his arms even tighter around himself, as constrictive as a snake.

'He kept grabbing at the wheel,' Richard said, as if that would absolve him of whatever was to come. 'Billy was being an idiot.'

'We'd just come up the road to his house when suddenly...' Don ignored him again and then paused, as though trying to collect his thoughts in a way that would put them in a better light. 'Someone stepped out into the road. There was a tremendous thump, and all the revelry sort of died. We thought we'd hit a deer, you see.'

Margery thought it highly likely that they might have hit a deer, remembering how narrow the path to Vivian's house had been when they had driven there. There were no streetlights on the quiet country lane. It must have been pitch black at night.

'But we hadn't,' Don said, his eyes wide, but not looking at either of them. Margery didn't even dare to breathe in, lest she break the spell he was under. 'We'd hit Eugene, he'd been at the house with Vivian.'

'Why was he with Vivian?' Clementine asked, slapping a hand over her mouth when she realised she'd interrupted his speech.

'It was Friday night, and the Golden Circle always met on Fridays,' Don said. 'This was a special one, of course, because Eugene was going away travelling. He'd told Billy and Vivian a few weeks before and it was his big going away party.'

'Well, that seems very convenient,' Margery said, her mother's voice screaming in her head that she mustn't forget her manners, even though Don was still standing in front of their only means of escape and didn't look likely to move at any time soon.

'You must believe me,' Don said, 'Gene was a very good friend of ours. He'd have been on the golf course with us if he hadn't been at the party. We should have been there anyway wishing him off.'

'Well, why weren't you at the party?' Clementine demanded to know.

'Because Billy wanted to golf and drink,' Don said, 'and I had to do what he wanted as his driver and Richard had to do whatever I wanted as my best friend.'

'You were part of the Golden Circle, though, weren't you?' Margery asked Richard.

'He was,' Don said when Richard didn't answer.

'Only because I was your friend,' Richard said. Don gave him a small smile.

'I really don't like the way Vivian and Billy had the whole town wrapped around their fingers,' Clementine said.

'I didn't always either,' Richard said. 'But it was better than not having a job and not being part of it. They had access to the high life and everyone else wanted in.'

'What did you do when you both realised it was Eugene?' Margery asked, wanting to move the conversation forwards.

'He was dead,' Don said. 'There was nothing else about it, we had been driving so fast... and Billy kept grabbing the wheel as a joke, like Rich said.' He swallowed before continuing. 'He'd broken his neck. No pulse.'

Margery and Clementine stood in horror.

'Billy said to put him in the back,' Don whispered. 'So we did. It was funny. It was as though Billy sobered up the minute we hit him. He was so serious. I can remember every little detail. There was a blue plastic sheet in the boot that they used to put over the seats if the dogs came with us. We wrapped Gene up in that and then I put him in the back of the car and then we drove to the house and parked the car in the garage.'

He took a gasp of air, like he was taking a much-needed breath after a long time underwater.

'Billy went and spoke to Vivian and then he came back and gave us some money... a lot of money... and he said, "This will stay between us and you'll both be well compensated."'

'That's grotesque,' Clementine whispered. Don nodded. Richard stared at the ceiling.

'Vivian came out to the garage, and they spoke for a bit. Hushed whispers you know,' Don said, his gaze far away as he recalled the details. 'Then she got in the car and she told us to come too and she drove us to the school.'

'Summerview?' Margery found herself saying out loud, though she already knew very well how the story ended.

'Yes,' Don said. 'We got there, and she'd got one of the builders to meet her there and between myself and him we got Gene into a hole they'd been filling and then he covered it enough so it wouldn't bring any suspicion before they finished the work the next day.'

'Who was the builder?' Margery asked.

'I don't know his name. I've never sought him out.' Don shook his head.

'Why not?' Clementine asked, flirting the line between danger and intrigue as always.

'Because Billy paid us every month after that. Hush money,' Don said, his face flushing in embarrassment. 'I'd imagine they paid the builder off too. And he looked nearly as old as Billy was. He's probably long passed.'

'And the payments stopped after Billy died?' Clementine said. 'So you blackmailed Vivian.'

The look on Don and Richard's faces told them that was true.

'Honestly, Evelyn must have had some suspicions before all this, she can't possibly think my pension's good enough for us to keep this house going and go on holiday four times a year,' Don spluttered. 'Christ, the golf club membership costs as much as a holiday abroad! She's an intelligent woman, she must know.'

'Evelyn probably saw what she wanted to see,' Margery said. 'She loves you. She sees the best in you. Did you know her before...?'

'Before we killed her brother?' Don smiled again. 'No, I knew of her of course. Gene had told me about her. But I didn't know her before he died, no. I met her because...' He took another breath, and then continued anyway. 'Billy and Vivian knew that she would never stop looking for him if he just disappeared and never wrote, so they sent me to get a copy of his handwriting. They knew he'd write to her, he always had before.'

'That's a horrible thing to do,' Clementine said. 'So, all this time she's thought she was receiving letters from her brother and really you were sending them.'

'Billy was sending them,' Don corrected her. 'And a few years ago, he moved to email, which made it even easier for him to keep up the pretence. He was a clever man, but she must have known something was up then.'

'That's why they stopped when he died.' Margery shook her head. 'Evelyn knew. She told us she was going to have you arrested, that she suspected you.'

'It didn't take a lot to convince her otherwise,' Don said. 'And I could prove I wasn't at the pool, couldn't I? I was at home when Richard took the car.'

'So you're the one who's been sending Evelyn those postcards?' Clementine said. 'And she wasn't suspicious about it at all until now? They had a big falling out, didn't they?'

Margery thought of the letters Vivian had sent to her family, the rude one she had sent Evelyn.

Don groaned. 'I didn't know about that until after I'd sent the first one. Honestly, they used to fall out all the time. Both so opinionated. They were like family. We all were – everyone in the Golden Circle. A big dysfunctional family.'

'But no one would have suspected you, surely?' Margery couldn't wrap her head around it. 'If you'd just left her body in the pool anyway. No one would put you both together in that way.'

'She told me she'd hidden the truth somewhere, and it would come out when it was ready.' Don looked haunted. 'I had to find it.'

'And have you?'

'No.'

'How did this all begin?' Margery struggled to put all the bits of it together in her head.

'Vivian obviously retired from all of that,' Don said. 'So, when she found out that the playground was due to be refurbished, she realised exactly what would happen. I told her that even if they found out who the body was, they'd never be able to connect us. But she rang me the night she died and said she was finished with running and there hadn't been a day since we'd done it that she hadn't regretted what she'd taken part in.' His eyes were haunted.

'She said it ruined her life and I couldn't blackmail her anymore.'

Margery felt her knees giving way a bit. She leaned heavily against the back wall of the room.

'What was your plan then?' she asked, determined to hear the full story. 'Were you going to kill her?'

'I really thought about it,' Don said, playing with the pool cue again, tapping it on the ground. 'But I'm not Billy, I couldn't have washed it away from my conscience like he could.'

'I think she must have been waiting for the right time to get out,' Richard said from the bar. He walked around it and poured himself a drink. 'Billy would have convinced her to forget about it.'

'What's next, then?' Margery said, dreading the answer.

'I've already told you,' Don said. 'We're going to find some evidence that we're sure she's left, and I'm going to destroy it before the police realise she has a second home. And then I'm going to leave here and go home. The police won't be able to find anything on any of us and they'll let it go eventually. Well, not for you. I'm sure they're at your house finding her car right now. You'd have gone down for it. Obviously now we're going to have to change plans, seeing as you've worked out what we're up to. Who's going to miss a couple of dinner ladies?'

He doesn't know that the police are already on their way here, Margery thought. We just have to hold on until they get here.

Even if they were wrongly arrested, that had to be better than being dead or kidnapped.

'I knew you'd be trouble the moment I saw you all doing whatever it is you were doing at the golf course. And then we talked in your office of course, and I thought

267

I'd scared you off looking into anything,' Richard said, looking to Margery. 'But when I saw you leaving the storeroom with all those school records, I knew exactly what you were up to.'

'You broke into our house and put the car there!' Clementine gasped, pointing down at the shiny leather loafers that Richard wore. 'It was your feet on the cat camera!'

'Yes, I did. How did you…?' Richard looked down at his own feet, confused for a second before he flicked his head back up to glare at her, obviously deciding it was of no consequence.

'It all looks very damning on the surface for us,' Don said, ignoring Clementine's outburst, 'but when you dive below, there isn't any evidence to prove we did a thing. I've already searched her entire house in Dewstow.'

The noise from upstairs got louder, and both Don and Richard glared up at the ceiling as though that would stop it in its tracks.

'We're going to go, then,' Clementine said, the trophy still hidden behind her. 'If you're going to be doing that, there's really no need for us to be here as well. We've got to get home for the cats, come along Margery.'

She took a step forwards, but Don blocked her way again. He drew out the pool cue in front of him as though it were a sword. Richard came around to the other side of the bar, and stood behind him as backup.

'Take a step back,' Don said. 'Unfortunately, you know too much. You're not going anywhere.'

'Yes, we are,' Clementine said, her voice trembling.

'Don't make me tie you up like we had to with William,' Richard said.

The thumping upstairs began anew. Don took a step towards them.

So many things happened in the next second that Margery almost had permanent amnesia about how events unfolded.

First, Clementine threw the trophy at Don's head, missing entirely. It landed on the floor and smashed into two, the gold cup separating from the base. At the same time, the door behind him slammed open, catching Don, who was flung forwards towards them, causing Margery and Clementine to jump backwards.

Margery nearly lost her footing, but managed to scramble back up, just as the police entered the room. They weren't any officers she recognised, but she breathed a huge sigh of relief when they handcuffed Donald and Richard instead of her and Clem, and began to read them their rights.

She turned to Clementine, but she was busily picking up a piece of paper that had been tightly folded and hidden inside the trophy, just as Vivian had said it would be.

Chapter Twenty-Nine

My dearest Evelyn,

By now you will have worked out my silly notes and you'll have come rushing here. And unfortunately, I know that in order for my plan to work out this way, I am long dead.

I do apologise for leaving you like this. I've come to the end of a long road I never thought I'd go down and I must admit, I'm very tired. Tired of running, tired of hiding and tired of covering up what happened to the one person I should have been honest with from the very beginning. But I couldn't. I could never bring myself to see the hurt in your face if I told you the truth and so it was easier not to. But every time I thought about telling you, I would think about how kind and loyal you have been to me over the years, and I just couldn't bring myself to it. I could not ruin your life like that and until recently, I had hoped sincerely that we would all be able to go to our graves without it coming out.

You will know by now about Eugene. I suspect that it won't be longer than a few weeks till they find out his identity and you realise that he's dead. It probably then won't be too big a jump for you to realise that his letters stopped several years ago

– when Billy died. I wish I could have the guts to have told you that Billy was the one forging his letters after all these years. Every time a friend went away on business or on holiday he would write you a letter as Gene, and ask them to post it for him. It became much easier, as you know, once Gene began to email you. Billy asked me to continue the emails after he died, to protect the family, he said. But I could never do it. Not least because I can barely see to write these letters, let alone use the computer!

I know that you will be upset with Donald, but he really does truly love you, and what happened was an accident. Billy panicked and forced both he and Richard to hide the body. Donald wanted to go to the police straight away, but Billy convinced him otherwise. I really don't know how he's lived with himself after all these years, especially as there has barely been a moment since it happened when I do not regret what we did. Richard is another story and I believe this would have all been out in the open much sooner if not for his input in the cover up.

I know that once this is all out you might not give a shred of a second thought to my death. You might even wish that I had suffered longer. But, my dear, I have suffered my own mind these last few decades, absolutely tormented by guilt for what I knew, for how I defended Billy and Donald and Richard. None of them deserved it in the end, but we all have to do our bit to keep the peace. I am hoping that the next life will not bring as much pain as this one does. It may be macabre, but I

am looking forward to seeing what's next. I believe
that there was a plan for this life, and I'm sure that
there is one for the next. I'm not afraid to find out
what it is.

If we confess our sins, He is faithful and right-
eous to forgive us our sins and to cleanse us from
all unrighteousness. I hope that you can find some
solace in the discovery of your brother. He always
spoke so highly of you – was so proud of his little
sister.

I will see you on the other side and I hope that
by the time you get here, you can forgive me.

Viv

X

The letter was damning. Vivian had included a separate page which contained the exact particulars of Eugene's death. It included lots of details that only the police had known before, along with several other things that they hadn't.

Vivian had secretly kept every bit of evidence that Billy, Richard and Donald had tried to hide over the years, including the receipt from when they had scrapped the car that had killed Eugene, and a letter from the school's construction management confirming the deed was done. It was as though she'd been planning this all along. Perhaps she had, Margery thought.

Don followed the police out to the car with his head bowed but Richard did not go quietly at all. Margery could still hear him yelling from their seat on Vivian's sofa as they put him in the police car outside on the driveway.

Officer Wilkinson sat down heavily in the chair opposite Margery and Clem. Vivian's letter sat between them in the evidence bag on the table. At some point during the chaos Evelyn had turned up and then been led into the kitchen by the startled police officers on site. William, who had been untied and looked over by paramedics, had been settled in the kitchen also. She had read the letter and then sat very quietly while Margery and Clementine were escorted away by Officer Wilkinson.

'Why didn't you arrest us?' Clementine asked as soon as they sat down on one living room sofa and he sat on the opposite, the coffee table in the middle of them as a buffer. 'I'm not complaining, but I was sure you'd let them go free.'

'You were very lucky actually. We knew you'd return here after we spoke to William and the rest of the family. So I arranged to have the house bugged with their permission,' Officer Wilkinson explained. 'I've had officers on standby for days. So, when Nigel rang to try and stall me, I just knew you were on the way here and we'd find something in your house. And we did, obviously. Her car in your garage with Mrs Black's suicide note in the dashboard. So off we set to arrest you, and imagine our surprise when Donald and Richard arrived and attacked William just before you got here.' A wry smile fluttered over his lips. 'We decided to hold back and see what would happen when you got here, we still weren't sure if you were all in cahoots, but then Mr Monroe confessed to planting the car as evidence! It's not every day a case falls into your hands like that.'

'Well, we are grateful that you haven't arrested us,' Margery said, not quite able to share in his triumph.

'So am I,' Officer Wilkinson said, shaking his head. 'There's not much left to say, but congratulations. How did you know the letter was in the trophy?'

'The postcards she sent Evelyn said to find a code. And there was a drawing of the trophy under a stamp,' Clementine explained. 'Donald posted them to Evelyn after she was dead. Just like Vivian's husband did with the forged letters from her brother Eugene.'

'A horrible thing to do to someone,' Officer Wilkinson said, shaking his head with his brow furrowed. 'And all for money.'

'Evelyn never realised,' Margery told him. 'They'd fallen out before and she thought Vivian was trying to wind her up. Don didn't know that they'd fallen out.'

Officer Wilkinson hummed, and they all fell silent for a moment, digesting the events of the day.

'Right, listen to me carefully here,' Officer Wilkinson said, turning to give them the pointed glare that Margery was used to seeing on his face. 'When you eventually bugger off to set up the old meddlers' detective agency, like I know you're going to—'

Clementine opened her mouth to speak, but he interrupted her with a look.

'Don't try and deny that's what's eventually going to happen,' he scoffed. 'I know enough about you to know I'm right. Listen, unfortunately for me it's perfectly legal for people to hire you to do that, but what isn't legal is trespassing and getting yourselves involved in police matters. Especially with a former police officer! You could have got him in big trouble if your plan hadn't worked.'

'Where is this going?' Clementine said. 'We just solved a million-year-old murder case for you!'

He rolled his eyes in such a spectacular fashion that it made them look like two loose marbles in his skull. 'Yes, but lots of that could have gone wrong, couldn't it? You could have died, William could have died, and also, there was a bit too much breaking into people's houses for my liking.'

Margery had to accede that it had been another very close call – a mystery solved by the skin of their teeth. She wondered what they would even call the detective agency that would never happen. The Former Dinner Ladies' Detective agency? Clementine would probably want to call it 'The Education Centre Nourishment Consultants' Agency', and that would never work either. No, it would never work. Especially as they didn't have any plans to retire yet. Officer Wilkinson finished dressing them down and then went to supervise Mr Redburn's arrest, taking the clipboard with the interview sheets with him, leaving Margery and Clementine in a pensive silence. Evelyn arrived in the living room doorway, her eyes red with the ghosts of former tears, but her face stony and steeled.

'Hello, ladies,' she said, taking the spot where Officer Wilkinson had been sitting. 'What a day.'

'Hello,' Margery said, wishing she knew Evelyn well enough to know how best to comfort her. 'How are you holding up?'

Evelyn gestured in a way that told Margery she had no choice but to carry on.

'I suppose it's all over now, isn't it?' Evelyn asked. It was less a question and more as a statement. 'I'm sorry the police nearly arrested you. Don was always so convincing, he had me really believing every word he said. Even when the police came to talk to me about him, he sauntered straight into the kitchen from the garden and shook that police officer's hand.' She waved over in the direction that Officer Wilkinson had left in. 'So confident, even though he knew it might all be about to blow up in his face.'

She looked at the letter and broken trophy sat in front of them on the coffee table.

'How did you open it?' she said curiously. 'I'd have never thought about that in a million years.'

'Well, she left you a code,' Clementine began. 'At least we thought it was a code. It turned out not to be one at all.'

'What was it?' Evelyn asked.

'4, 7, 1, 1,' Margery told her. 'Like the perfume you buy her.'

Evelyn's face broke into something nearing a smile.

'But that wasn't the code?'

Margery and Clementine shook their heads.

'I wonder,' Evelyn said, jumping out of her seat and rushing from the room. Margery and Clementine exchanged looks of concern as they wondered where she had gone. Barely a few minutes later, Evelyn sat back down, this time clutching another blue, old-fashioned bottle. Evelyn tapped the bottle dramatically with her finger.

Margery took the bottle and gave it a closer look to read the label, but that didn't give her any clues. It wasn't a spray bottle – it was a splash. So she unscrewed the lid and opened it, just as she had for the bottle in the gift bag. Inside the bottle top was a carefully laminated piece of paper with the numbers '8875'.

Clementine oohed and reached for the broken trophy, inputting the numbers into the still intact lock mechanism. It clicked open easily.

'Well,' Clementine said, putting the trophy down again. 'This puzzle was certainly meant for you.'

'Oh, poor Vivian,' Evelyn said, putting her head in her hands. She sniffed once and then regained control of herself, as if she had decided that she'd had enough of a pity party. '1975 is when Eugene went missing. The police just told me that in her notes she wrote that it all happened on the eighth of August.'

They sat and thought about it, listening to the police wandering around the house. The haunted look Evelyn had worn had gone and been replaced by something much more pensive. Margery couldn't even imagine how she must feel, the betrayal must have been devastating. If she had been being sent letters for years by a loved one and then found that he was dead she thought it would probably be enough to destroy her, and Evelyn had gone through that twice in one life. Her heart ached for her. Margery wanted to reach over and comfort Evelyn, tell her it would all be all right, but she knew that her words couldn't promise such a thing.

'I'm sorry about all this,' she said finally. 'I let Don tell the police you were blackmailing me and of course, I gave you that money of my own accord.'

'That's quite alright,' Clementine said, though she bristled at the mention of the accusation. 'We should give it back really, seeing as we didn't solve your problem.'

'Well, you did,' Evelyn joked. 'He certainly wasn't having an affair.'

'No.' Margery smiled weakly.

'Though I really wish he had been now,' Evelyn laughed. 'I never thought I'd say that!'

They chuckled at the joke, but Margery felt that there was a darkness lying underneath it that sucked all the humour from the moment.

'Do you think you'll be alright?' Clementine asked her.

Evelyn sucked in a breath, obviously hoping not to be asked that question, as though if she didn't ever think about it in any capacity, then it wouldn't really be happening.

'Yes, I do,' Evelyn said. 'It's just such a relief to know what happened to Eugene. I don't have much family left, and my mother passed a long time ago now, but what's left of us can give him a proper funeral now. Set things to rest. As for Don...' Her face darkened as she glared at the thought of him. 'I'm just so angry at him. I don't think we can fix this, and hopefully he'll go away for long enough that I'll have time to sort everything out.'

'I've got everything crossed for you,' Clementine said.

'You should really think about opening a proper detective agency,' Evelyn mused, as much to herself as to Margery and Clementine. 'You've really helped me. Think of all the good you could do for the town.'

'We might even find Martha Mugglethwaite's other missing shoe,' Clementine said. They all laughed. 'We are getting a knack for it, aren't we?'

'Maybe,' Margery said finally, though she thought that for the time being she would have had enough of all of it. Another murder solved, two deaths even. But at what cost? She looked around the room till she found something blue and took in a deep breath. She wondered what they would say back at school – their reputation was beginning to precede them. She was sure the headmaster would find it assembly worthy at the very least.

Epilogue

Seren and Gary's wedding was supposed to fall on a beautiful August day, without a cloud in the sky. Instead, the school field was a barren hellscape of heavy rain, high winds and errant crisp packets from the school playground billowing past. Margery desperately tried to continue leading the troops from inside the catering gazebo that had been set up next to the main marquee.

They had managed somehow to move most of the equipment they needed from the kitchen to the tent the previous afternoon, when the weather hadn't looked quite as grim. Now Margery worried that the oven and long folding tables would blow away with the rest of the tent. The wind howled through a gap in the tarpaulin and the ten kilo weights on each of the four marque feet were struggling to hold it down. In all the other more important preparations for the day, Rose had forgotten to bring the pegs that would usually pin the gazebo down into the earth.

'Don't worry, Sharon!' Karen called over the wind as they all held on for dear life. 'Rain on a wedding day is actually good luck. It's going to wash all their troubles away!'

'It's going to wash us away too!' Gloria cried, with one hand firmly on the handle for the gravy pan and the other on the nearest tray of par-cooked vegetables.

It was anyone's guess why the weather had changed so much in the few hours since they had watched Seren get married at Dewstow church at ten that morning. It had still been a bit windy then, but nothing like this. Margery suspected that they were being punished for expecting a British summer day to be nice. Wales was known for being green and lush, and constant rain was the reason for that.

'We need more canapés!' Mrs George shrieked, bringing in the empty serving tray. 'They all blew off the tray when I was walking to the tent!'

Karen and Sharon leapt to attention. Karen let go of the tent to begin piping whipped cream cheese onto the homemade blinis. Sharon topped them with smoked salmon, but when she went to top them with a sprig of dill the entire bag blew away, whipping from her hands out of the tent and disappearing into the cloudy sky through the open tent door.

A few hours later, they sat comfortably inside the school hall, after everything had been relocated. It had not been an easy feat, but once the catering tent had well and truly disappeared across the field, the decision was taken – for the safety of all involved – that being inside a real bricks-and-mortar building would be a much better plan. Margery just hoped the gas oven would still work after its ordeal. They hadn't had time to plug it back in once they managed to heave it back into the kitchen, its wheels covered in mud and grass. The food had been a disaster. The crates they had taken the food up to the field in had blown away too and the ones they had managed to catch were a disorganised mess. Rose had taken one look at what remained edible and then called the local pizzeria, ordering one hundred meat feast and one hundred margarita pizzas. Gluten free be damned in an emergency.

'You're looking very short,' Mrs Blossom said to Clementine, who looked up in surprise, the slice of pizza in her hand flopping over under the weight of its own grease.

'I'm sitting down?' Clementine murmured. Mrs Blossom had already sashayed off to join Rose, Ada Bones under her arm. Something was happening, Margery thought to herself – she could feel the energy in the air change. Ignoring it, she turned to look at the DJ booth as the music stopped.

'It's now time for Mr and Mrs Matthews' first dance!' The DJ called excitedly. Margery recognised him as one of the Media Studies group B students.

Gary and Seren took to the floor and began to glide around the hall in each other's arms. Clementine took Margery's hand on top of the tablecloth.

'Remember our first dance?' Clementine said.

Margery smiled at the memory of Ceri-Ann accidentally playing the Cha Cha Slide over the village hall speaker system instead of 'Something About the Way You Look Tonight' by Elton John.

The music suddenly stopped. Gary and Seren turned toward the DJ table where Rose was waiting in a sequined outfit that she hadn't been wearing twenty minutes earlier. Margery suddenly realised in horror what was about to happen.

To the other side of the table stood Rhonda Blossom, wearing a matching outfit. They raised their arms up in what Margery was sure was supposed to be triumph and then the music started again, this time many beats per minute faster. Margery and Clementine shared a look as Rose and Rhonda began the bizarre, coordinated dance routine, which was obviously supposed to be the big surprise that Rose had planned.

'Good Lord!' Gloria said what they were all thinking out loud. 'First, we nearly all get blown away with the tent, and now this! When will it end?'

'Not till the sweet release of death I imagine,' Clementine said, chuckling at the sight of Rose pirouetting around the room. She'd brought out some ribbons from somewhere and now the dance had turned even more theatrical.

To her credit, Seren took being upstaged during her own wedding dance with good humour and she and Gary were both clapping along in time to the music as they span. Mrs Blossom's tiny dog Ada Bones twirled around behind them and yapped, wearing her own sparkly leotard.

Margery jumped as someone grabbed the back of her chair – she whirled around to find Ceri-Ann staring at her.

'Christ, it's just as well I sold them Taylor Swift tickets,' Ceri-Ann said, pulling a face. 'She's basically here with us.'

Margery and Clementine chuckled, but then Ceri-Ann's face turned serious. It was jarring under the lights from the DJ booth and the dance routine still ongoing in the background.

'Have you heard about Mr Barrow?' Ceri-Ann hissed, her face suddenly serious.

Margery turned to watch as Mr Barrow clapped along to the music, oblivious to their eyes.

'No?' Clementine said.

Ceri-Ann sat back down in her seat, her eyes flitting over to Symon, who was holding baby Nicholas across the room and bobbing along to the beat. The dinner lady team leaned in to listen.

'He's been forced to step down at the school,' Ceri-Ann told them. 'We're going to have a new headteacher.'

'What?' Margery and Clementine cried in unison as Gloria gasped. Karen and Sharon looked on the verge of tears again.

'You are joking?' Sharon asked. Ceri-Ann shook her head.

'Deadly serious mate,' she said. 'Apparently we're all going to get a letter to go to a governors' meeting before school starts next month.'

'You don't think it has anything to do with our confrontation with Richard?' Clementine gasped, throwing a hand over her mouth.

Ceri-Ann shook her head, 'No, well. That probably didn't help, but I think there was loads of stuff wrong.'

'He did say he'd already sent in his report,' Margery explained, trying to remember exactly what had been said. 'I can't imagine it was very good.'

It had been so many months since the incident that she had entirely forgotten about the audit results. She hadn't even thought to ask Mr Barrow about them. Margery looked over at the dance floor again where Seren was now spinning with Rose, Gary and Mr Barrow clapping along happily and had the horrible sinking feeling that a lot of things were about to change.

Acknowledgements

If you'd told me three years ago that I'd write five books I'd have asked you to get out of my house, but here we are!

As always, I have to start by thanking my family and friends for always believing in me. Especially my Mum – one day I'll believe you when you say how much you like reading the series.

The biggest of thank-you's to my wife Robyn, who I would have shriveled up and died without. Thank you for being there for me and for growing Baby Hendy – who I haven't met in person yet, but I'm sure will be just as lovely as you are.

Thank you to Francesca Riccardi, my excellent agent, for all your help. I promise that the next book won't have so many potential endings, (probably!).

A huge thank-you to all the team at Canelo and Canelo Crime but especially:

- Siân Heap, who somehow manages to get these books from the awful first drafts to the slightly less awful, published thing.

- Thanhmai Bui-Van and Kate Shepherd for supporting and promoting the series so well.

- Ami Smithson, for another delightful cover!

- Thank you also to Russel McLean for his excellent editing and writing advice and Laurel Sills for the copy edit. Editing can sometimes feel like a never-ending nightmare, but you both made it seem so easy.

In other workplaces, thank you, Pickled Pumpkin Catering for employing me part time so I can keep one foot in the kitchen!

A special thank-you to Alis Hawkins and Crime Cymru, of which I am proud to say I'm a member, and a thank you to all my fellow crime writing authors as well. I think the crime writing community might be the nicest group of people you could ever meet.

Last but not ever least, thank you for reading this book, so I can continue to write them! It brings me immense joy that so many people are following along with Margery and Clementine's adventures, and I hope you enjoyed this one.

Until the next time!

CANELOCRIME

Do you love crime fiction and are always on the lookout for brilliant authors?

Canelo Crime is home to some of the most exciting novels around. Thousands of readers are already enjoying our compulsive stories. Are you ready to find your new favourite writer?

Find out more and sign up to our newsletter at canelocrime.com